The Edge of Destiny

The Edge of Destiny

Forever Warriors Book 2

M.J. Sewall

ALSO BY M J SEWALL

Contents

To Christopher James Mayer,
A friend and colleague who made every page better

PART 1

"Much is buried inside The River."
- Rigel of Athens, Amartus Elder

The Simoom

June 17, 1859, California

Unna quickly brushed her long black hair behind her ear, not caring if it was streaked with blood.

She had no time. She glanced back over her shoulder, as she flung the weighty satchel onto her back.

Damn, I'll never make it, she thought to herself. *Not if that's really him.*

The dark figure appeared, a hundred yards out, on foot. Unna's mind raced, along with her horse's heart. She could feel the blood rush through the animal beneath her. She shifted the weighty satchel on her back and allowed a look back through her crooked elbow.

The Elder stood there and raised his hands. He had no weapons, but he didn't need any; he was the weapon. Una rode faster.

Pentoss, my love, where are you? She soothed her own mind with the thought of him. *No time for that,* she scolded herself, *you are no damsel. Save yourself.* Unna dug in her spurs, as hard as she dared without hurting her horse. *Run like our lives depend on it because they do.*

She could feel the horse lurch beneath her, but she could also feel the dark figure framed against the horizon. Her steed pounded away at the soft earth, giving distance between herself, her cargo, and the elder.

She stretched out her mind farther, ahead and all around for any place to escape, hide. California was a beautiful place; Rancheros as far as she could see, cattle everywhere. From the vantage, she saw the valley of farmers, ranchers, and their workers. She felt them all, but that's not what she was looking for. She needed a way out, away. Her steed galloped furiously toward the hills.

Unna didn't know how he'd found her, but the curious ways of Elders were nothing to ponder now. Her horse jumped a low rough wooden fence as the hill became steeper.

She stretched out her mind behind her, to feel if the elder had moved closer. He hadn't, but something reached for her. Heat. A wave of blistering heat. *A simoom.* The ancient word rang in her head, sent ahead by the elder. A warning, mocking her.

Her mind conceived it, but it didn't make any sense. Simooms happened naturally in the middle east, in the desert. Or, whenever Elder Yarro unleased his terrible power. She climbed the hill faster. She felt the sweat pour from the horse. Just a little farther.

The satchel weighed on her back. That was all that mattered, getting these out of the elder's hands, anywhere, just away. Ahead, she saw the group of cows, a few stragglers, too small to be called a herd. The cows objected loudly as she galloped past them, two scattering as she raced up the hill.

She noticed her own sweat, and knew it was more than the effort of the ride. A wave of nausea wrenched her stomach as the tendrils of heat reached for her. Unna had no idea how far from the elder she was now, but the heat still came. Faster. Hotter. Oppressive. She heard a noise, looking back left through her riding arm again, and watched in amazement as a low copse of trees exploded in flame.

The cows expressed their displeasure, then one of them caught fire too. An otherworldly shriek came from the others as they ran, nowhere to hide.

Her steed faltered. Unna swooned but stayed on her saddle, forcing it to gallop. It slowed, the heat pushing at her from behind and above. Her horse screamed as its tail caught fire, swishing it madly back and forth like it was battling a barrage of flies made of flame.

The earth below them seemed to shimmer, then the wall of heat pushed harder, the super-heated air igniting the scrub grass behind them. The ground leveled out. They had reached the top of the hill, a plateau.

Unna spotted strange wavy lines to her left, along a small rise of earth and turned toward it. Her steed collapsed, pitching her forward. Her dark hair caught fire. She managed a rough roll over her shoulder, but could not get up to run, could not even imagine how to stop the heat. The world was an oven.

The heat was like nothing she'd ever felt, not even in the desert lands she'd explored. She was inches from the sun. She tried to draw breath, but she could no longer breathe. She had swallowed fire. None of her past lifetimes prepared her for this sweltering hell. Unna dragged the satchel under her body. The clothes on her back caught fire.

Then the earth gave way beneath her. She fell into darkness. She didn't register it as a crevasse. The earth just consumed her. She only knew it was cool, so dark and cool. She clung to the satchel, not knowing how her arms still worked. She felt only the cool rushing air over her blistered skin. *Is my hair still on fire?* Unna didn't know.

The heat had scorched her lungs, her hair, her skin. She couldn't speak. The darkness rushed into her. Unna's last thoughts were, *Pentoss, Pentoss, my love.*

Two hours later, the fires had burned themselves out, and Elder Yarro stood on the hill. He swept past the charred remains of the horse, ignoring the charred smell of dead flesh.

He scowled at the crevasse below him. It was no wider than three feet across but might be a hundred feet deep. More dirt had collapsed into the crevasse with the woman.

No tools he knew of would penetrate that split in the earth. But at least he knew they would not be going anywhere. He had time, and no matter how many lifetimes it took, he would return and claim what belonged to him.

CHAPTER ONE
A Night Mission

Present Day, California

The five teens stood on the flat roof. This side overlooked the alley of the long-closed department store they stood on top of. They all took turns peering over the short half wall, down on the tagger spray painting the back wall of the building. Lucas seemed disinterested as he leaned his thin frame on the large air conditioning unit. Ariana stood next to him. Zacke, Katie and Cody whispered by the half wall overlooking the criminal.

"This is stupid." Zacke folded his arms. "I'm not wearing that." He handed the mask back to Cody.

Cody sighed and scratched his short brown hair in frustration. "If you don't, they'll see who you are. This is classic secret identity stuff."

Katie snatched it and compared it to her own. "Are they Ninja Turtle masks? Where did you get these?"

"After Halloween." Cody pointed to his own dark blue mask, with two eye holes cut out. "Half price."

Zacke looked over the ledge, keeping it to a loud whisper, "We're not ninjas, or superheroes. Stop trying to..."

"Shhh." said Cody, finger over his mouth, very serious, glancing over the wall "Mirror man has..."

"Mirror Man?" Katie whispered to Lucas.

Lucas put his hands up, "Not my idea, I wanted Cody to be Electron."

Ariana furrowed her brow at the name.

Cody straightened up. "Mirror Man is all I could think of. Name doesn't matter."

"Then I'm calling you Electro boy." said Zacke.

"Stop it." Cody leaned over the roof ledge, making sure not to be seen, "If we don't do something soon, he'll move on and damage someone else's property."

Katie shot side eyes to Lucas. "What do you think, Viking Boy?"

"I'm definitely not going to be Viking Boy." Lucas shrugged. "What's the plan again, Cody – umm, Mirror Man?"

"We've been over this," answered Cody, concerned over the volume of their voices. "The masks are to hide our identities. The names... the names don't matter, I guess. But we need to act. Do something. This is our team's first mission."

"What team?" asked Zacke. "It's been months since the fire tower. John and David still haven't contacted us. There is no team."

Cody pointed to the tagger. "Yeah, I know. That's why we need to do something. We can't wait for John or my dad."

Katie asked, "Still no word from them?"

Cody just shook his head. "We can't just wait around. At least we can do this."

"Fight petty crime?" asked Zacke.

"You were the police explorer. Better than doing nothing." Cody shot back. "This will be easy."

"Does this seem dangerous to anyone else?" asked Ariana. "Maybe the guy has a weapon."

Lucas smiled "Hmm. Not a problem."

Zacke said, "There's a big difference between doing training and these 'missions,' or whatever."

Katie touched Zacke's arm. "Let's just give this a chance. Cody worked really hard on this plan."

Zacke kept his arms folded.

Lucas joined the rest of the teens. "Come on. We all agreed. Let's just do this. If we don't stop this crap, no one else will."

"Except the police. Let me just call them." Zacke pulled his cell from a back pocket.

"No!" said Cody, too loud.

"Hey!" a shout came from below. "Hey, who's up there?"

They all froze.

"Who's up there?" shouted the tagger from the alley. "I hear you!"

"Stop what you're doing!" Cody said, his voiced deepened.

Lucas finished, "Or I'll pull your lungs out through your shoulder blades."

Ariana smacked Lucas. "Lucas? What the heck?"

"What? It's a real thing."

"Lucas? Lucas who?" shouted the tagger.

Lucas' inner warrior said, "Hey, I wasn't joking, criminal. It's a very effective ancient way to kill."

"We're not here to kill him!" Zacke shook his head and reluctantly put on his mask, "never mind. Lucas, you better stay here. Katie and Cody, with me."

Before Lucas or Ariana could object to being left behind, Zacke had taken flight, a tight arm around the waists of Cody and Katie. They adjusted their masks as they flew over the roof's edge.

"What the fu..." started the tagger.

Zacke touched down in the alley, Katie and Cody awkwardly finding their feet.

"Come on man," said Cody as he tripped and almost went over, not finding his feet well at all.

They had landed in between the tagger and his "art," a large stylized "Never" emblazoned on the cinder block wall. The tagger dropped his can and casually grabbed for his cell phone. Before he could find the camera button, Cody had fried the phone with his ability.

"OWW – son of a whore." The phone dropped to the ground, sparking wildly.

Zacke tried to follow Lucas' script, "Sir, you need to stop destroying personal property." He noticed that the tagger was no older than he was, maybe 16. He changed the script, "Man, just stop destroying other people's shit."

"Place is derelict. Owner got insurance," the tagger shot back. "Mind your business."

Zacke shook his head, "Dude, the guy that owns this business works probably works really hard, trying to find someone to rent it." He pointed to the "art."

"Who's going to rent it now? You ever heard of a deductible? He pays that out of pocket."

The tagger wasn't listening. He casually reached down for his can of paint and reached for something else in his other pocket.

Before Zacke could react, the tagger has pressed the button on the spray can and lit his lighter at the same time. The flame shot out at Zacke's head. Just before it reached him, it curved back toward the tagger as though hitting a curved shield.

Just then, a wild cry came from above and Lucas landed behind the tagger.

Marveling at the perfect landing from two stories, Cody began, "How did you?" when he saw Lucas flick his wrists. The twin extendable metal batons clicked in to place.

Katie acted fast, throwing a shield ball at the tagger's face. He took the impact, spun and splayed back five feet, also hitting Lucas.

Lucas made a "what did you do that for?" motion as he slid the batons back into their handles. He put them in his back pockets.

Ariana shouted from the roof, "We wanted him to stop, not get his head bashed in!"

A faint smile played across Lucas' lips. Katie winced. *Is that Lucas or his warrior?*

Moans came from the tagger boy. They went to him. He was face down in an unnatural posture on the ground.

From the roof, Ariana asked, "Is that guy okay?"

The guy on the ground moaned his response as they turned him over.

Zacke asked, "What did you do, Katie?"

Katie couldn't speak, starting at the boy's face. The light from the streetlamp above lit his face and showed the damage. They all stared.

The boy tried to speak, "Uww oke my yaw!"

"I... I just threw a shield ball." Katie sputtered. She went to yank off her mask but stopped.

Zacke winced as he looked at the boy, "Well, it looks like he took a cannonball to the jaw."

A siren wailed, only blocks away.

"Damn!" said Cody. "Battle stance 13!" shouted Cody.

"What is that? We aren't fighting the cops." said Zacke, the siren closer. "Never mind. Katie, shield ball. I'll lift us to the roof."

Lucas, Cody, and Katie bunched close together. An invisible ball surrounded them all, like they were in a giant invisible bubble. Zacke lifted them all as the cop car swung their lights into the alley. He landed on the roof, next to Ariana. Katie dropped the shield, and they all found their feet. They waited.

The siren stopped, but they saw the lights flash in the alley, throwing colorful lighted shadows on them.

"Umm Ugg!" came the incoherent sounds of the tagger. He pointed to the roof.

"Hey, who's up there? Come down right now," demanded the authoritative shout of a policewoman.

"He ratted us out," said Cody.

"You fried his phone, remember?"

"Oh yeah, how did they get her so fast?" asked Ariana.

"No idea," said Zacke. "We better go. Katie broke that guy's jaw," said Zacke.

"I didn't mean to!" shouted Katie, too loud.

"I know," said Zacke.

"Units are surrounding the building right now. There is no way off that roof," came from the policewoman below.

"Uhgg ummm!" said the tagger, probably hoping the cop would pay more attention to his pain.

Zacke didn't hear any more sirens. The policewoman was probably exaggerating, but more cops were coming. "Okay. We'll run to the other side of the roof and bubble lift out of here."

Lucas chimed in, "Escape plan 17! You did read my playbook."

"Shut up!" Zacke said louder than he meant to. He crumpled his mask and crushed it into his pocket. "We just better pray no one saw us."

Cody didn't say anything else.

They ran to the far side of the roof. They huddled in close together. Katie threw up her shield ball and Zacke lifted them in the air. He hoped he chose a direction least likely to be seen. Since they were in a busy part of the city, no one could be sure. Katie chose a thick green shield in her mind, though only Ariana and Cody were able to see it. To everyone else, it was totally invisible. She promised herself more experiments and training later.

They floated away into the night. No one noticed the shadowy figure across the alley with his high-res digital camera.

CHAPTER TWO

Elders Meeting

Present Day, Italy

Elder Ordway stood in her white pant suit and blood red pumps – made, coincidentally, at a factory just a hundred miles away in Le Marche. Her feet hurt like hell, climbing all those stairs up to the palazzo, but Elder Zamma had made it impossible to use magic to approach his former lair.

She'd been watching from a distance. His palazzo was a palatial estate on the Amalfi Italian coast. Expensive, private. Ordway was surprised there were no guards and few defenses left. Just old magic fading after Zamma's death. He also had that weird aversion to elevators, so the gruesome climb up all the marble stairs was unnecessarily exhausting. Ordway promised herself she'd have an underling massage her feet after this meeting was done.

It still stinks of him, she thought. She stood at the massive door, scanning for traps. Inside, his sanctum. He had been, perhaps, the most cunning of them. She repeated words of power in her mind, scanning the nearly invisible bonds of magic for any last traps. She spotted the swatch of color over the door as she felt a new presence behind her.

"Well?" spoke Sorrento, as though he'd been present the entire time. She didn't give him the satisfaction of whirling around. He was safely five feet behind her by the stairs. No knives in the back, yet. Plus, it was Sorrento. Not much to worry about.

"Still sneaking up, I see," said Ordway. "Of course, at your height, how could anyone see you coming?"

"Short jokes, really?" He looked down at his own short frame, "You know I've always hated this body, but your jibes don't penetrate. Let me through, I'll scan for traps." Sorrento produced a curious object from his coat pocket of his custom-tailored suit. She wondered briefly if they had the same tailor. The object resembled a screwdriver and glowed green.

"Oh Sorrento, watching Doctor Who again? You and your gadgets. Just focus the magic yourself." She smiled. "Did you come here in a red telephone box, as well?"

"It is a blue police box now, troglodyte. My device focuses magic in ways you couldn't even understand." His device made no sound, glowing the same eerie green. He put his gadget away. "All clear, no traps."

"Are you sure?" asked Ordway as she reached up into the air above the door. She pulled the swatch of color off the elaborate door casement.

Sorrento shrieked.

Ordway pushed the large door open with magic, then flung the splotch of color into the room, like a scoop of muddy snow. It tumbled onto the floor, getting caught on the carpet.

The wash of color laid like a pile of jelly until an arm popped out, then a leg. The wad of colorful jelly flopped over and was soon in the form of a tall man. He wore board shorts and a flowery Hawaiian shirt.

"Hahahahah," the man rolled on the carpet, as he reformed into himself.

Sorrento sniffed. "Yarro. Why is that funny?"

"You shrieked!" said Yarro, laughing through his thick gray beard. "It's a wonder you both survived this long. I was above you the whole time."

"I saw you the minute I arrived. Hard to miss that... whatever that is on your body."

He indicated his colorful shirt. "Gotta stay comfortable." Elder Yarro was still on the rug where he'd landed. "Nice rug. I might take this. Feels Persian, maybe Kazak?" He rolled onto his side, eyeing Ordway. "Care for a quick roll on the rug? Been a long time."

Ordway rolled her eyes. "Last time I was a man and you were a woman, as I recall. Eons ago."

"How do we know you aren't a trap, Yarro?" said Sorrento.

Yarro rolled his eyes this time. "Ever to the point, Sorrento. We are at war, granted. This is a peace conference. Relax." Yarro rose and made his way to the desk by the window, a mess of papers and ruined books. "Besides, if it was a trap, you'd be dead. But you're not, so let's cut the crap."

"Let's," echoed Ordway.

Sorrento entered the room fully, still looking around as if there may be a hidden surprise. He surveyed a curious full-length mirror on the far wall with a few cracks in it. Yarro took a seat at the desk, and Ordway took off her shoes and sat on an antique couch, French, Louis the IV, she guessed.

"So, here we are," said Yarro, "the last three Elders."

"That we know of," added Sorrento.

"You mean, the weak-willed Amartus elders? They are dead and gone," Yarro said, riffling through papers. "Not many Amartus warriors left, either, by my count."

"Oh? And how do we know?" said Sorrento, surveying the far side of the room. "Even the Sect won't say where things stand."

Ordway clicked on her phone. "Talk to the Sect much, do you? What do you think happened here?" she asked, gesturing around the ransacked room. "If you'll notice, not much left of value."

Sorrento had noticed. "You think so? But, the Sect are neutral. They can't!"

"I saw a disciple after he'd murdered his elder Zamma and stolen his power." Ordway rose from the couch. "It's a new world, my friend. Things may be changing."

"Friend? How can you forget we are at war?" Sorrento pulled out his device, but before he could wield it, Ordway used her power. A wall of water erupted out of nowhere, crashing over Sorrento and knocking the device and him across the room. Sorrento got to his feet soggily, the water soaking him, the bulk of the wave disappeared from whence it came.

Ordway stood on her bare feet, ready to defend or attack.

The Palazzo shook with a voice like an Olympian god, "ENOUGH!"

The mini earthquake caused Ordway to stumble over. Sorrento swayed and turned to Yarro.

Yarro's power echoed away and the room stopped shaking. "Now, that's better. We are here to decide what comes next. Forget the war."

"Forget?" growled Sorrento.

"For now! Elder Zamma has been killed. His disciples, the brothers, have been killed. Because of Elder Ordway, we know there are at least five new players on the board."

Ordway nodded. "Yes. A new break out. I'm sure of it. And Pentoss is back, out of hiding."

Yarro laughed. "Of course he is. With Zamma gone, why not? He doesn't have an elder hunting him."

"No," Ordway said, "now he'll have three."

Yarro smiled, leaned back in the desk chair, hands behind his head. "I suppose. That's what we're here to decide."

No one spoke.

Yarro looked between them. "Well, we are palavering, so palaver. Ideas on strategy?"

Sorrento retrieved his device. "It's obvious. Attack with all we have. They are five. We are the Rageto. We are legion."

"Are you, Sorrento?" said Yarro. "Not what I hear. How many warriors do you have? Twenty? Less?"

"More than you, I hear," Sorrento said grimly. "Want to find out?"

"Ugg," said Yarro. "This is why we never get together. Pissing contests! We are elders, not children. We have not lived all of these lives, been born into this power to simply bicker. Yes, we war on each other. It is in our nature. Time to change."

"What do you suggest, oh great Elder Hawaiian shirt?" mocked Ordway.

Yarro came around the front of the desk. "The Amartus is weak. Their annoying dagger in our side is almost gone forever. The River seems to be flowing with us and not against us."

"For now," Sorrento huffed. "Until it changes its mind."

"Yes, the ways of the River are mysterious. We are not meant to know... blah, blah, blah..." Yarro stroked his beard. "We need a final blow. The Amartus Elders are gone, their warriors have dwindled. We wipe these new children out, and we win."

"Then begin fighting each other for eternity." Sorrento suggested.

Ordway said quietly, "Oh no, surely not that long."

Yarro walked down the steps to join the others. "Don't you see? The River is giving us a clear sign, for once. Not war. Instead, it is time for us to finally unite."

"Unite our power? How would that work?" Ordway motioned to the three of them. "We hate each other."

"We compete with each other. I don't hate either of you," said Yarro, with his palms up, as if in peace.

"Oh no, I hate Ordway." Sorrento pointed.

"Feeling's mutual," she gave a little mocking wave.

"Think! Look at this room. Zamma's other disciples have scattered, ready to rally to a new Elder."

Ordway thought, *Oh, I know where a few are stashed. I've almost worked out how he did it.*

"The Sect may be a problem," said Sorrento, indicating the ransacked room. "They have finally shed that annoying pretense of neutrality."

Ordway reasoned. "But that's good. They are just inferiors, after all, scribbling in their little books. There is less check on our power, or even better, if they have chosen sides, they are now fair game."

"Out with it! What do you propose?" said Sorrento.

Yarro regarded him silently. He took a step closer to Sorrento. Then another.

Sorrento wiped his brow. "Respectfully, Elder Yarro."

"That's better. We have two choices. One – attack these five new ones. Problem? They killed the brothers, one of which had all of Zamma's powers. None of us liked the monster, but we all knew his power. Plus, even Elder Ordway had to escape them."

"Retreat," corrected Ordway.

"Retreat. Yes, of course." Yarro put out his hand, respectfully. "Nothing wrong with that. But, Ordway, no matter what body you are in, I know your power, too. If you had to retreat, that gives me pause."

"I had to." She'd been saving this bit of news for just such a meeting: "They linked."

"No!" shouted Sorrento.

"Yes! They linked as we have all dreamed of doing, like the old stories. They became one, like one warrior with all the powers shared."

Yarro's brow furrowed. "You didn't mention that alarming detail."

"Wait, you two spoke before this?" Sorrento began. "I thought..."

Yarro put up a dismissive hand. "Briefly, on the phone, as we all did. Ordway also said they had the power of flight."

That forced Sorrento to fall into the nearest chair. "Flight? I... I had no idea."

"That's because we don't talk to each other," said Yarro, standing between the two. "Always fighting, angling. Now we must take a lesson from these children. We can't link our powers, but we can join forces."

"That was the first option. What was the second?"

"Well, that's where it gets interesting. Instead of an overt offensive, I have some other ideas."

"Let's hear it," said Ordway.

Then, Elder Yarro laid out his multi-fronted plan of attack to wipe them all out of existence.

CHAPTER THREE
The Garage Room Lair

Back at Lucas' room, the friends caught a breath. The converted garage that was Lucas Sandler's bedroom resembled a gym, with machines of all sorts: weight station, treadmill. It also was very much a teenage boy's room, exploding with pop culture objects and posters. The mirrors that used to hang on both walls facing each other were now replaced with just one.

In the mirror, Katie adjusted her make-up, a nervous habit of hers. "I can't get the sound out of my head, when my shield ball hit that kid's jaw."

"Yeah," Ariana put her hand on Katie's shoulder, "that was really bad."

"Hey! I thought you were comforting me."

"I am, I was." Ariana dropped her hand. "Sorry. I mean, we just need to be really careful. It's been only a few months since the final battle."

"Final Battle?" Lucas laughed. "You sound like Cody."

"Hey, Lucas, come on." Zacke was getting sick of being the voice of reason. "Cody tried something. Didn't work. That's okay. We're all trying to figure this stuff out."

"Yeah, well," Lucas threw his mask in a garbage can. "I told you this super-hero stuff wasn't the way. That's not our story. We are Amartus. There will be bigger fights."

Ariana added, "Plus, it was danger we looked for. Zacke almost got fried. That kid will be drinking liquid for months."

"Yeah, that can was a surprise. Do all taggers had a backup blow torch?" asked Zacke.

"And the cops? Did they see us? Did someone else? I know we aren't a big city or anything, but like forty thousand people live here. They all have cell phones with cameras."

"And someone called the police. They got there too fast," offered Katie.

"We can't be doing these things." Ariana sat on the weight bench. "We're still just kids in high school."

"And that guy can fly," Katie pointed to each person in turn, "and he can fry cell phones..."

"And she can break people's jaws," said Cody.

"Hey! Too soon. We're not superheroes," Katie said.

"But we're not normal, either," Ariana said with a sigh. "Yeah, I get it."

Lucas said, "We're also not technically in high school. Winter break still has a week left."

Zacke blurted, "I wish John was here."

"Me too," said Lucas.

Ariana asked, "Anyone tried to call or text lately?"

"Yeah, like every day," said Zacke. "What is that about? He was supposed to come back and help us."

"Nobody knows," Katie shrugged.

Zacke asked, knowing the answer already. "Cody have you heard from your Dad?"

"I already told you no." Cody said, the words barely escaping through his gritted teeth.

"Okay," said Zacke, "just asking."

"Guys, we can't... I mean, we have to do something." Cody's next words came in a flood. "After all the crazy shit... I don't know what to do now. I feel stuck and, I don't know, angry all the time."

"Me too. After the fire tower, I thought I'd be stronger. But I'm just scared all the time. What if someone comes after us, like that Elder lady? Lucas may be activated, but I'm not." Ariana slumped. "I don't even know what I am."

"Yeah, me neither," echoed Zacke.

"One thing we can't do is give up." Katie stood up. "Especially not to fear. I'm scared too, guys, but I'm also tired of being scared. We stick together. Not as superheroes, but as friends who have each other's backs."

Cody said, "That's a superhero speech."

"Shut up, Electro boy," said Zacke with a half-smile.

Cody retorted, "Mixed-race Superman."

Zacke cocked his head to one side, considering. "I like it."

Cody shook his head but smiled anyway.

Lucas said, "Sorry guys, nearly eleven o'clock." Curfew for most of them.

"I'll drive you guys home," said Cody. "Unless you want to fly."

"Don't start," warned Zacke but was cut off from a knock at the side door. Zacke smiled. "Looks like I have a ride after all."

Lucas answered the door to find Victoria.

She asked, "Hey guys. Hey Babe, you need a ride?"

"As if you read my mind." Zacke walked to the door and kissed Victoria.

"Ughh. Gross," "Boo" and "Get a room" were heard from the other teens.

"Yeah, yeah. You're all just jealous. Bye guys." Zacke said as he and Victoria left.

Mutual goodbyes were said. Cody left with Ariana and Katie to drop them off. Lucas said goodbye and closed the door to his garage room.

He frowned about how the night had gone. It was clear the others didn't understand what the Amartus struggle really was.

Lucas stood at the cheap mirror he had bought after all his large ones were destroyed by Zamma. He let the warrior awake in him. Elgisard, the ancient Viking warrior said through Lucas, "I should have taken over."

"I still can't get used to your blue eyes." Lucas stared at himself in the mirror.

"They are your eyes too, now. They have always been."

"That's not confusing at all." Lucas said to his own reflection, and two beings becoming one.

They both laughed at their reflection. Lucas internalized his thoughts and the warrior answered. Elgisard thought, *We are one, Lucas. There is no you or I, there is only us.*

Lucas thought, *It still doesn't feel that way.*

It takes time. I will always be here.

All my memories, all my lifetimes.

I can show you more

Not yet. I'm still... still not ready to see it all.

That last time really...

Yes. I know. I pushed too hard last time.

Am I fully activated?

My mind still feels separate from you, like you're an...

Like I'm an invader in your head.
I know. It may feel that way for some time.
If John was here...
Pentoss must have his reasons.
He's a complicated warrior.
Aren't we all?
Not really.
They both laughed as one.
There is an old saying –
when the mind is stuck, move the body.
Are you really done for the night?
Lucas looked at the clock, 11:13.

He glanced at the door connecting his converted garage bedroom to the house.

Beyond it his awesome and concerned parents were likely in bed already.
Nope, not even close.
Good.

Lucas reached for the leather bandana. He'd cut large eye holes in it, ready for just such a night. Much cooler than a ninja turtle. He put black grease makeup around each eye. He'd seen similar stuff used in baseball and football. Supposedly it was to reduce glare. Lucas used it to help hide his identity. He also thought it looked cool as he put on the bandana and looked in the mirror.

Elgisard thought, *You look like a racoon.*

As Lucas tied a knot at the back of his head as tight as he could, he said to his reflection, his warrior, "An ancient Norse warrior racoon. I'll take it."

He left by the side door, not bothering to lock it. John had said that all of their houses had been building quiet protection, a kind of immunity. The home bases were safe, just like in some kid games. John hadn't explained fully, which seemed to be a John trait. Lucas didn't know if it was his ancient, the River, or if it just happened naturally. He'd gotten no straight answer from his ancient warrior either.

As he left, he wasn't worried about tracking down criminals. He'd found out where they would all be, all in one place. His ancient warrior Elgisard had been gone from this plane of existence for a while, stuck in the River instead since 1964. Coming back deep into the twenty first century was a continuing education. Technology was amazing, information available at a fingertip. They had found the chatrooms and social media trail. It wasn't hard to find at all.

In his small city, the crime was limited to small, contained areas of two to three blocks. Mid twentieth century apartment buildings filled with struggling lower income families, and of course a criminal element. If there was a shooting or stabbing in Sea Valley, it was in one of these seedy pockets. What he needed tonight would be found there.

As he approached the alley, he saw the glow to the left. It came from between two apartment buildings, three stories tall. He scanned for the layers of "security." Though he knew many Hispanic young men lived in this neighborhood, the first layer of bouncers was a couple of strung out skinny white guys. The sole light pole shone down on them.

The tallest of the two asked, "What are you, homie?"

Lucas was shirtless, fifteen, and scrawny. Although he'd been working out for a year and knew martial arts, his small frame with a sinewy layer of developing muscles. He wore his not-superhero racoon mask. He said just two words, "Fight Night."

The layers of tattoos roiled like a snake as the youth on the left covered his mouth to snigger. Lucas produced a $20 bill. The one on the right looked Lucas up and down. "Your funeral, dude." He waved him through.

As Lucas walked through the two tattooed guards-of-sorts, he felt Elgisard under his skin, filling his frame, making him feel taller. Through the warrior's eyes, he saw the glow to the left. From between the buildings, Elgisard imagined a scene like his first homeland. He expected to walk into the scene of warriors ready to do battle, sensors, torches, and open fire pits all around, lighting the scene. As they turned the corner in their small, teenage frame, the lights came from modern LED lights.

Not unlike an ancient fighting pit, light came from all around and shone dramatically. Lanterns strewn the scene laying on the tough scrub grass between the buildings. Several large modern pop-up canopies were tied together to make a series of fighting tents. There were no more guards, just layers of shirtless warriors about to do battle.

Brown flesh, white flesh, all mixed together. The outer ring was made up of watchers, shouting. Chanting. The action had already begun, two warriors beating on each other with their fists. Lucas caught the eye of the one that was winning. His losing opponent swayed, confused, his back to Lucas.

As Lucas stepped closer, the crowds stopped. About three dozen boys and men of all ages stopped. The winner put his arm around the loser, who flinched. Lucas figured he was just about to go down when the winner locked his arm around his shoulders and spun him toward Lucas. The loser couldn't believe what he was seeing at first. With a bloody smile, he was the first to laugh. The winner joined. Then the whole crowd joined in, as Lucas stood there, the object of everyone's attention.

He's wanted a fair fight. Lucas scanned from right to left, the peals of laughter echoing through his mind. He felt the warrior Elgisard just under his skin, just under his mind. *No such thing as a fair fight.* The warrior and he smiled together and bit their tongue, releasing the berserker blood rage.

They shouldn't have laughed.

CHAPTER FOUR

Fighting Ancient

In Cody's minivan, Katie was doing most of the talking. "I'm not dissing you Cody, it's just that the idea of fighting crime is not what we should be doing. There are cops for that."

"Hey. Come on, at least he's trying something. None of us know what to do." Ariana didn't even know what to call her abilities. *Freeze things in mid-air? What's the use? And what John said about me being a hub. What did that even mean?*

"Yeah," Cody said, "my ability is useless, too. I'm surprised I can drive this long without shorting out this van."

"You knew I was thinking about my ability?" asked Ariana.

"Hey. Yeah! I did." said Cody. "John said we may hear each other's thoughts again. I've kinda missed that."

"Yeah well I can guess some of your thoughts with two hot girls in your van." Katie said, looking around. "Why do you have a minivan exactly? I mean, crank windows? How old is this thing?"

"2001 Caravan," Cody smiled widely.

"Oh my God, that's older than us!" yelled Ariana, giggling.

"Yeah, I know." Cody shifted in his seat. "My mom bought it off a co-worker. It's all she could afford, okay? Besides, it has room for all of us, so that's cool."

"Uh huh," Ariana's giggles got worse.

Katie giggled too. "Yeah, totally cool murder shag van."

"At least I have a ride." Cody wouldn't be baited about his van. His mom worked hard.

Katie quieted, thinking about how the night had gone. "Think that guy's okay?"

"You mean the tagger?" Cody shrugged. "Serves him right."

"Katie broke his jaw!"

"Do you have to keep saying it like that?" Katie asked.

"Sorry, you didn't mean to – but you did." Ariana's lost her giggles. "I just wish John was here to help us control all this."

Ariana was in the middle seat, just behind the others, but could feel Cody tense at the wheel. The minivan sped up.

Katie put a hand on Cody's arm. "Hey, Cody. It's okay. Sorry I made fun of your van."

"Huh?" He realized they were referring to his speeding up. "Oh, no. I have to rev up to make it over this hill."

That broke the mood. They all laughed as the minivan finally crested the hill, the last one before leaving town on the way to Katie's ranch house at the edge of town.

Ariana rolled her eyes. "Good. I thought it was about you dad. Not hearing from him and everything."

Katie swirled around to look at Ariana, a non-verbal chiding.

"Sorry, I just meant John and your dad left together, so..."

Katie's face betrayed her thoughts. "You don't get the non-verbal cool it signal, do you? Cody doesn't want to talk about it."

"I don't? Who says?" The van sped up again. "Why would I not want to talk about my dad leaving again. No word at all. No calls, no letters. Did he get taken again? I don't know. How would I? Why wouldn't we talk about that?!"

"Oh my god, blood," spurted Ariana. Her breaths got louder. She put her hand over her mouth.

"What's wrong?" asked Cody.

"Ariana, what is it?" asked Katie.

The van slowed, and Cody pulled to the side. They hadn't made it over the hill.

"We have to go back." Ariana said, breathing heavily.

"Why? What is it?" Cody demanded.

"It's Lucas. He's... he's in trouble. I got a flash. Lots of blood."

"How do you know?" Katie asked, her breathing matching Ariana.

"I don't know. I just do. Quick. I don't know where."

Katie tried to understand. "Are you seeing something?"

"No." Ariana searched her mind. "Yes. I mean... it's like it used to be. I'm inside his, like I'm where he is, seeing through his eyes. I see apartment buildings. Tents. Wait – a sign. It's torn. Noche Lucha. Oh no!"

"I take French," said Katie, "What does it mean?"

Cody said, "I know where he is. Stupid kid. Hold on."

The van made a surprisingly smooth U-turn, headed back down the hill. Cody said. "This baby has its own superpower. Corners like a dream."

As they drove faster than they should, but not so fast they would be pulled over, Ariana realized which neighborhood they were headed for.

Katie did too. "Not the ghetto. Why would Lucas be there?"

Cody and Ariana said in unison, "Fight Night."

Only two blocks from their school, Sea Valley High, these few blocks were notorious. They parked two blocks out from where Cody figured Lucas would be. "Not to sound racist, but you do speak Spanish, right?"

Ariana shrugged. "Of course. This is California. Don't you, wedo?" She didn't mean to crack a joke. The sense of Lucas was fading. "I don't feel him anymore."

"It's okay." Cody began walking. "This way."

"How do you know where he is?" asked Katie.

"A couple of my friends paid to go to Fight Night. It's like a bunch of gang members that beat up on each other for money. Happens once a month if the police don't break it up. They usually don't."

"Why would Lucas be here?" Katie asked.

"Failed mission? Feeling antsy, maybe?" Cody steeled his nerves. He was a bit older than Lucas, well-muscled from his high school football experience and he remembered the wild stories his football buddies brought back from Fight Night. "That Viking warrior is gonna get Lucas killed."

Ariana hit Cody in the shoulder. "Don't say that." She rushed ahead. She realized how dangerous these blocks were. Some cousins, aunts, and uncles lived close by.

They were all rushing now, seeing the likely alley. A glow to the left was a clue, between buildings. Faint, upbeat Hispanic music drifted toward them.

Ariana didn't mention everything she'd seen in her – vision? Feeling? It was still a jumble. She shook her head for clarity. Was she having visions now? Or was this reminding her how much she didn't want to have feelings for Lucas?

There was no one to stop them from entering, no guards of any kind, though there was a small table there. They saw the first young man on a strip of crab grass, a blood trail coming down from his ear and covering his torso. He didn't seem to notice them as he clapped his own ear, trying to stop the bleeding.

The music got louder as they came upon several white canopies tied together, like little circus tents. The music blared, drowning every other sound in the sonic sea. All Katie, Ariana, and Cody could see was a wall of bare backs.

Then a high-pitched whistle. The crowd of men – Ariana actually noted most of them were boys, though many bodies were heavily tattooed and covered in blood.

Ariana pushed in, saying, "Compromiso," as she shoved. The boys parted reluctantly, mostly confused by the new Mexican girl with the two white teenagers. Cody tried to do the macho head jerk at some random boys as though they were part of the same club. Katie assumed it was classic jock training.

Ariana saw Lucas' back, a thin white frame. It was covered in blood and sweat. As she reached for him, his head jerked back. The crowds went wild. "Campeón de Wedo!" Lucas slowly turned around, his chest a mix of blood and sweat, a thin cut on his right chest.

"Lucas!" Ariana shouted, then noticed a sickly sweet scent over the sweat. "Wait, is that Tequila?"

"Hey! My friends! Amigas, amigo!" Lucas downed the contents and crushed his red plastic cup dramatically.

"Oh shit," Cody muttered to himself.

Ariana didn't know what to say. Katie was quietly revving up her shields, just in case. She noticed a wad of cash in Lucas' other hand.

A hand slapped on Cody's shoulder. It was the young man standing next to Lucas who had shouted his new title. He said to Cody firmly, "Hey friend, time for Senor Wedo to go."

Cody nodded, as the man squeezed his shoulder tighter, driving home the point. The man whispered in his ear, "I don't know how he won. But he comes back again, they're gonna kill him."

He met Cody's eyes to emphasize. Lucas didn't hear any of this. Slurring his words, he shouted, "Viva la..." He clearly knew no Spanish, "Viva la... deniro!" And he threw the wad of money into the air.

Cody said to the girls, "Time to go."

"Cody," Lucas shouted, as though he just noticed him again, "I won!"

"Yeah, buddy, I see. Let's go home now."

He reluctantly took Lucas under his arm, knowing his own shirt would be ruined by Lucas' bloody sweat. Was that Lucas' blood? He noticed a line of weathered boys all looking worse off than Lucas. They glared at the teens as they left.

Katie smiled politely as they carefully made their way out of the alley, away from the crowd, most of which were fighting over the money Lucas had thrown. "Is okay, I can walk," Lucas said confidently. "Tequila is the awesome!" he said as Cody let him go.

Lucas listed to one side but recovered. "This way?" he asked as they walked.

Cody resumed helping him, trying to corral Lucas toward the van. "What were you doing, Lucas? Is this Elgisard? Is the warrior there? I'd like to talk to him, please."

"He's here. Always here. Wow, Tequila burns at first, but now…"

"Focus, Lucas," said Katie, "how many guys did you fight?"

"All of them, I think. Not sure. Lost count. Fun."

They had reached the van. Cody flung Lucas into the side, sliding door. "Not fun, Lucas. Dangerous. They could have killed you."

"Don't push me again." Lucas sounded one hundred percent sober, all at once. Cody couldn't tell if it was him talking, or the warrior. It was getting hard to tell anymore.

Cody yanked off Lucas' bandana. "This was stupid. Anyone could have yanked this off. Then what? What if they'd had a gun?"

"One of them had a knife." Lucas indicated his cut. "Not a problem."

Cody pointed behind Lucas at the open sliding door. "Get in. I'm taking you home."

Lucas nearly tumbled in, the drunk taking over again. He grabbed Cody's arm. His voice sounded younger, "Wait. I don't want… I don't want my parents to see me like this."

Cody looked down at Lucas' hand, then back to his 15-year-old face. "You can stay at my house tonight. Unlock your phone and Katie will text your parents." Indicating the blood, he added, "You're buying me a new shirt."

Lucas could only manage a smile, the tequila catching up with his 130-pound body.

"And no puking in my van," added Cody.

They got the girls home, Ariana silently furious the whole way home. Lucas did not vomit, half-sleeping the entire way. Luckily there was a gym towel to protect Cody's seat from blood.

Cody's mom was already in bed after a long double shift. Cody woke Lucas and got him into the shower. "I'm not doing this for you, so you'll have to undress and shower yourself. I have some PJ's that don't fit anymore. I'll leave them here, got it?"

Lucas nodded, only saying aloud, "Hey no mirrors in your bathroom. Oh, yeah, I remember now." He trailed off and Cody closed the bathroom door.

Lucas came out a while later and immediately crashed onto his bed. It was okay, Cody planned to sleep on the couch later. When Lucas was snoring, he pulled three cans of beer from his mini-fridge and headed to the living room. Cody knew how to hold his liquor. *I mean, it's just beer.* Cody felt it helped when he was alone. He was all alone now. In the living room, one beer drained and a second half empty, he propped up the mirror in front of him. It was only one-foot by one-foot square, but it would do the trick.

No longer afraid of the glass, since the elder he had seen in it was long dead, he gazed deeply. His reflection didn't stare back. Instead he saw other places: A dark field, a random room. *Maybe a dusty attic? Why would you be in an attic?* Somewhere. He couldn't be sure. He wasn't even sure how to use this ability, despite trying hard each night. He thought of one thing and concentrated, like a chant.

Dad, where are you?

CHAPTER FIVE

Planned Attack

The tree lined street was bathed in the warm light of streetlamps. Lines of cars were parked for the night on both sides of the quite residential street.

Victoria's windows fogged against the crisp night air. In the car, they broke, panting, searching for they own breath.

"Wow," said Zacke.

"What, too much for you?" asked Victoria, their bodies entwined in the back seat of her Toyota, she was currently on top but they'd switched positions a few times.

"Nope. But I mean, it's a Toyota. We're gonna get hernias back here." Zacke moved his arm around Victoria again.

"Don't worry about me, kid. You know we can't hang at my place. Too many roommates."

"Oh, yeah? A bunch of cougars at your place? I'm still underage, you know," Zacke smiled.

"You're almost 17. I'm 18. Calm down. It's not like we've actually done anything yet anyway." Victoria rubbed her nose on his. "We could go to your place."

"No! I mean, respectfully, no. My brother's back and he and dad are at it all the time."

"Maybe we wouldn't be noticed sneaking in, then." Victoria kissed him, then sat up on the seat. "I like your dad." She pursed her lips, "Your brother Deke. Intense."

"Yeah, he's a lot."

"I don't think he likes me."

Zacke shrugged the best he could. "He's got a hang up about females."

"Misogynist?"

"Does that mean he doesn't like women?" Zacke smiled. "Or white girls?"

"Women!" Victoria poked him in the stomach, a recent ticklish discovery. "Wait, does he care that I'm white?"

"I don't know. He's angry, confused. Let's not talk about him." Zacke bent in for another deep kiss.

Victoria pulled back. "We could talk about your mom instead."

Zacke untangled himself, raising his knees and putting his feet on the floorboards.

"Or not. Sorry."

"Oww." Zacke felt on the floorboard. "What is...?" He withdrew a small device with two prongs sticking out. "Is this new?"

"Oh yeah, I just ordered it. It's my taser."

"For what?"

"For protection," she smiled. "I close the restaurant late sometimes."

Zacke couldn't imagine her using this thing. "That's why you use the buddy system to leave."

"I'm in management. I don't want to pay others to wait around for me while I forget the safe combo for the seventeenth time."

There was a knock at the window.

Zacke got a sudden flash. He turned around but it was just a homeless person near them.

"Shit. He scared me. Hold on." Victoria looked for her wallet but couldn't find it.

"Seriously?" asked Zacke.

"What? He's probably just hungry."

The side door opened, and the homeless man grabbed Victoria, pulling her out. She squawked as she left the car.

Zacke fumbled for his door handle, forgetting if it was high or low or where it was. He finally found it and jumped out, racing around the back of the car. He stopped. To his happy surprise, Victoria held her own. The man had dragged her out by the leg, where she'd landed on her butt. Now she was up and the man was groaning, bent over and holding his stomach. Her hands were raised, ready to punch, but Zacke guessed that she'd kicked the man in the privates. He looked at his own hand and realized he'd grabbed the taser.

The man grabbed for her weakly, but she swatted his hand away and kicked the man again. He went over, onto the pavement, still doubled over.

"In the gonads?"

"Gonads," she confirmed.

Zacke handed her the taser.

Victoria arched an eyebrow. "Not defending my honor?"

"You're doing just fine," he held up his own hands. He'd never used his strength in a fight. Zacke was afraid to, even to defend her. He reached for his phone. "I'll call the cops instead."

"No," she said sharply. She softened it with, "The guy is just confused. Let's go." She turned away, headed back to the driver's side.

The man grunted, his hoodie obscuring his face and he lurched for Victoria again. His arm shot out to grab her. Zacke caught it. "Bad move, man." Smoky anger tendrilled into his chest.

Victoria whirled, taser in hand. The man tried to move, pull back his arm, but Zacke held it like it was encased in cement. The man looked from Victoria to Zacke, frantic.

"I got this," Zacke said, staring at the man's hooded face, but Victoria got the message.

"Just don't kill the guy."

Zacke nodded and pulled the man closer. With his other hand he put it flat on the man's chest so he was almost stooped over it. He pushed. Zacke was careful to use a fraction of his talent.

The man let out a whoosh of air as he flew over two cars parked behind them. He bounced off of a third car's roof and landed out of sight.

Zacke looked after, seeing if the man would get up. He did. The hooded man popped up as if nothing had happened. He walked toward them again. Zacke said, "Get in. I'll stop him."

She stood and watched Zacke.

He saw the man was just about to scramble between cars. Zacke ran to the car directly behind Victoria's and pushed. The car slammed bumpers with the one behind and pushed the next car into the man, pinning his legs. The man yowled in pain.

Zacke stared down the man, making sure he couldn't get out. The man cursed and pulled, but he was stuck. Zacke didn't think he'd broken anything. He turned to Victoria. "You okay?"

"Yeah. Are you?" She analyzed what was in his eyes but wasn't sure.

"Let's go." He walked to the passenger door and looked back. The man looked like he was starting to unpin himself. Porch lights along the street were coming on.

As they climbed in and buckled up, Victoria looked back in the rear view. The man had got himself free. He stared after them as they sped away.

They both checked their mirrors. The man was limping toward them, but neither could see his face. Zacke had a sudden urge to bolt from the car and rip the guy's head off. He felt that urge when he pushed those cars. A flash came of his mother. *I will not become the demon she said I was.*

He glanced over to Victoria, who was constantly checking her mirrors. Zacke put his hand on Victoria's leg. "You sure you're okay?"

"Yeah. I'm fine. You? What were you thinking when you did that with the cars?"

He couldn't tell her. He said the only version of the truth he could, "I was thinking of you."

She gave a smile and squeezed his leg.

Zacke was not okay. Anger swirled in his chest. He looked in the side mirror but could no longer see the man. *They didn't come for me. They tried to hurt her.* John said that their houses were safe from attack, *what would stop them from attacking my dad, brother... Victoria?*

He squeezed her hand. "Just keep that taser close, okay?"

She nodded.

The anger changed to cold fear. *I have so much to lose now.*

CHAPTER SIX

Long Hidden

Julien Aarden cut a classic figure of an industrial man. His lithe, strong masculine frame was not overly tall at 5'9", but he was surely in command of any room he entered. He wore tailored white shirt and gray slacks. His shoes were black leather, though no one could tell as they were covered in fine white dust at the moment.

A black folding notebook in hand, he held onto his hardhat against the stiff breeze. Overlooking Sea Valley, Julien smiled at the gorgeous view. Though it was different in many ways from his Belgium homeland, he overlooked the valley from his small mountain and saw only the similarities. Cityscape beneath, framed by rolling hills in front and behind, and the purple mountains looming behind the hills.

Julien came back to reality when the vibration stopped. He pulled out his earplugs and swiveled to look behind him. He listened. Nothing. The secession of vibration to a miner is as jarring as a sudden noise to a civilian.

"Mr. Aarden," called Steve, the site manager, "You need to see this, sir."

Julien put his sunglasses back on and trudged through the swirling, fine white powder. "Something interesting?" asked Julien.

"We think so, yes," answered Steve, leading him to the edge of a deep slice in the mountain.

Julien peered down. "A crevasse." It was not a question, though Steve took it as one.

"Yes." Steve nodded. "A deep one. We won't know until we send spelunkers down, sir. That could take a while. We have the gear back at HQ but getting qualified divers here might take a while. I know some guys in Santa Helena, but they are usually booked solid this time of year."

Julien smiled. "I'll go down."

"Sir, we... we don't know how far down this goes. You know the diatomaceous earth could collapse. Too risky."

Julien put a hand on Steve's arm. "I'm a world class diver and spelunker, my friend. I was in Neptune's Caves back home when you were in diapers. Please have the gear retrieved."

"There's also the protocols, Julien." He couldn't whisper on the hillside, but only a few other men were around, so he spoke so only they could hear. "If there are Chumash artifacts down there, this could get messy quick. Proper authorities need to be called."

"Of course. You have my word they will be notified if Native American items are found. *If* there is anything down there, at all." Julien smiled his black-tie-event smile. "I don't get much chance at adventure, my friend. Allow me this, oui?"

"I suppose. I better clear this with the boss." Steven turned away from Julien.

"If you must." Julien smirked.

He turned back to Julien. "Is this okay with you, boss?"

"Oui. Yes. Once again, it is good to be the king."

Steven smiled and called on his radio for the cave diving supplies. Shortly, a truck pulled up the path with nylon rope, harnesses, LED flashlights, and a lighted helmet to replace Julien's standard hardhat, along with a mask to filter out any fine diatomaceous silt. He kept his spelunking backpack with him at all times, ready for this moment. *It is finally here*, he thought.

"Take this, too," said Steven, "the two-way walkie is good for 2000 yards."

Julien made a tisking sound. "You mean 914 *meters.* I would change company policy on this archaic Imperial measurement business..."

"But us good old American yanks would revolt and throw your waffle eating company out on its ear."

Julien laughed. "No respect. Is waffles all my beautiful Belgium is known for?" He put on his filtered mask.

"Around here, yep," said Steven as Julien was lowered down, still smiling behind his mask.

Julien turned on his helmet light and focused on discovery. The crevasse was shaped like a broad sword, the walls like a tapering blade as he got deeper. The light from above disappeared quickly, like a setting sun. He looked down, to judge how far he'd gone. 20 feet (6.09 meters – he did the conversion in his head), 30 feet, 40. He paused and held a handheld LED light downward. At least another 20 feet, maybe more.

He continued down and the walkie came to life, deafening in the silence, "You okay Julien?"

He paused and fumbled for the walkie. "Yes, about halfway to the bottom, I'd guess."

The walls made a dull sound that cavers know well. It could mean anything: natural shifting, a reaction to a new factor in the space like himself, or a cave-in about to happen. He smiled. How cruelly ironic a cave in would be here, now.

55 feet, 60, 63. The crevasse was getting thinner, coming to the point of the sword. At 67 feet (his gauge read 20.42 meters), his feet touched bottom. There was not much room to move. He was only four inches from the wall in front of him, perhaps six behind him. He'd been in tighter squeezes. A chill ran through him as he surveyed this space.

He shined his handheld light in all directions and was met will only large veins of white diatomaceous earth. There were a few outcroppings to his right, so he headed there. He tugged on his line for more rope and got a few feet's slack.

Steve's voice cracked in, "You aright, boss? Any trouble?"

"Fine. Fine. Just hit bottom. Going for a short walk."

"I'm getting pretty nervous up here."

"All is well." Julien said, and shone his light over a new texture in the wall. Leather.

He wondered if an old wagon had tumbled down here too, maybe a sack of dry beans. He smiled at the thought of old west artifacts. That would make a good cover story.

He pulled the cloth, but it wouldn't budge. He knew this was no Chumash Indian artifact. He tugged again and it moved a little.

He shone his helmet light on the cloth and pulled harder. The corner of the leather bag came loose in a rush of white dust. As he pulled, the corner of the bag revealed a hood. As he tugged harder, the bag opened and the skull inside flashed white as it tumbled out.

He started through his dust mask as the bag of bones tumbled to the sword-like crevasse floor. White dust splashed up like a cloud and covered him, reburying the pile of bones. On top of the bones was a leather satchel, winched tight.

It was still intact, well preserved by the silt. Like a fossil, he thought. But this was no fossil. This had been a person, a woman. A woman someone loved, and who had loved fiercely. He closed his eyes and gave a moment of respect for the bones. Then he gathered what he could find of the remaining skeleton and shoved them into a bag he'd brought. He would rebury the bones where no one would ever find them, in a private solemn ceremony just for the two of them.

Glints of gold shone immediately. These were mostly metal things, some horn and bone and one ancient book. *Everything is here.*

Unable to help himself, Julien burst into tears. He wasn't sure if it was for the woman, or the long time that had passed since anyone had seen these things. Or for what finding them meant for the future. They were wonderful things. They were hope. At last. At last, it was time to act.

CHAPTER SEVEN

Boy, Lost

"Ugghhh." Lucas awoke to a bed that wasn't his. He tried to look around, but it felt like a small gold brick had been smashed just behind his eyes, still smashing for that matter. He opened them anyway. A new sensation took him. "Ahhhh. What died in my mouth?"

Fighting the weird headache, he got up anyway and realized he was in Cody's house. The small plastic license plate on the wall announced "California CODY" proving he needed no detective skills. He found the bathroom, annoyed there was no mirror. *Oh, yeah, of course Cody would have no mirrors.* Lucas washed his face and slowly realized Cody had given up his own bed for him. *That isn't like Cody. Or is it? We don't really hang out. Where is he, anyway?*

What happened last night? Just then, Lucas sucked in air, feeling along his right side. A long bandage was there. He peeled it back carefully, revealing a line of congealed blood. He cursed again at the no mirror thing.

Elgisard? What happened?

Fighting and liquor, came the mental reply.

He wasn't sure if his warrior was sharing his memories, or if the memories were filtering back naturally. He still wasn't sure how this really worked, but they came back alright, all at once.

Lucas started to remember. *Fight Night. Blood. Tequila. Oh Shit.*

Elgisard rallied Lucas, *We did well. You should be proud.*

Three of them pulled knives.

You disarmed all three, Elgisard reminded.

Lucas touched his bandage and winced.

Well, you did... eventually.

Oh, we have a new honor, a grand title – Campion de Wedo.
Know what it means?
Lucas did. *It means champion of the white boys.*
Never learned Spanish.
Didn't get along with the moors.
I don't think it was meant as a compliment.
Why did you drag me there?
As I keep saying, we are one.
The decisions are made together.
You wanted to go as well.
And the tequila?
Well...
Uh huh.
We couldn't refuse our hosts!

Lucas shook his head, which was a bad idea. The gold brick smashed inside his head again. He swore never to drink Ever. Again. That made him think of Cody. *Where is he?*

Lucas looked around for a shirt but couldn't find one that didn't belong to Cody. Thankfully, he still had PJ pants on, though they weren't his. He spotted his bloody clothes in a pile.

He passed by an open door, presumably Cody's mother's room. The bed was made and light strewn in through the window. He continued onto the living room, where he finally spotted Cody, but just the back of his head. Cody was seated at a coffee table in front of the couch, staring at a black screen. "Hey, Cody?"

No answer.

Lucas came around the back of the couch and was startled to see Cody's eyes open. He stared at his black screen. Lucas looked over and realized it wasn't a screen. Propped up in front of Cody like a picture frame was a mirror about the size of Cody's face. There was no reflection. It was cold black nothingness.

A tingle zipped down Lucas' spine, but it quickly warmed to curiosity. Cody had recounted a few things about his mirror viewing, even the story of how he'd gone through the mirror into Elder Zamma's lair, but he was short on details.

Lucas stared at the glass, which wasn't glass. It was solid black, but for a second, he thought he saw a wisp of cloud or... something. He heard something, too. He thought it might be a sound coming from Cody's cell phone, then remembered Cody couldn't have electronics – that weird zapping ability of his. Lucas leaned in, listening to the mirror. It sounded like wind. Wind through a...

Cody's hand smashed the mirror flat, shattering the mirror. Breaking glass cut short the ghostly sound.

Lucas' head jerked to look at Cody.

He didn't see Lucas – Cody was looking at something else, beyond him, through him. A tear ran down Cody's cheek. He whispered, "I can't find him. Where is he? I can't find him."

Lucas didn't know what to do. He started to speak, then noticed the deep lines around Cody's eyes, dark bags under both. Cody's face scrunched up, his eyes closing. Cody's hands covered his face. He began to sob. No words just sobs.

Lucas reached out to touch him, help him.

A guttural voice answered him, "Go. Just go."

Lucas began "But I..."

"Go!" shouted Cody, his arms now wrapped around his eyes, the sobs convulsing his body.

Lucas slowly backed away, left out the front door and walked home.

* * *

Zacke woke from an unpleasant dream of homeless guys in hoodies chasing him. There were too many of them and his strength was gone. He couldn't fly. Randomly, his mom was there, shouting. He couldn't see her clearly, but Zacke felt her just out of sight. He couldn't see the homeless guys' faces, just felt them grabbing at him from all sides. No escape.

As his mind focused on reality, he realized it was Deke and his dad yelling. It came filtered through his wall. Wait, nope. Just Deke was yelling.

Through the walls, Zacke heard, "I don't need this. Who are you to talk, anyway?"

He couldn't hear his dad's voice clearly. He must be talking in calmer tones.

Deke: "You don't want me here, that's cool."

More reasoned tones, an undistinguishable low humming.

"I got friends. They..."

Response.

"They are my friends. What do you know?"

Zacke walked down the hall, the opposite way from the predictable fight. Deke had never moved out, exactly. But he'd only wandered back to the house in recent weeks sporadically, after months of absentee partying with "friends," mostly out of town.

Zacke brushed his teeth, thinking of putting ear buds in to drown out the fight. About to hop in the shower, he finished his teeth and started the water for the hot shower.

Deke's howls got louder, but he couldn't hear the words anymore. Witnessing plenty of recent fights, he knew that when his dad got more reasonable, Deke got louder. It drove Deke crazy. Zacke smiled, sadly. He wondered if Deke missed the old days when dad's drinking fueled a tennis match of shouts. Dad's recent sobriety had thrown Deke off balance, maybe even thrown an unwanted mirror up to Deke's behavior.

Mirror. Window.

Zacke felt he was being watched. He pulled the shower curtain back, checking the window for hooded homeless guys. The glass was frosted, but he saw no shapes looming in the morning sun.

He glanced at the mirror. He didn't have Cody's abilities, but after the crazy story Cody told him, it would make anyone paranoid. Nothing. Just a steamed over mirror. Still, the feeling persisted. He thought of all the jump scares in horror films where you turn around and there is a monster right behind you. There wasn't. He was in a very small bathroom with a shower, toilet, and sink. He looked around anyway. Nothing. He still couldn't shake the feeling.

Someone was watching.

* * *

Katie and Ariana stood in the clearing. Katie knew her stepdad Jason was doing his ranch chores, but this copse of trees stood at the outside of their property, shaded from prying eyes. At least, she hoped so.

The fallen tree at the center of the clearing was perfect. Along the dead trunk, Ariana placed the last of the assorted bottles. She placed the small hot sauce bottle at the end of the line.

"Thanks Ari. I appreciate the help training."

"No problem." Ariana mused, "I like Ari. No one else calls me that."

"It suits you." Katie concentrated on the bottles. "Which one should I try first?"

Ariana eyed the rows of plastic and glass bottles. "We're trying for control, so I think you should lift the largest, and try to shoot the smallest, maybe float the middle one"

"So, lift the largest, float the middle one across the field and shoot the smallest. Got it."

Ariana stood behind Katie's shoulder as she placed a shield bubble around the largest bottle, a liter jug of water. Unlike most of the other friends, Ariana could see the color of each shield. "Why green?"

"Huh? Oh yeah, you can see them." Katie scrunched up her face. "Umm. Green feels the... easiest, most natural."

"Not the strongest?" asked Ariana.

"No." She continued to the next bottle, a glass root beer bottle. "I'm still trying to figure it out. Blue is like for stronger things – if I want to put a shield around a door, for example – a barrier? I use blue shields. Yellow feels right for organic things. Like if a guy was chasing me, I'd wrap him in a yellow shield."

"How do you know that?"

Katie thought, but had no answer. "I wish I knew. That Derek jerk called me Zhanna at the Mission, remember, that night with the spiders? In that moment, I had a rush of memories. I felt her inside me, like it was me."

That reminded Ariana of the flash from last night, seeing through Lucas' eyes. *Or maybe that warrior jerk*, she thought angrily of Lucas' ancient.

"But since then I can use the shields – they are stronger, too. But no other memories."

"Any dreams?" asked Ariana.

"No bad ones. Why? You having dreams?"

"Not really." Ariana said, and even believed it herself. What she had lately didn't feel like dreams. Not exactly.

Katie continued, "I thought when John said we were nearly activated, that the answers would just come." She lifted the second bottle and hurled it forward, out of sight.

"At least you know you are an ancient. I still have no idea what my abilities are, or what they mean."

"Yeah, so you freeze things, right?" said Katie. "Anything else?"

"No!" Ariana said with too much force. "Yes. Kind of. Things freeze in midair, but only for a minute, then unfreeze. What good is that? And nothing else except that weird make-people-throw-up thing I did a few times."

"Hmm. You also do that hub thing," offered Katie.

"I guess. I don't even know how I linked us over the fire tower, not really." Memories flooding in of how it felt, the connection they all shared through minds and bodies. "It felt so natural, once I saw all of our minds, the way to connect us..." The memories clouded, like a mental fog just rolled in. She growled in frustration. "Then it just slips away. I just wish John was here. He has a lot more explaining to do."

"I know. And David's missing too. Cody's doesn't say anything, but I'd be super pissed if my dad left again after everything that happened." That caused a twinge in Katie. How long since she'd seen her real dad? Talked to him, even? *Since my last birthday?*

"Okay, Chica. Focus." Ariana pointed, "Last bottle."

"Shoot it, right?" Katie smiled. She looked at the tiny hot sauce bottle and had a better idea. She spied the other bottle lying on the ground. She put a shield around each one and they floated together. The empty hot sauce bottle floated up too, then they all joined together. Ariana noticed the colors replaced by a dark sphere.

"What happened?"

"Nothing. Black shield. The hardest one of all. I imagine all the color strengths layered together.At that tree over there." Katie pointed behind her, not even looking, sure of her aim.

Ariana followed her finger, then yelled, "Katie, wait!"

The bottles were already moving as one, nearly faster than Ari's eyes could track. Ariana flung out her hand, instinctively, and the bottles froze. There was no visible shield around them, but as Katie swung her head, she saw a distinct shimmer around the bottles, like a rising heat wave. It formed a perfect circle and was suspended right in front of Megan's face.

"Hey!" Megan shouted, putting up her hands instinctively, then realized the bottles were inches from her face, frozen.

Katie had nearly slammed them into her little sister's face.

"Megan!" shouted Katie. She dropped the shimmering sphere straight down, where all three bottles crashed into the hard-packed dirt. The plastic bottle jumped as the glass ones shattered.

Megan stood frozen. Both girls ran toward her.

"Megan!" shouted Katie, just reaching her. "Are you okay?"

"Yeah. Look where you're throwing, sis," said Megan.

"I'm so sorry. I..." Katie thought fast. "Yeah, crazy for me to throw those three bottles at once. You probably didn't even see me pick them up..."

"I know you have powers, Katie." Megan crossed her arms. "Duh."

"What? No. Powers? Crazy! What do you mean?" Katie sputtered, hearing how she sounded. Even she wouldn't believe herself.

"What are your powers?" Megan turned to Ari. "You freeze things, or what?"

Ariana did an exact imitation of Katie's bad lying. "Come on, Megan, don't be silly."

Katie sighed, knowing her little sister sniffed out her lies as well as her mom did. "How long have you known?" Katie asked.

Megan's face scrunched up, thinking about stretching out the moment. Instead she blurted, "For months! It's been so hard not to ask like a million questions."

"I've been careful!" Katie was more annoyed her stepsister had figured it out than if a stranger did. "What tipped me off?"

"The snake you saved me from. The stadium. Something not right about that, but I don't think that was you. I've seen you do stuff around the house, too. You do stuff all the time. You're kinda lazy about it."

"Hey!"

"Closing doors, locking me out of the bathroom when I know that lock is *not* broken. I saw you float the saltshaker once."

"You saw that? Sneaky little monster," said Katie.

"Siblings see things," said Ariana, hands on hips, thinking of all her brothers, "like sneaky security cameras,"

Katie asked, "Mom knows, doesn't she?"

"Yes," Katie blurted, "I mean no."

"You are such a bad liar." Megan shook her head.

Katie looked in Megan's eyes. "You can't tell anyone."

Megan replied, "I know! Again, duh."

"Wait. Do you hear something? A buzzing sound." Ariana looked around, through the trees. "Katie, Megan? Does your dad use a drone on this ranch?"

"No. Why?" Katie pivoted to see what Ariana saw.

Ariana pointed to a drone flying away from them. Katie threw some shield balls at it, but it was too far away. Soon it was out of sight, taking the buzzing sound with it.

Ariana said, her voice rising, "That isn't good. If it recorded everything..."

43

Katie was already ahead of her, dialing Zacke.

"Wow, she's calling someone? On her phone?" Megan reasoned. "This must be serious."

"Hey Zacke. We need to meet. No, not over the phone. Can you gather the others? Yeah, we'll meet at Lucas' room."

Ariana thought of the good luck they'd had. No one had bothered them in over two months since the battle at the fire tower. If the Rageto were watching them the whole time, they were just waiting for the right moment to strike.

Katie and Ariana exchanged glances. They'd agreed as a group to keep any stray thoughts to themselves until John and David came back.

But they were both thinking the same thing.

They would never be truly safe ever again.

CHAPTER EIGHT

Challenge Accepted

Back in Lucas' room, everyone shared what they knew.

"A drone? Are you sure?" asked Lucas.

"Yeah, but it got away," answered Katie.

Zacke put it together. "I felt like someone was watching me at my house, too."

"John said we're safe in our houses, right?" Ariana asked. "Like ingrained protection, or something? I've been depending on that."

Cody reasoned, "I guess they can still watch from the outside."

"Who are they?" Katie asked, with a shiver. "That Elder lady?"

"Or her henchmen," said Ariana, "her, I don't know... minions?"

Katie smiled as she thought of a cartoon banana with one eye. Then she remembered how they all nearly died on that tower. That was just two Rageto agents. *If there are more watching...*

"How many Rageto are there?" asked Megan.

"Why is she here?" asked Cody.

"First, rude," said Katie, then continued, "Second, I told you, she saw us. She knows we have abilities. The little monster is smart. Plus, I'm kind of babysitting."

Megan stiffened at the old nickname little monster. She decided to focus on the smart compliment. "Do you guys know how many there are?"

They were silent. Nobody did.

"No. We don't," admitted Zacke. "Which means we need more information. Lucas, how's the project going?"

"Tricky," Lucas replied. "I've been searching, very carefully, for information on the Rageto and the Amartus. I'm a geek, but I'm not the stereotypical computer hacker. I've found vague hints and references going back to ancient Samaria, but nothing concrete. The Amartus and Rageto – both sides have hidden themselves really well, like spooky well. I've found out more stuff about the Illuminati, which are not real, than what the River actually is."

"What about the Sect?" asked Ariana.

"That's even worse. The word 'sect' is generic for so many things: ancient Christian cults, splinter groups of all kinds. Like every major historical movement has 'sects' from their main belief system. I've found nothing about the Sect that Pete belonged to."

They all paused. Not everyone had met Sect agent Pete, but those that did mourned his loss. He was killed by the brothers, Sazzo and Caron, before the battle on the beach.

Cody exploded. "Dammit! Where is John? Where's my dad? They promised to contact us. We're still in the dark. Every day!"

"And we have no idea who's hunting us." Zacke said, no answer for Cody.

A loud pop sounded and startled them all. A high-pitched sizzle erupted at the door to the outside. Lucas thought of the stormtroopers cutting through a blast door with lasers. He hoped Darth Vader wasn't coming through.

Green sparks washed the door, then it transformed into a shimmering green plate, like a chalkboard hovering where the door had been. They all instinctively grouped together, facing the eerie green rectangle.

Letters swirled into being.

Hello there, newbies.

Some of us have met before, but you may not remember, yet.

Each sentence swirled into existence, then disappeared as though wiped with an invisible eraser.

"What do you want?" asked Zacke.

Fly boy, right?

We want to talk. That's all.

"About what?" Cody took a step closer. "Who are you?"

Warriors. Champions.

But those are just titles. The names change.

Best we talk in person.

"To take our measure," said Lucas.

The Viking.

We missed you.

Heard you had a true death.

"Heard wrong."

Apparently.

Then come out to play.

All of you are invited.

The words disappeared and a map took its place.

The map was all glowing green lines, like vintage vector video game graphics. It was clearly of their city, with a glowing dot of bright green.

"Where is that?" asked Zacke.

Lucas answered, "Edge of town. The riverbed."

"Why there?" asked Cody.

Ariana asked the obvious. "Ambush?"

"Probably." Zacke got closer, studying the strange magical map, the size of Lucas' door. As he approached, a new message appeared –

See you soon.

Then it fell away, like green sand sliding off. All that was left was Lucas' plain door.

"Okay, I know we aren't supposed to say this, but magic is cool," said Cody.

"Elgisard, does this magic look familiar?" asked Zacke. Lucas' ancient was always there, they all knew. But Zacke felt when he addressed the ancient warrior directly, Lucas' whole body changed.

Elgisard said, "Hmm. Might be Ansool. He always liked messing with your head. Or maybe Mellis. She likes to lure people into traps. Neither works alone."

"Why there, of all places?" asked Katie.

"Hmm." Ariana watched Lucas move as he retrieved his laptop. He moved like Lucas, but also like a confident man, much older. It was sometimes surreal when Lucas was so engaged with his warrior. It made her feel strange. She wasn't sure she liked it.

Lucas/Elgisard flipped open the laptop. "Well, it's secluded. That's obvious. Except for the homeless folks that wander around, there shouldn't be anyone there this time of day. I wonder if..." He clicked some more keys. "Yes. Look there. It's near an old line." He pointed to the maps on his screen.

They gathered around. There was a split screen, two open windows. One was a map of their modern area, a Google map. The other was the same area with a bunch of crisscrossing lines with strange names.

"What are those?" asked Katie.

"Ley lines," answered Lucas.

"Wait, aren't those like a myth?" asked Zacke. "I've read about ley lines in fantasy books and stuff."

"No, they're real." Lucas traced his hand over the lines for emphasis. "They run all over the world, mostly between ancient monuments and places of power. But I've seen maps of ley lines that go all over the place, no rhyme or reason."

Silence.

"That's it?" asked Cody.

Lucas shrugged.

Cody sighed. "Why do we get the one ancient that never read a book?"

"Hey!" said Katie. "Not cool. Do you know anything about ley lines, smart guy?"

"No!" Cody said, "But I haven't lived like two thousand years either."

Elgisard laughed through Lucas. "Not quite that old, but it's true. I'm a fighter, not a scholar. Lucas is the brains here." Lucas spoke, "And I've only heard of ley lines from fantasy books, too."

Ariana ignored the odd bisected response and asked, "Do you know how these ley lines work, at least?"

Elgisard shrugged.

"Great," said Katie.

"I mean, I know that some Amartus and Rageto can travel along them." Elgisard said, "The Rageto by magic, I assume."

Zacke managed, "You assume."

Elgisard shrugged. "Most teams kept me around to break things. Sorry guys."

"We're not going, right?" Ariana asked. "This is obviously a trap."

"Of course it is, but don't we need to go?" asked Cody.

"We could be captured like Cody's dad," said Katie, "made to work for them."

Cody clenched his teeth at the mention of what his dad had been through. "They don't know what we can do."

"What about that drone? People watching you?" Megan said. "They probably know a lot."

"Smart kid," Katie said, smiling at her sister. "But, wait, they can use magic. Why would they use a drone?"

"That's true," Ariana answered, "but if not them, who is it?"

"Doesn't matter," Cody insisted. "Dad's missing, John's missing. If there's a chance they know something, we need to go!"

"Cody, I know. We all want answers," Zacke said. "But it's an obvious trick. We need information before we walk into their trap."

Elgisard picked up Lucas' phone. They were the same person, but it was clear there were still internal communication problems. "Of course, Lucas. Good idea." He said to himself as he opened his phone. "We know the terrain better than they do."

Cody nodded. "Home field advantage."

Lucas announced, "I have an idea."

The others gathered around his phone as he explained the strategy.

The Shifting Battle

The Santa Innes riverbed was bone dry. The dusty, snaking trail was once full of fresh water for the area around Sea Valley. Then the dam was built. Thirteen miles east was the Gibraltar-Bradbury Dam, and the large lake beyond its massive concrete structure. The lake was now the local place for camping, fishing and most of the local water supply. The dam that stood at the gateway only let water into the dusty riverbed when overcapacity. With a history of California droughts, the bed had been bereft of water for years.

Sea Valley was built around this old river and had three bridges over it where the snaking river cut into the city – one on each end of town and the other near the center. The riverbed curled in and around Sea Valley, mostly hugging the outer edge. Now it was filled only with sand and miles of scrub brush.

The ley line location was just north of the first bridge on the north edge of town. They decided to approach it from half a mile from their green "X" on the map.

Katie, Cody, and Lucas walked through the dusty bed, now only a few hundred feet from their meeting place. They spotted the Rageto warriors right away. There were two, standing dramatically in the center of the riverbed. The sides of the empty river climbed up twenty feet on each side, framed by scrub grass and wispy bushes. Not many places to hide.

The teens walked confidently toward the Rageto warriors.

The two men seemed confident too, both in their early to mid-twenties. One was dressed in a black suit, white shirt, and razor thin tie. He wore sunglasses. Katie thought he might be auditioning for a Matrix reboot. Cody eyed the other one, standing to the Matrix man's right, sweating. He was short and wore a constant smirk. His eyes kept sweeping over all of them, his eye glancing skyward occasionally. Cody wondered if their strategy might be compromised. They barely took notice of Lucas, the thin wisp of a teen, bringing up the rear.

The teens got to just fifty feet away and stopped in the sand. Short man spoke first, "Where are the rest?"

"We could ask the same," Katie said. "You didn't bring just two, did you?"

"Yeah, didn't go well with just two of you last time," finished Cody.

Matrix man shot them a nervous look. Maybe the fact that they'd defeated the infamous brothers had rippled through the Rageto. Cody hoped so. Matrix scratched his wrist. Cody noticed what looked like a cell phone in his hand. Probably a signal for the others to pounce. Perfect.

"That's close enough," said the Matrix-wannabe.

Katie and Cody stopped.

Lucas didn't. He walked to Cody's right, flanking. "What's the plan? Snatch us? Fight us here? Tell us what you want."

"Stop there," said Matrix man.

Lucas didn't. He was only twenty feet away now. He cocked his head. "Hmm. New Birth? No..."

Matrix scratched his other wrist again but didn't answer.

Lucas smiled and motioned for Katie and Cody to join him. Elgisard was in full command now.

"Funny how the River decides our fates," Elgisard said. "Never the same, but sometimes the same thing comes through – maybe a mole in the same place on the face, life after life. Sometimes, a nervous habit that repeats. Always a hint."

Matrix stopped scratching his wrist.

Elgisard said, "Hello, Cimo."

Cimo glanced into Lucas but wasn't sure who he saw there. Lucas just smiled.

Cody asked, "We asked a question. What do you want?"

"Our Elders have a message," said Cimo, glad to have his focus off the small one with the bold words.

"Join us, or die? We've heard that one before," said Katie.

"Dissemble – or we kill everyone you love."

"Dissemble?" asked Katie. She wasn't even sure what the word meant, certainly not in this context.

"Never," growled Elgisard.

Cimo looked over all three, the clear confusion on Katie and Cody's faces. "You mean…" Cimo laughed, "we suspected you didn't know *everything*, but they didn't explain your options?" The man laughed again. The small man joined him, but his eyes kept darting between them.

The laughter trailed off. The small man said, "You are in real trouble, newbies."

Elgisard clarified to his friends, but stared at his foes, "It means deny the warrior, live outside the struggle."

"We can do that?" asked Katie.

"I can't," said Cody, anger flaring, thinking of his father.

"Too bad," Cimo said, "that means we get to kill your families." He looked at Katie. "We'll start with Megan."

Katie flinched.

He continued, "Then your parents, Lucas."

Elgisard and Lucas growled together. The small man stopped smiling.

"Then your mom, Cody," finished Cimo.

Cody went white hot. Rage flooded his system. *You took my dad. I will not let you take my mom.*

Katie's system flooded with fear. *They have been watching us.*

The small man touched his phone. Cody shot a curtain of electric air at them both. The cell phone sparked. The man dropped it like a firework had gone off in his hand. Cimo was knocked back a step.

Katie followed the plan and made a shield bubble around the men. They couldn't see the bubble shield around them but felt the air pressure change. They banged on the walls to break free.

Lucas pulled out his retractable batons but kept them collapsed. Scanning the area for more Rageto, he thrust his right hand in the air, the signal for Zacke.

Ariana ran to join her friends from her hiding spot.

Airborne, Zacke flew from behind the Rageto men. He lifted the two inside Katie's bubble, straight up into the air. Ten feet, twenty, thirty. The sudden rise made the two collapse onto the bubble's floor. They clung to the invisible floor like giant hamsters in a wheel. They tried to stand, but Zacke shook the bubble. "Where are the rest?"

Cimo began to speak, a spell. Zacke shook the bubble, "Wrong answer. Where are the rest?"

They went silent. Zacke stopped, floating in place, the bubble above his head.

"Still no answers?" With no warning, Zacke let the ball roll off his hand. He caught Cimo's terrified eyes as the ball fell. The screaming began as they dropped straight down.

Both men pushed at the walls of the bubble, screaming. It was no use. The men plummeted. The earth loomed but suddenly Zacke's hand shot out to the side of the bubble and pushed hard. Instead of smashing into earth, they careened horizontally. The sudden change in lateral force punched into Cimo's stomach. It gave way. The inside of the bubble was covered in Cimo's lunch, coating both men.

Just then, the bubble disintegrated, and the two men tumbled to the sand, flipping like drunk acrobats. Cimo's vomit made the sand stick to them. The small man got to his feet, shakily. His voice squeaked, "Amartus scum." Then he began speaking another language, another spell.

"Ariana. Now," shouted Lucas.

She put her hands out and the little guy froze in place.

Just then, the teens felt the world *move*. It felt like the air around them was grinding.

Lucas thought it was an earthquake at first, and he spun around to look for Caron. He knew he was dead, of course, but as he spun Lucas spotted another person – a teenage girl he hadn't seen before. *Where did she come from?*

The world moved again. Not an earthquake, but it shook their bones. The sound was awful, low and guttural and vibrated through all of them. Cody looked down. The earth wasn't spinning. It felt like the air around them was.

Lucas remembered the maps he studied earlier. "Step back!" he ordered.

When they didn't move, Lucas got in front of his friends, pushing them all back a few feet. The Rageto men also scurried father away from them.

Elgisard kept pushing his friends back, away from the strange movement.

Ariana got a flash. She saw through John's eyes, just for a second. He sprang to his feet... then the vision was gone. She shook her head. *Wishful thinking. We need to save ourselves.*

The world cranked again, the air pressure like stone grinding stone. Lucas was sure it was the girl across the sandy field doing it. He flicked his hands and the twin black baton extended.

"Wow," said Ariana, though no one could hear her. Cody saw the colors, too. A wall of shimmering colors, like the world in front of them was a painting and the colors were smearing horizontally, colorful reality blurring and grinding.

The grinding was slowing, coming into focus, the color fading.

Dad! Cody got a flash, saw his father. He was screaming. Cody ran at the wall of color.

The grinding slowed again. Katie blinked. Cody was gone, winked out. In his place stood four new warriors.

They stared at the teens and smiled.

CHAPTER TEN
Attack

Ariana's teeth ached. The grinding, reality shifting still danced across her nerves. She shook it off and focused. She looked left and right for Cody. He was just gone.

The new warriors stood before them, three men and one woman.

"Children, children. Never stand that close to a ley line when one is active. Anything can happen." This came from the tallest of the newly arrived warriors. "My name is Pyken." He jerked his thumb to the woman who'd moved the world, far behind him, "That young lady is…"

A howl of rage rang out. It startled Pyken, who spun to face the new player.

The young woman screamed, but stopped abruptly. Her head rolled away as her body fell to the sand.

Shocked by the sudden act of violence, Ariana her hand shot to her mouth. The warriors were shocked too. Pyken said, "Who is that? Get him!" The man to his left obliged, as did Cimo, still covered in puke and sand.

The newly arrived warrior, holding a sword at the ready, ran for Pyken. He was a black man in his thirties.

Zacke yelled, "John!"

The Rageto warrior that got to John first pulled his gun and fired. John's sword moved so fast he either knocked the bullet away or dodged it. Zacke couldn't tell.

John charged the man. Before he got off another shot, John had run him through the chest with the sword. The man fell to the sand.

Zacke didn't wait. He flew straight into the tall man at the center. Pyken was facing away, toward John. Zacke slammed into Pyken's back and flung his arm around the man's waist at the same time. Zacke smiled at the yowl of surprise. He didn't stop, but curved into the air, lifting Pyken straight up. He flailed his arms and legs, but the g force was on Zacke's side. Pyken's back arched into Zacke until they were thirty feet in the air.

Then Zacke unlooped his arm and just stopped in midair.

Pyken's momentum kept going up. He pulled away from Zacke and flew another few feet up over him.

To Zacke's surprise, the man twisted in midair just as gravity pulled him earth bound again.

How did he do that? Zacke wondered as they faced each other, Pyken falling fast at Zacke.

Pyken's face changed to a hard snarl.

Zacke froze.

Pyken's arms stretched out, his fingers becoming bright points of light. The light stretched out, like bright snakes reaching for the teen.

Zacke let himself fall back, hoping the free fall could outrun whatever was coming at him. The bright fingers of light left images on his eyes that disoriented him, like looking at the sun. Zacke covered his eyed as he fell straight down, his back to the ground, falling fast. He didn't know how close the ground was, but instinctively knew he didn't want these things to touch him. He felt a sizzle as one passed close to his face, like angry hornets of light.

One landed on his left arm and stuck. Before he could claw at it, another landed on his chest. They both exploded at once. It blew him harder toward the ground. He twisted around, all the way until he was facing down. Zacke plummeted toward the sand. He pushed back but was only able to soften the landing. He landed face down in the sand. It was not as soft as he hoped.

Three of the new warriors had surrounded John. Katie had thrown small shield balls at all of them. John was in close proximity, at the center of the fight, but they all kept shifting around.

Most of the shield balls missed. The woman warrior must have felt the ball whiz by and turned to face her attacker. She ran at Katie and started shouting, probably a spell. Katie let a volleyball sized shield ball fly. It slammed into the woman's shoulder, comically spinning her like a human tornado. She fell to the ground. John leaped and stabbed her.

Lucas was engaged with another Rageto warrior, apparently winning.

Ariana had frozen Cimo in place again. She ran for Zacke. The clump that was Pyken laid in her way. She ran around him. A hand shot out. Pyken grabbed her ankle hard. She tumbled over into the sand, but his grip held. A howl sounded near her and John's blade went through Pyken into the sand below him. His grip loosened.

Ariana saw John, covered in blood. "Help him," said John, pointing to Zacke. She stumbled over to Zacke a few feet away.

Ariana reached Zacke. He didn't move. She shook him hard. "Zacke!" He laid on his stomach. She turned him over. Blood covered his arm and chest. It looked like his t-shirt had exploded. It was in shreds, his chest wound a bloody mess. More blood coated his arm, the same wound there. It looked like something had taken bites out of him. She didn't know what to do. She froze Zacke. He stopped bleeding, at least for a moment.

She looked around to the others. Katie ran toward Ariana. There was a Rageto warrior chasing her. She could see he was saying something, but she couldn't hear what. A look of surprise overtook him as he stumbled forward, crashing into the sand. John stood over him. Ariana saw the slash in the man's back, as he turned to face John. As John stalked toward him, the man raised his hand. John gave him a matching hole in his front. Ariana shut her eyes tightly. She'd never seen this side of John.

Lucas ran at Cimo. The man panicked, talking to himself, probably a spell. Lucas shouted in rage as he neared the small man. His batons fully extended, Lucas lifted one arm to swing down, but stopped and held the sides of his head instead.

Blue lines appeared next to Cimo. They stretched until they formed a square of glowing blue outlines, a gateway. A dark void filled the square. Cimo stepped into it. Lucas stopped holding his head, Cimo's spell broken.

The small man had hung back, observing the battle. He stepped in the gate too. Blue lines, like living electric vines, shot out to each of the bodies. They wrapped around arms or legs and pulled the bodies into the gate.

Out of the three in the first wave and the four warriors in the second wave, only Cimo and the small man left the battle alive. All that was left was a trail in the sand where the bodies had been dragged to the gate. And drying blood. The gate collapsed into two blue lines, then those winked out.

Zacke unfroze. He screamed, the pain ripping through him. He tried to hold his two wounds, but it seemed to hurt more when he touched them. John arrived by Zacke's side. He spoke to Katie, "Call an ambulance."

"What? John, are you sure? How will we explain?"

"Ambulance, Katie. Now! These wounds won't heal on their own. Tell them it was..." He looked around at the terrain, saw all the Rageto blood. "A mountain lion attack."

Katie didn't know if that would work, but she was already dialing. John assessed the teens, all gathered around now. Lucas had streaks of blood in several places, not his own. Ariana was clean, just sweating, scared, and dirty. Katie seemed okay, at least unmarked physically.

John said, "Okay. Ariana, you and Katie stay with Zacke and wait for the ambulance. Tell them it was a mountain lion. It attacked out of nowhere. Tell them you think..." John's mind was whirling. "That it got some homeless people, but they ran off. That will explain all the different blood." John seemed confused, struggling, distracted. "Lucas, we need a safe place to clean up."

"What about Cody?" asked Ariana. "Where did he go?"

John shook his head. "Elsewhere." John didn't elaborate. "He should be fine."

Ariana looked to where Cody had vanished in front of them all. "Elsewhere? What does that mean?"

"There's no time. Zacke needs a hospital now. We're covered in several people's blood. Lucas, is there a car?"

"Yeah, Cody drove. Damn, he had the keys."

"Of course he did. We'll go on foot. This city isn't that big. We'll take side streets. Is your room safe?"

"Yeah, I guess." John shot him a serious look.

Lucas swallowed. "Yes."

"We just need to clean up," said John, scowling. "Then I'll form a plan. We have to go. Will you girls be alright with Zacke?"

"Should I freeze him again?"

John thought for a moment as Zacke cried out again. "I don't think it could hurt. Just don't let him be frozen when the ambulance arrives." It might have been a smart-ass comment under different circumstances. But it was no time for jokes. "I'll contact you later."

John assessed the scene. There was no time to clean up anything else. Luckily, most of the evidence had disappeared through the Elder's gate.

The only thing no one noticed was the woman's severed head, still in the bushes.

PART 2

"This fight is eternal
until the River changes."
- from the Sect Novel,
The Warriors Asunder

CHAPTER ELEVEN

Elder Plans

Cimo, and the small man kneeled on the hardwood floor in Ordway's giant ballroom. The pile of failed warriors laid in a heap just a few feet away.

"Thank... thank you for healing us, our esteemed elders," said Cimo.

Yarro stood over the remains of the others. He summoned an intense magical heat and the bodies glowed red, then became flecks of gray ash.

Ordway studied the floor. "You couldn't do that outside? Even magic won't get the stains out of those parquets." She turned to Cimo. "Explain."

He responded, "My elder, we met the teams for the trap, delivered your message. Baldina set the ley line in motion. The next team arrived as planned." He looked at the pile of ash. "They were waiting on the ley line near London. All positioned flawlessly."

Yarro chimed in, "And were bested by five teenagers."

Cimo winced. "Not exactly. There was another. He..."

"I was watching, imbecile," Ordway said. "I know there was another. Pentoss."

Cimo scratched his wrist nervously. "That was Pentoss? No wonder we..."

Ordway pointed to the pile of smoldering ashes. "Do I need to tell you to be quiet?"

Ordway turned to the small man. "Janus, what did you observe?"

"Pentoss attacked, cut off Baldina's head and slew several more. The flying boy took on Pyken and was injured."

"Zacke. Be precise." Ordway corrected.

"Zacke, yes. Pyken wounded him badly, I believe."

"Yet he lives. What else?" Ordway demanded.

"They did not seem activated, except for Lucas," Janus answered. "I know you think two are new births."

"You know what I think now, do you?" Her eyes flashed a dangerous blue.

"No, Elder Ordway." Sweat poured down Janus' brow. "I mean no disrespect. You have said you believed two are new births. I think you are right. The girl Katie wields the powers of Zhanna, but they are not fully activated. She appeared a teenaged girl the whole time."

Yarro said, "Good. That could be useful. What happened to the boy Cody? He left the field and I can't see him anywhere."

"I'm not sure." started Janus, "Cody disappeared when the shifting ended. I believe he was swept into the vortex of the Ley line."

"And because Baldina is dead," said Ordway, "he could be anywhere."

Janus agreed, "Yes. Since we didn't anticipate Pentoss, that may be how he arrived."

Silence hung in the air. The two Elders exchanged glances.

"If I may ask," Cimo shifted on his knees. "have you found Cody's father, yet? The one the brothers called the Witness?"

A cold blue gaze met Cimo's. "Not your concern. We three have another task for you."

"Three?" Cimo spun around, bad etiquette when kneeling in front of an Elder. He couldn't help it. He'd felt someone just behind him and was shocked to see another Elder standing there. Sorrento.

Ordway said, "Sorrento, these are the two that survived."

Sorrento asked, "Just these? Will they be enough?"

"No." Ordway stated. "We will add more warriors to the team."

"Begging pardon, your excellencies," Cimo felt Sorrento looming behind him. He looked straight ahead, facing the other Elders. He did not meet their eyes. "May we know the plan?"

"They refused our offer to Dissemble." Yarro smiled, but not with mirth. "Time to get personal and take some players off the board."

Sorrento added, "Now the fun begins."

CHAPTER TWELVE

Suspicion

Zacke couldn't focus his eyes. He closed them and tried to open them again. Each time they struggled open for just a moment. The world blurred, unfocused. The sounds that filtered in changed each time, like falling asleep watching a movie then waking up again. He finally forced his eyes open and thought the blur might be Katie, sitting in a chair.

The pain hit Zacke afresh. He felt on fire, like hot irons had scorched him. At first it felt all over, then he localized it to his chest and his arm. *What were those things?*

Katie sprung up. "Zacke!" She lowered her voice. "Zacke, they only let us in for a few minutes. You need to remember the story. Mountain lion."

"Is he awake?" a new voice entered the room. It sounded familiar. "Katie, why don't you wait in the lobby with your friend."

"I can stay." Katie offered. "Zacke's been through a lot. I want to be here for him."

"We have your statement. If I need anything, I'll call the nurse or the doctor."

Zacke recognized the cadence, all kindly business, but no BS. Officer Jack, Zacke's sponsor at the junior police explorer program. Zacke winced as he tried to raise himself up. "Hey, Officer Jack." Zacke tried to sound normal, but the pain was bad.

"Hey Zacke. Go ahead and lay back.," said Officer Jack, looking over Zacke's bandages. "You got banged up real good. Can you tell me what happened?"

Zacke's thoughts swam in a pool crashing into icebergs of pain. *What was the story?*

"It's okay. Take your time." said Jack. He noticed that the officer didn't sit or pull up a chair like a friend. This was official business. Zacke had a sudden clear memory of lying to Jack only a few months before. He reminded himself, *that was to protect everyone from what was going on. Nothing has changed.* "It was a mountain lion, Jack. I didn't even see it coming."

Jack nodded, obviously the story he'd heard before. "Were you near any bushes? Do you think it snuck up on you and your friends?"

Zacke heard the police question and reinterpreted it – Zacke, did a mountain lion really sneak up on three teenagers and single you out, in broad daylight, in the wide-open riverbed? He was tempted to tell Jack the truth, even if only to see his face: *You see, Jack, I had this guy about forty feet up in the air. I released him so he would come crashing down—probably to his death— but his fingers lit up and shot this white-hot crap at me that seemed to explode when it hit my skin. If burns like hell, by the way, and probably looks nothing like a cat scratch or bite. Do you buy it, Officer Jack, do you?*

Zacke shrugged instead.

Jack looked Zacke over. "I don't accuse without evidence, Zacke. You are a good kid and a good explorer. You will make a good officer one day." He shook his head. "But I know there's more going on than you're telling me."

"Zacke!" His dad rushed in. "I got here as fast as I could. What happened? They say a mountain lion attack? How do you feel? Crap, that was stupid... Oh, hi Officer Jack. Have they caught the mountain lion yet?"

Jack shook his father's hand. "No Oliver. Not yet." He looked at Zacke, pulling his father in close, a confidence of three. "Zacke is lucky. No one knows this yet, but we found a woman's head near the scene."

Zacke froze.

"What?" said Zacke's dad, Oliver. "Oh my God."

Officer Jack stared at Zacke. "Taken off so clean, it looks like a knife did the job. Must have been very sharp claws."

"That's awful." Oliver shook his head.

"The local press don't know yet. We want to keep it quiet until we can identify her. Even stranger..." Officer Jack looked into Zacke's eyes, "we haven't found the body yet."

Dad asked, "Wait. You mean, the mountain lion dragged it away?"

"We aren't sure. Just be glad your boy survived the *animal* that did this. Zacke, you have my number if you remember any details." Jack paused. "Anything could be useful to figure out what's going on here. Anything you want to tell me."

Zacke swallowed the lump in his throat. It wouldn't go down. He managed, "Yeah... will do, Officer Jack. Thanks."

Officer Jack nodded sadly and left.

Zacke's dad gently put his hand on his son's forehead. He did this whenever anything was wrong, like feeling for a fever was universal in all situations. Zacke closed his eyes. Whatever magic parents had, he did feel a little better. Then he heard the voice.

"Zacke?"

The sound hit his spine and froze it to the bed.

His dad squeezed his son's hand, then released it slowly, not wanting to disengage with Zacke to turn around to the door. Zacke saw his father's face frozen, turning toward the door.

The woman stood at the door, a vision in purple. She was dressed in dark purple dress suit and skirt below her knees. She wore a ruffled lace at the neck with a purple hat. Her skin was the same hue as Zacke's. His dad said nothing. Zacke finally spoke.

"Hi Mom."

CHAPTER THIRTEEN

Cosplay

"Doesn't quite fit, does it?" said Lucas.

John looked in the mirror. His bloody clothes were changed, tucked away in a bag he would dispose of later. He now wore a pair of corduroy pants that belonged to Lucas' dad. The shirt was Lucas'. John's short sword was attached to his back by leather strap. He made a strange sight as he checked himself in the mirror.

"It will have to do." John adjusted his sword strap. "I'll get clothes that fit at the nearest thrift store. I'll head there next."

Lucas thought of the woman's severed head and wondered if he should point out John's phrasing.

A knock sounded at the door from the connecting garage room and house. Before Lucas could answer it, it swung open into his converted room.

"Dad!" said Lucas, far too loud. His dad was in before Lucas could stop him. What he saw was his son with no shirt, actively changing standing next to a black man in his thirties in his son's very tight tank top. The man also had a sword swung over his back.

Dad didn't know where to begin. He looked over the strange man again. "Wait, are those my pants?"

Lucas quickly scanned around for any bloody clothes his dad might spot. Then Lucas realized how awkward the scene looked. He tried to think of a reason, any reason. Nothing came. Help me, Elgisard. The ancient inside stifled a laugh.

"Oh my *GOD!*" John rushed at Lucas' dad, hugging him. "Lucas has told me all about you. Hi dad!"

"He has?" he tried to get out of the hug and couldn't. "Who... who are you, exactly?"

"Oh my God! I'm Johnny." John released the hug and over gesticulated. "Lucas was a lifesaver – such a good friend! I was passing through town on the way to a comic book convention..."

"Sili-con." offered Lucas.

"Silicon – yes!" He motioned to the sword. "We share some interests. We like to dress up like our favorite characters."

"Cosplay," offered Lucas.

"We call it cosplay. And Lucas. Well, can you keep a secret?" John leaned in close to the dad's ear.

His dad looked baffled but nodded in agreement.

"I have a little... this is so embarrassing... I have a little," he took it down to a whisper, "a little irritable bowel syndrome. Anyway, I had an issue on the road and messaged my good online friend Lucas here. Oh! He saved me so much embarrassment." John indicated the bag full of his bloody clothes. Lucas was glad he chose a thick black lawn bag, instead of a white one from the kitchen. He could not have explained bloody clothes at this point.

John continued, "I promise when I get to my hotel..."

"In Simi Valley."

"Simi Valley. Exactly! Then I will launder these fine clothes and post them right back to you. I'm so sorry to borrow. I hope you understand how much a life saver Mr. Lucas here has been."

His dad just stared.

Lucas had nothing. Elgisard smiled inside, enjoying the awkward moment.

"He's a great kid," said Lucas' dad. Lucas couldn't tell if he's bought the story or not.

"He is!" John indicated his new "costume" and said, "Now all I need is a hood and I will go to the convention as my favorite comic book character..." John froze. He'd said too much and got stuck.

Dad looked at John expectantly. John smiled wide, but nothing came.

Lucas saw the sword strapped to John's back. "Deadpool, right?"

"Exactly!" John winked at Lucas. "Love that dead pool!"

"No problem. I'm glad Lucas could help." Dad turned to Lucas. "Son, are you okay?"

"Yeah, sure." Lucas wondered if he forgot a detail. "Why wouldn't I be?"

"I just saw it on the news." His dad elaborated, "A mountain lion attacked someone at the riverbed."

"Oh, that's awful." Lucas still scanned the room for anything he missed. "Did they say if the bo... if the *person* is okay?"

"They aren't releasing names. Said it was a minor, that's all. But you're okay?"

"Yeah, Dad. Thanks for checking. If I see any mountain lions..."

John objected. "Lucas! Don't be a smart aleck. Your dad is worried about you. My goodness, do you get a lot of mountain lions around here?"

"No, not really." Dad shook his head. "A few are spotted every year in the hills, but they never attack. Scary."

"Very! Well, I better be off. I need to get to that convention." John shook dad's hand, not too firmly. "Thanks again for letting your son help me. Bye now!" With that, John left out the side door.

His dad looked after him, saying nothing. He turned back to Lucas. "You sure everything is okay?"

"Yeah." Lucas panicked as he spotted a bloody sock peeking out from behind his dresser. "Dad, Let's go inside. I'm real hungry. I could eat a Kalakukko." The word slipped out. Lucas blanched. Elgisard said in Lucas' mind, *that sounds delicious.* He flashed an image of the delicacy.

"Okay," his dad laughed, "me too. What is that?"

Lucas shook his head and knew he couldn't answer that it was a Finnish dish, in essence a fish pie. "Sorry, I've been practicing with... my friend John. It's Klingon for pizza."

CHAPTER FOURTEEN

Travelling

Cody had no idea where he was.

There was still sand, much like the riverbed he'd been standing in, but this was more of a ditch. There was trash strewn all around him. As he breathed in, his breath caught. It felt like he was breathing fire. For a second, he though a bucket of warm water had been dumped on him, then realized he was sweating in sheets. *Is this... humidity?*

Cody had travelled all over the state with his mom. She'd tried to make his childhood as normal as possible, despite her many jobs and his dad's absence. The California desert was hot, but this felt nothing like that. He climbed out of the ditch and stared at the sun. "Bad idea," he said aloud, thrusting his hand to block the disc. He looked down and realized people were staring at him. As he scanned around, there were people everywhere. Some gave him dubious looks, most ignored him. He felt like a giant. Everyone he saw was much shorter than he.

He also saw a strange mix of buildings. In front of him were houses, very close together. The mix of architectural styles, even building materials, was jarring. Some of the houses looked more like shacks. Looking in the distance, modern skyscrapers loomed. He noticed everyone around him had brown skin. He wondered to himself *is that racist?*

It suddenly began to rain. But warm, not like California rain at all.

His first thought that he was in Mexico, then realized that might be racist too. He wiped his brow, but the sweat kept coming. His t-shirt was sopping wet even before the rain started.

Then the rain stopped, just as abruptly as it started.

An older man passed. Cody asked, "Excuse me sir? Where am I?"

The man stopped, scowled and said, "Saan ka nagmula?"

"Sorry, I don't speak..." but Cody had no idea what language that was.

"Tagalog." The man smiled, an infectious warm thing. Cody smiled back. The man said, "I speak English. I asked, 'where are you from?'"

"Oh. California."

He looked around. "Lots of Californians here. They all know where they are," he winked. "Why not you?" Cody couldn't tell if the man was joking or not. His smile was warm, but hard to read.

"Sorry, I'm just a little confused." Cody said, the sweat pouring down his face got in his eyes and he blinked furiously.

"Be careful," he said, looking around, a whisper, "They take drug use very serious in Manila."

Cody racked his brain, trying to remember his geography. *Is Manila a country in South America? Wait, does this guy think I'm high?*

The man finally smiled. "Joking. Island humor. This is Manila, capital city in the Philippines."

"Holy crap, isn't that near The Orient?"

The man frowned. "We don't really call it that anymore. The Philippines is near Asia, yes. About, oh, seven thousand miles from California. But you must know that. You had to get here somehow. Need some help?"

"No. Yes. No..." *Yep, he thinks I'm high.* "I mean, thank you. Is there an international phone nearby?"

"Most people have cell phones here." He said, still smiling, pointing to people walking about with phones in their hands.

"I'm sorry." Cody did feel like an idiot, saying all the wrong things. He tried not to freak out at the news about where he was. He said as calmly as he could, "Sorry again. I'm just a little confused. I'll go find my family."

The man gave another wary look, then went on his way. *His family.* Cody froze at the thought of his mom and what that Rageto warrior said. *I need a phone, now.* Cody looked around again and saw where the main part of the city must be. He walked towards the skyscrapers. He realized he had no money. He'd left his wallet in the car, again. *I have to stop doing that.* He dug into his pockets. *Well, I have my van keys, like that will help.*

As the sun beat down, Cody walked slower and slower. He tried to walk close to the buildings for shade, but the people were endless, all around, also hugging to the shadows.

He was very thirsty. Cody figured he must have lost gallons in sweat alone. He walked for an hour, seemingly getting no closer to the skyscrapers. The houses were now studded with small shops and restaurants. The food smelled amazing. *Great, I'm a pasty white boy from Cali and I'm going to die starving and dehydrated in a foreign country. No one will even know who I am.*

He spotted another restaurant and got an idea. He walked in and asked at the counter, "Bathroom?"

The middle-aged woman just stared, shaking her head. He remembered the Spanish word, and tried again. "Bano?" he said. He'd never envied anyone else with a cell phone as much as he did right now. The woman shook her head again but smiled and waved him to a back corner of the building. The look clearly read "dumb American."

He found the bathroom, thank God for international symbols, the male and female figures on the doors, otherwise he'd have made another blunder. Cody washed his hands, then greedily slurped from the tap. It didn't taste great, and he wondered briefly about drinking water in foreign countries. *Wait, isn't this an American territory, or something?* He didn't remember and fleetingly wished he'd paid more attention in school. *Aren't you supposed to get a shot and stuff before leaving the US?* Had he already contracted Malaria, or some other horrible disease? He splashed cold water on his face to calm himself.

You have more immediate problems. Like no money, no ID, and no way to contact anyone or get home. He wondered if he looked as desperate as he felt. There was no mirror over the sink. He thought, *Screw malaria.* He took another gulp of the tap water.

He looked around the room. The full-length mirror on the wall to his right caught his eye. He stood before it, studying his face. He was already red from the sun, still covered in sweat. He thought about wringing out his shirt but didn't have the energy. The mirror reflected his image back to him, thankfully not showing some random location. He thought of his father again.

Why had he not come back? Contacted him, even? Why was he staying away? Cody felt the urge to touch the mirror. His hand raised, but he hesitated. He still didn't know if going through the mirror before was the Elder's magic or something to do with him. The Elder wasn't present when Derek threw him through the mirror at school, but the Elder was waiting for him on the other side. *How did any of that work?*

He'd wondered on it plenty in the past months. How could he not? But he'd never gotten the courage to try to go through a mirror. Every time he thought of it, he felt crazy. Like a kid who thinks he has superpowers. But all those things really happened. He was suddenly in the Philippines, after all. There was no turning back from these crazy things, even if he wanted to. Cody touched the glass, pressing against the image of his own finger.

He touched. Glass, solid. His finger touched only his reflected finger. He dropped his hand to his side, his other hand over his face. He couldn't help it. He smiled. Then laughed. He was laughing in a bathroom 7000 miles from home and he thought he could walk through a mirror. He raised his head and ran his fingers through sweat soaked hair.

When he looked back up, his reflection was gone.

Cody felt a cool breeze. It came from the mirror. The image was a place he'd never seen. It looked like a short stone wall with a solid gray sky behind. He raised his hand again, tentatively. He pressed his whole hand at the glass. It wasn't there. His hand went through. It didn't feel like there was anything at all, just air, like the mirror was just a frame around a door in the wall.

He remembered the flash of his dad, the reason he went into the grinding wall of color.

Maybe I can finally get to him.

Cody thought of his father and stepped through.

CHAPTER FIFTEEN

Stranger Still

Lucas ate with his father. The conversations lately had become more strained. These days, he spent most of his time in his room, either training or just lying in bed going through Elgisard's memories. He began questioning why he was even going to school, with so much knowledge in his head. He wasn't bullied anymore, but school now just seemed pointless. He had checked and Elgisard had rarely gone to school during his many lifetimes.

"Okay, Dad," he stood up from the table, "thanks for the sandwiches. I gotta go take a shower."

"Yep, buddy boy, you do." His dad took a dramatic whiff of the air near Lucas. "I wasn't going to saw anything, but all your mom's flowers have wilted." He hooked a thumb at the imaginary flowers behind him. Lucas knew that both his parents killed any plant they tried to cultivate – the "black thumb," they called it. Lucas smiled at his dad's joke and headed for the shower.

After he got out, he saw the dozen texts from Ariana and Katie. Before he could answer any, the knocking came at his bedroom side door.

"Where have you been?" Katie asked as she entered his room, not waiting to be invited.

Lucas looked down at his bare chest, only a towel wrapped around his lower half. "Umm, taking a shower after the battle."

"Oh, well..." Katie noticed he had no shirt and looked away. "Yeah, well, put a shirt on. Is John here?"

"No. He was here, then my dad... it was actually kind of funny..."

Ariana stepped right up to Lucas' face. "Not funny. Zacke is in the hospital. What did John say? Where has he been all this time?"

"Why did he only show up now?" added Katie, crowding Lucas.

"He didn't mean to. One of those Rageto, the girl off to the side, could somehow turn Ley lines. I've never seen anyone do that before." Lucas dropped into his serious voice. It was getting harder to tell if it was Lucas or Elgisard. Then he brightened. "In fact, even Elgisard hadn't used a ley line in centuries..."

"Lucas, focus," said Katie.

"And please put on a shirt," added Ariana.

"Yeah, yeah," said Lucas as he grabbed a shirt from a pile, along with pants. He left them alone in his room while he changed in the bathroom.

"So, John just appears, but he didn't mean to? What the hell?" Katie bombarded Lucas when he reappeared.

"Katie, I didn't have long with John, and he didn't answer all my questions, either," Lucas said.

"Just like old times," quipped Katie.

"That's not good enough," said Ariana. "Where did Cody go? Swept up in this Ley line, or whatever? Do we need to rescue him? Is that possible? How do we find him?"

"I don't know. John seemed worried, distracted. Not about Cody – he didn't even mention him, actually. Something bigger is going on."

Katie stood firm, in Lucas' face. "Where is he?"

"A hotel, I guess. He said he'd contact us soon. Told me to tell everyone to stay home, stay safe, and wait for him."

Katie snapped, "No. I'm done waiting. I'm sick of being in the dark."

A knock came at the door to the outside.

"John?" asked Ariana.

Lucas shrugged and headed to the door. A large man stood there. He didn't say anything to Lucas, just handed him some mail. It was late afternoon, and he was clearly not a mailman.

"Thanks," said Lucas. The man did not smile, just nodded and left. Lucas noticed he had a limp. Nothing about the man got Elgisard's hackles up, so he probably wasn't Rageto. The man was around the corner and gone before Lucas thought to stop him.

There were seven unstamped envelopes, addressed to each one of them – including David, Cody's dad. They looked like invitations.

"Well," said Lucas, "so much for our secret lair." He handed the invitations to Katie and Ariana.

They opened them. They all read the same thing: "You are invited to a safe place. I will provide answers to many of your questions. You have not been told the whole truth. Everyone needs the truth." It gave an address in Miguel Canyon, a few miles outside of the town proper.

Ariana's said, "This address is way out in the canyon. There are only a few scattered ranches. Rich people country."

"What is this?" asked Katie, holding the same invite.

Lucas shook his head. "No idea. Good way to get us all together willingly."

"Another trap, you mean." Ariana rolled her eyes.

Lucas nodded. "Probably."

"Pretty dumb one, though," said Katie. "Hey, rats, you are cordially invited to come and out and get the cheese."

Ariana read her invitation again. "But it's not offering us power, or threats – just answers. How would they know that's what we want more than anything?"

"Games. Sounds like the Rageto," Lucas said, tossing the invite on a table nearby.

Ariana wasn't sure. "Whatever it is, I'm not going to any secluded house out in the middle of the canyon blind. Besides, there's no date or time. Are we just supposed to show up anytime we want? This is too weird. We need to talk to John."

She threw her invitation on a stack with Lucas', so did Katie. A text message appeared on Lucas' phone, then Katie's and Ariana's.

Hello. John here. I hope none of you changed your numbers. Do you remember the first place we all met? Meet me there tonight at sundown. Has anyone heard from Cody? He needs to hear this too.

"Does he not know that Cody vanished into thin air?" asked Katie.

Lucas said, "I told him. Like I said, he seemed preoccupied. Wait, does he mean to meet at the Mission?"

"No," said Katie, "the high school football stadium was where we first met John."

Zacke group texted them back. Sorry, can't make it. Just released from the hospital, but I got family stuff now.

"Great," said Katie. "Well, I guess it's just us three."

* * *

The high school campus had a roaming security guard at night, but the stadium was next to the campus and had only flimsy chain link all around. They walked by it every day, slowly seeing twisted ruins of the stadium bleachers hauled away each day. Now the field was full of new construction materials, waiting for the new bleachers. It still felt eerie as the sun went down, the construction supplies and equipment making strange shadows. The earthquake that the brother Caron created brought the bleachers down, but this was the next chapter. Ariana said, "Did all that really happen just a few months ago?"

"Yeah," said Katie, remembering her sister Megan all bloody and buried under twisted rows of wood and steel.

Lucas noted, "Looks like they're ready to build."

"Almost. I asked a teacher why it was taking so long," said Ariana, "They rolled their eyes and said 'budget cuts.' "

Katie hesitated, then said, "Do you ever think – I mean, I know it all really happened, but sometimes it feels like..."

"A dream?" asked John, walking up to them.

"John! I really wish you wouldn't do that," said Katie. "Will we ever hear you coming?"

"Maybe someday," said John.

"Where's David?" asked Ariana.

"David is safe for now, but he isn't well."

"That's it?" Katie was in John's face now. "Not good enough. You and David disappeared. You promised to come back and help us. You didn't. We needed you!"

Ariana put a hand on Katie's shoulder, but addressed John. "How did you get here? Why now?"

John shook his head. "I wish I could say it was on purpose, but I was pulled here."

"You were that close to a Ley line?" asked Elgisard.

"Yes. Too close, apparently. I needed the Ley line's power to help David."

Katie shook her head. "Okay, what does this Ley line do? And no mansplaining and keep it short. I'm still super pissed."

"Ley lines are many things," said John, "Most cultures believe they are ancient lines that connect religious sites, famous landmarks and special places. They are much more than that. There's a reason there are pyramids in Egypt, South America, and Cambodia."

Ariana smiled. "Yeah, aliens, right?"

"No. But funny." John continued, "The first Elders and other talented members of the struggle constructed these lines, and most of the culture you've read about. It just turns out the books are wrong about the origins of those histories."

"Got it." said Katie, "What's wrong with David? And where is Cody?"

John rubbed his chin. "Yes. I'm very worried about Cody. He could be anywhere. I've never heard of a warrior that can shift Ley lines like that."

Ariana remembered seeing the woman's head roll. She would never forget that. Never. *Are more things like that going to happen?*

John turned to Lucas. "Have you seen it before?"

Elgisard answered, "No. There was that boy in Sumatra. He could see all the Ley lines, and he was a kind of guide. But this?" Lucas and Elgisard shook their head. "Which elder did this? That blue gate was Ordway's, of course."

"It was. But it didn't feel like an Ordway attack, somehow."

"I agree," reasoned Elgisard. "The gate was hers, but it feels like there is more to this."

John smiled. "Another Viking hunch?"

"It's been right once or twice." Elgisard smiled back.

"Focus!" Katie shouted. "Answers!"

"Yes, please," Ariana interrupted. "Nice ancient to ancient chat, but focus."

"Sorry. Of course," said John. "I was close to a Ley line, to pull power for David. I knew it was risky for David, but I had no idea I'd be pulled out until I felt it coming. I only had a few seconds to grab my sword."

"What's wrong with David?" asked Katie.

"He's... what are those?" asked John.

"Oh," said Ariana, her hands full of the strange invitations. "These were delivered by an odd limping guy. Here's yours." She handed him the envelope labeled John.

John opened it and read. Inside, John was crossed out and Pentoss was penned in with masterful handwriting. The last line, "Everyone needs the truth," was underlined. At the bottom the letter was signed with the letter U. It was circled.

"Where is this address. Is it far?" shouted John.

"Jeez." Katie took a step back. "Yes, it's out where the rich folks live. Miguel Canyon."

John insisted, "Take me there. Now!"

"Calm down. Don't you think we have enough mysteries to worry about right now?" asked Ariana.

He turned to Lucas. "Do you have a car?" He looked down at Lucas' thin body. "Of course you don't. You're all still children."

"Hey!" shouted Katie.

Lucas' hand shot out and grabbed John's shoulder. "John. Pentoss. None of us are children anymore. Tell me."

John pushed the invitation at Lucas. Elgisard read it and understood. There was a tear in John's right eye, threatening to spill.

Lucas checked the address again, grabbed his phone and found the app. He put in the information.

Katie asked, "What are you doing?"

Lucas scowled, as though there were no stupider question. "Calling an Uber."

CHAPTER SIXTEEN

Family Reunion

Zacke sat in his kitchen, stunned, unable to process the scene.

His father sat quietly, passively.

Zacke focused on his breathing. It hurt to breathe, so he focused on the pain. It kept the anger at bay, for now.

"I can't get over how much you look like your father, more and more," said Zacke's mother as she stirred her tea. His father must have made it for her, but he didn't remember when.

Zacke had a million questions. None of them came to mind. The ride home had been surreal. His father drove, his mother in the old familiar passenger side and he in the back seat. His side was still on fire, though the prescribed anti-inflammatories had helped a little.

His mother talked the entire ride home, commenting on how the town had changed or hadn't changed in the year she was away.

Zacke thought, *When you left us.*

Now they were in the kitchen, his mom still droning on about the curtains being the same, like she was some welcome visiting aunt, chatting away. Zacke wanted to scream, *Dad has been devastated since you left, of course he wouldn't change the damned curtains.*

He didn't get the chance. Just then, his brother Deke strolled in. She stopped dead in the middle of the kitchen.

Their mother stopped talking.

Deke folded his arms. "Get out."

Their dad spoke weakly, "Deke, let's give her a chance."

"No, Pop." He turned their mother. "You left us!"

"I'm here to explain," she said.

Deke pulled out a chair and sat directly in front of her. "Okay, *Mommy*. Explain. Explain how a mother could walk out on her own children. Her husband. Who never did her any wrong. Explain, *Mother*." Deke made the last word sound like a curse.

Zacke saw the old anger flash on his mom's face. She was the disciplinarian, and those cold stares use to terrify him. She never exploded. It was a deeper power. Mother Earth herself. A volcano you never wanted to see erupt. Her eyes darted to Zacke and softened.

Mom said, "I, I was confused. I was scared. I won't deny it."

"Why Mom? Because you saw a demon in your own son? Crazy shit like that?"

"Deke," Zacke finally spoke.

He stood, flinging the chair back, wheeling on Zacke. "What? You gonna defend her now?" He turned back to their mother. "You wanna call him evil to his face, *Mom*?"

Mother Earth awoke. Zacke saw it for just a flash, then it was gone. What replaced it wasn't contrition. Zacke thought it looked painful for her to tamp down the old anger. Instead, she smiled strangely. "I know you're not a demon, son. Like I said, I was confused. I found people that helped me. They showed me the truth."

"Your crazy church?" asked Deke.

Dad put his hand in front of him, the old peacemaker. "Deke, let's..."

"What are you gonna say?" he said to his dad, then turned back to their mother. "You know what you did to *him*? Kicked him straight down the bottle."

"Stop!" Dad shot up.

Deke started to say something, but he shook his head and walked to the counter, his back to everyone. Dad sat back down.

At that, she reacted, perhaps a tinge of regret. Maybe not. Zacke thought she recovered too quickly. Her face was a mask of pleasantness again. Zacke almost wished she's become old hard-ass Mother Earth again. This was too strange. His emotions couldn't find a handhold. He felt like he was still in a dream. Then he pulled a sharp breath and felt the pain again in his side. *Nope. This is really happening.*

Deke looked around at his brother, so only Zacke could see. There was a tear there, but it rejected gravity and stayed just under his eye. Zacke wasn't sure he had the strength to see that.

He saw Deke's shoulder's tense again. He was choosing rage again. Before he could turn around Zacke rose up. "I think you should go."

Deke's posture changed, turning slowly to face her again. "You heard him."

She looked from son to son, pain to rage. Whatever spell she'd cast by showing up had been broken. She looked to her husband. He stayed seated, but nodded in agreement.

She stood but didn't meet anyone's eyes as she said, "I see I'm not wanted. I wished to explain, at least, but I suppose this isn't the time. I'll go."

Deke crossed his arms, a last defiance. Or perhaps a way to stay angry, without it turning into something else.

She left, closing the kitchen door behind her.

Deke collapsed back into his chair. He looked over, a real look, brother to brother. "You okay?"

"Yeah. I'm alright," Zacke sniffed.

Deke looked at his bandages. "Damn. Mountain lion? For real? I told you to play with those pussy cats, but that's not what I meant."

Zacke laughed involuntarily. His pain volunteered all over again. "Oh, man. Too soon, bro."

Deke had run out of things to say. "Yeah, well I'm gonna go to my room, I guess."

"Yeah, me too," said Zacke. He stood and made a loud wince of pain. Deke grabbed for his arm, in support.

"Hey bro, I got you," he helped Zacke down the hallway.

When they got to Zacke's door, he stared hard into Deke's eyes. "Thank you."

* * *

Cody peered over the waist high stone wall. If felt cold to the touch like any other stone but had no clear signs of age – no cracks, no green moss, no crumbling stone dust, but it still seemed ancient. He looked farther over the wall, down into what must have been a valley or moat, or nothingness. It was covered in thick fog. The sky was no help – no sun, just gray. The central coast of California, his home, had lots of days when the thick marine layer covered the city, hung up in the sky, a thin gray coat of paint. This was different. The light seemed diffused perfectly. He scanned the vastness of gray but could detect no direct light source. *That's makes no sense. The sun shines everywhere, doesn't it?*

There were no landmarks beyond the walls. He looked to his left and right, identical stone walkways that lead off farther than he could see. It wasn't straight, it had some architectural detail – a few pillars occasionally, some steps down to break up the lines, and open doorways that must have led inside. *But where?*

He'd wandered into a few rooms, but there wasn't anything to find. Just empty stone rooms of various sizes.

His first thought was that he'd been roaming a castle, but if so, the architect was off. Some stone pathways led nowhere, some stairways led up to a stone wall, all the stone exactly the same color of gray. *This is something weirder.* When he wandered into a passageway from the main walkways, the interior hallways were lit – he just didn't know how. There were no light fixtures, not even torches. It was like looking at a painting where you couldn't see the source of light.

He'd imagined castles would have torches along the wall like in movies. A light existed, in half circles on the walls, like a torch was there, but it wasn't – just the light, no source.

"Don't try to figure it out." a voice said on his right.

Cody yelped. He hoped it sounded manly, but he was pretty sure it hadn't. A woman stood about twenty feet away, down a corridor. She was a dark-skinned woman and spoke with a heavy accent. Cody couldn't tell from where. She wore jeans and sneakers, but a leather shirt, almost like armor. There was a short sword at her right side, and a gun holster on her left side.

"Did you just arrive?" she smirked. "We thought we felt someone new."

"We? There are more people here? Where is here?"

"That is a matter of debate." She motioned with her arm. "I'm Amina. Come, join the others."

Cody's mind didn't alarm. He only just realized it, but there had been no sense of urgency. He'd almost been filled with calm. No, that wasn't it. When he arrived, it just felt stopped, like time didn't work here. He looked at the woman. Amina smiled. Cody thought, *why not?*

"You're young," Amina said as she led him down yet another generic corridor.

"I guess," he offered. "I'm Cody."

"Young and polite. Rare."

"This place. I'm trying..." He didn't know what he should and shouldn't say. He was too weary to care. "I'm looking for my father, David. Is he here?"

"Hmm. No David. What is his ancient name?"

"He doesn't have one – I think he's a new birth."

"And you are his son? Very unusual for two family members to have powers."

"So I've heard." Cody thought, *She used the word powers, not abilities. Must be Rageto.* Though this thought strangely did not alarm him either.

She led him down a complicated set of rooms and corridors. Each place was lit by the same mysterious non-light, even as they descended. Or he thought they were going down. He kept thinking of an art book he'd seen where the stairways go every which way, even upside down, defying all physics. *Of course, I did walk through a mirror to get here, so I probably shouldn't judge.*

"There are a famous pair of brothers, of course. Both Rageto." She cocked her head. "Very dangerous."

Cody could hear talking from up ahead, just around another archway. "Yeah, the brothers. They won't be a problem anymore."

The walked into the room, men and woman of all ages – a dozen that Cody could see – were talking in small groups.

Annis asked, "Oh, why is that? You've met the brothers, Sazzo and Caron, have you?"

"Yeah," Cody answered, "my friends and I killed them a few months ago."

The room fell silent.

A shout came from a large man who'd been taking a drink. "What did you say, boy?"

"We killed – umm, destroyed? The Rageto brothers a few months ago."

"Lies! Many have boasted that they killed Sazzo and Caron." But the man seemed hopeful. He put down his cup. "True deaths?"

"Well – one was a true death, one wasn't."

A stout middle-aged woman marched across the room, "How was it done? Which one got a true death?"

"Sazzo, with a sword – a relic sword. Caron died by lightning storm." Cody smiled as he said the last, thinking of his father's awesome ability. He was half talking to the woman and half scanning to make sure his dad wasn't one of them. He didn't see him.

A bellow came from the large man, a deep laugh that forced his head back and came from pure joy. A cheer rose too, from the whole room. "At least

Sazzo is gone forever! Come, young slayer of ancient monsters. Let's sit on the ground and tell tales of dead kings."

Another man bellowed, "Sazzo weren't no king."

"It's Shakespeare, you dunce," replied the man.

The man grumbled back, "Bah. Give me the classics. I'll take Cicero any day."

"Stuck in the past. You probably knew Cicero back fifty bodies ago."

"Nah. Dated his son," a woman laughed.

"Don't crowd the boy all at once." Cody's new friend wore glasses, but ones from a different century. "We'll have plenty of time to hear all his stories."

Cody asked, "You will? Umm, why?"

The man looked down his glasses. "Because no one leaves here, my boy."

Another woman offered, "But we don't seem to age, either, so there's that."

Cody remembered all the corridors and the crazy art book with pictures of stairs that led nowhere. "You're all trapped here?"

"Afraid so," offered the bespectacled man. "I'm Bevan. Who are you?"

"Cody," he answered absently. *This place has nothing to do with Dad. Why did I see this place in the mirror?* thought Cody. "Wait! I may be able to help. Where's the nearest mirror?"

They all laughed.

Bevan offered, "No mirrors here."

"There must be a way out," said Cody, looking around.

"There's good news, though," said Bevan. "Whoever designed this place has a never-ending supply of food – nothing fancy, but it never runs out."

"The Elder that trapped us here, you mean," called a nearby man.

"I've told you a thousand times, that makes no sense. Why would they trap us here then feed us?"

"The River provides!" announced a woman across the room. A few echoed the cheer.

"Screw the River!" yelled another. He was shouted down by the others, apparently an old, tired battle.

"You haven't told him the best part," the man stood aside to reveal a large keg on its side with a wooden spigot. The man cranked it into a cup. He handed Cody the frothy liquid, who could smell what it was before he tasted it. Beer. He looked around suspiciously. No one stopped him, so he took a swig.

"Lotus eaters! The lot of you!" said Bevan.

"Are you in charge here?" asked Cody.

The room erupted in laughter again.

Bevan sneered. "Philistines, all. Actually, a few of you probably were literally Philistines!"

A few laughs, a few boos.

Bevan replied, "No, young man, I'm not in charge, But I should be."

"Who are you, then?" Again, no adult stopped Cody, so he swigged some more beer.

"Can't you tell? Glasses, holding a book? I'm the scholar here." Bevan became serious. "You said mirror before. Are you by any chance a mirror walker?"

The room hushed.

"I don't know. I got here through a mirror, so... I guess?"

Bevan rubbed his chin. "Rare. Rare. Usually requires magic. Are you Rageto, then?"

"No. Those guys are dicks," stated Cody. A few laughs around the room. He noticed not all agreed and met him with angry faces.

"Careful, now. There are Rageto and Amartus here, even Sect," Bevan said. "The River sometimes gives us gifts at just the right time. Tell me everything. Maybe you are the key to get us out of this place."

CHAPTER SEVENTEEN

Hearts and Bones

The Uber driver, Chet, was confused.

The teens girls seemed fine, but the teenage boy was off somehow. He gave off a weird vibe. The adult man was clearly agitated, sitting next to him in the front seat. A fake sword sat on the floor between his legs, but none of the others were dressed up in costume. They were all stuffed into Chet's Toyota Prius, not made for four passengers. Chet glanced at the sword again and said, "Nice sword."

He stared ahead. "We coss-play."

"Cosplay," corrected Lucas.

"Right," agreed John but offered no other comfort to the driver.

Sea Valley was flanked by hills and mountains on both sides to the North and the South. The valley faced the west, the mighty Pacific Ocean, and the mountains and hill scape funneled the ocean breezes into the city. They were headed South now, into one of the few canyon roads that cut through those hills. Miguel Canyon Road was curvy, tree lined, and dotted with ranch properties and a single park. To the left ran a rail line that had seen better days. The only thing it served now was the diatomaceous earth plant called DioTerre.

They had just passed the plant on the left and the park on the right, headed for the address on the invitation. Past mile ten on the road, the ranches got bigger and farther between. They arrived at the address, and a locked gate met them. There was a call box, a silver box with a speaker, LED screen, and button.

John got out.

"Umm, do you want me to wait?" asked Chet.

John said, "No," and shut the door.

"Thanks for the ride," said Ariana. Lucas, Katie, and Ariana all got out. Chet left, his Prius silently departing back towards town.

John pressed the button. He spotted the camera and looked into it.

The gate buzzed and swung out toward them. John kept his sword out. They walked down the path. The house was visible after the first turn on the long the driveway. The entire path was well lit on both sides, visibility in all directions.

Katie asked, "Are you going to tell us what we're about to walk into?"

"I'm not sure," said John.

"That's reassuring," said Ariana. "John, you're doing that thing again when you tell us next to nothing and expect us to follow you."

John stopped. "You're right. I'm sorry. The invitation. That phrase was code between... between someone I thought died a long time ago. If they've returned – here, now – I'm not sure what it means, but I must know."

John walked ahead.

The three teens walked a few paces behind. Lucas at the rear, with his collapsed batons in hand.

"Okay, ancient Viking guy," started Katie, "wanna fill us in?"

Lucas/Elgisard spoke in hushed, respectful tones, "I don't think we are in danger, but we must be on our guard. If it's who John thinks it is... well, I'm not sure what it all means."

A large man stood on the porch. The house was only one story – a ranch style house, obviously very expensive. The man said nothing, just opened the door and nodded his head. He eyed John's sword but said nothing. Ariana recognized him as the man who gave them the invitations.

John entered the house. A bronze statue of a horse stood on the entrance table. John spotted fine objects everywhere – a real Ming vase, a Roman era marble statue, fine art on the walls from many eras. Music was playing.

A man stood in front of a mirror, just next to the high-end sound system. He turned off the music as he spotted John in the mirror.

John took the man in. He was thin, but fit, about forty. His clothes seemed tailored, expensive.

He turned and their eyes met. His eyes pierced John. There was no way to tell from outside appearance who lurked inside. John thought to himself, *can it be?*

"Explain this," John held out the invitation.

"I am Julien Aarden. This is my home in California. I was born in Belgium and have houses wherever my work takes me. I own the mining company DioTerre just down the road, among many other businesses around the world."

John said, "Thanks for the biography. How did you know about us? What do you want? Who are you, really?"

"I want to share with you, for I've been building this important knowledge a long time. I know many things. I invited you because it's time for truth."

John thrust the paper in the air again and walked to the man. "And this? What do you know about this?"

"Don't you remember what it means?" Julien touched John's hand.

"That person died a long time ago," John looked down, but he didn't remove Julien's hand. He twisted Julien's hand palm up. A small tattoo was there. e the sign of rebirth. John stared at Julien.

"You didn't come back to me," John whispered.

Julien stroked John's arm. "I'm here now."

He hugged Julien fiercely. Julien hugged back, just as hard.

When the long embrace ended, John took Julien's face in his hand. "Is this really you? How? Why didn't you..."

Before waiting for an answer, John kissed Julien deeply on the mouth.

"Oh. Okay," said Katie, "wasn't expecting that."

The kiss lasted a long time. They all looked around, awkwardly.

"Umm, sorry," interrupted Ariana, "John, who is that?"

Elgisard just smiled, hoping this was a good omen for the following days.

The kiss finally ended. Julien and John were covered in tears.

Julien said, "It's me, my love."

John took Julien's hand and turned to the others. "This is my wife, Unna."

CHAPTER EIGHTEEN

Father and Son

"That's quite the tale, boy," said Bevan.

"It's all true, umm..." Cody struggled. "I forgot your name. Sorry, I'm pretty tired."

"Bevan. I'm surprised you remember anything after that adventure. Plus, you just met all us strangers. Can't expect you to remember all our names. So, Elder Zamma was killed by his own henchman, and Sazzo, no less. Thank the River that maniac is gone forever."

"Which maniac – they were all crazy."

"All of them!" Bevan laughed. "Yeah, the two names thing gets very confusing. Imagine going through a few dozen lifetimes, two names each? It must get ridiculous – especially if you remember most of those past selves. I don't know how they do it."

"They?" asked Cody. "You mean, you aren't Amartus?"

"Me? No, I'm Sect. Name's been Bevan McDermott since I was born sixty-two years ago. These lot are mostly Amartus, a few Rageto."

Cody looked at all the warriors. "Why aren't they fighting?"

The room laughed. The men and woman sat around, stood in groups, most eating and drinking. Cody thought of a Roman feast, everyone lounging on couches. This was sadder than that. They all just seemed bored.

Bevan said, "Oh, they fight all the time!"

The room cheered.

"Well, they used to." Bevan sighed. "There's still a dust up or two, but most of us have been here so long, we're just bored and tired."

Cody looked around to the others, "Why are all of you here?"

"Stupidity," said a nearby man.

"True," Bevan laughed. "We all got trapped here one way or the other. I've been here since 1997."

Cody sputtered, "Holy crap. That's longer than I've been alive."

"Never say that to old people. We hate that."

"Sorry."

Bevan said, "Doesn't feel like it though. Time works different here. This is the King's Road..."

"Bah!" He was cut off by jeers from those around him. "Fairy Tales!"

Bevan shouted back, "King's Road, I say!"

"Just old stories," shouted someone else.

"King's Road, Elder's Peace, Mirror High Road, call it what you want." Bevan stood, announcing, "It says it in the book *Secrets of the Elders.*"

"You wrote that book," shouted a woman.

"Yes, but I'm a Sect scholar, so shut your trap." Bevan sat.

"King's Road?" asked Cody, sipping some more beer.

"The King's Road is a place built by an ancient. Some called him the Raven King, but there's no evidence that he ever existed. Sect scholarship says this place was created by two Elders, one Rageto, one Amartus to make the peace."

"Between the two sides?" Cody thought of the several battles he'd been in. "From what I've seen there's no peace."

"True. Wasn't when I was out there, either. But everyone says they *want* peace. Long ago, they tried for it. It lasted for quite a while. There were lots of smaller wars – there always are – but the peace brought us the Renaissance. Not bad. The problem is that there are always troublemakers rebirthed out of the River." Bevan scratched his head. "The Sect has spent it's entire history trying to figure out the logic of the River, it's ebbs and flows, the reason it spits out these monsters and heroes that wreck history."

"I wish John was more help." The beer tasted sour at the thought of John. "Seems like he only ever tells us half the story. I always feel like he's hiding something."

"This is Pentoss we're talking about?"

"That's him."

"Pentoss is a great warrior of the Amartus. Goes back to the beginning. Sumerian, I think – or Phoenician – I forget which. He's been around a long time. There's even a great Sect epic written about him: *The Warriors Asunder.* It was written in the late 1800's, so it's dripping with Victorian romantic imagery."

"John? In a romance novel?"

Bevan tipped back his head, as though searching for the story. "Pentoss and the lady Unna. A fierce warrior. The story goes that they met life after life, always finding one another across the wide world. They fought in the war with Attila, and lost – very romantic, died in each other's arms. They fought in Britain. She was a Lancastrian, if I'm remembering right, he a York — or maybe vice versa. Then, they met again after Columbus came. He was a native girl, she was a rather nasty Conquistador."

Cody cocked his brow.

"Oh yes, the multiple name thing is bad enough, but warriors are born into male and female bodies higgledy-piggledy. The River has quite the sense of humor."

"So, what happened? Where is she now? John seems like a loner. Never mentioned a wife."

"That's the tragedy. She hasn't been for a long time. Unna disappeared out west, late 1850's. An Elder claimed he killed her, true death, but no body. Pentoss searched for her. Never found her. The book ends with another war – Battle of Chickamauga – American Civil war. He thinks he sees her across the lines, then dies trying to reach her. Tragedy. Wasn't even her. The epilogue has him scouring the streets of 1880's London, never finding her."

Cody nodded his head. "That's why he's moody."

"I can see why," Bevan snorted.

"That," Cody said, "and the fact he's the last Amartus."

"What's that now?" Bevan's brow furrowed.

A man nearby stood up. "What did you say, boy?"

"John – Pentoss, he says he's the last Amartus left. That's why he was so desperate to activate us."

"What did he say, exactly?" Bevan asked.

"He said he'd searched everywhere, that he was the last Amartus left."

A crowd gathered around them. Bevan asked, "What do the Amartus Elders have to say?"

"I don't know. It seemed like they are gone, too."

"No!" shouted a woman.

A man opposite added, "Lies!"

"Calm down, all of you." Bevan raised his arms gently. "Calm down. Are you sure of this, Cody?"

"Yeah. John actually hid it from us at first. Didn't want to tell us. I thought he'd lied to us. My father knows a lot more, but I can't find him."

"Well," Bevan shrugged, "We're all prisoners."

Cody glanced about, "You're sure there are no mirrors here. Not in any of these rooms and corridors?"

Bevan laughed. "Boy, many of us were trapped here by mirrors. Zamma made sure there was no way out."

"There must be..." Cody looked down and spotted his cup. He asked the room, "Where does this beer come from? Can I see the source?"

An Amartus warrior led him there.

Arriving at the source, there were twin basins. The bowls were made of stone, like everything else here. They were both fed from a pour spout with a decorative image of a mountain pass. The water sources flowed through these mountain passes and trickled into the basins. Cody looked at the imagery. "Oh. I get it. A river, right?"

"Yep." said the warrior.

The basin on the left was foamy, while the other was clear.

"Why two?"

"Duality of the River, we think. The ancient struggle, two sides." said the warrior. "Oh, and one is beer. One is water."

"So you gave me the beer?" asked Cody. "Dude. I'm sixteen."

The warrior shrugged. "Beer is better."

Cody shook his head. "Help me stop the water." He didn't notice, but a group of warriors had gathered behind him.

The warriors laughed at him again. Cody was getting tired of that.

A warrior loomed in the back, near seven feet tall. "Boy, this place was made by magic. The flow never stops."

"Some of you are Rageto." Cody looked at them, extending his arms. "All of you have powers – or talents, or whatever. You mean all of you can't stop a little water?"

"What good would it do, Cody?" asked Bevan.

"I may be a boy, but I got here walking through a damned mirror. I can find people through mirrors... well, sometimes. Anyway, my point is," he pointed at the water basin.

"Yeah, it's water," said the warrior next to him. "I don't get it."

Cody pointed. "When the water is calm, what does it look like?"

Bevan stopped smiling. "A mirror. By the River, help him!"

They gathered closer. One Amartus warrior used their shield to keep the water from pouring into the basin. It ran off the shield to the floor. No Rageto magic needed. They all watched as the flow to the ground stopped. It ran straight into the basin again. To the warrior's surprise, the water was pounding straight through the shield, like it wasn't there.

"Told you." A warrior hooked a thumb at the stream. "Magic water."

"Give me the shield. Better idea." said Cody.

The warrior handed it to him, reluctantly. Cody removed the strap until it resembled a round shallow bowl. He flipped the shield upside down. He dipped an edge into the basin and water filled the shield. He had a few of them carry it to a flat stone bench nearby. He steadied the shield, letting the water calm.

When it was a clear surface, becalmed, he thought of simply going through it. But the last time it had landed him here. He needed help. Cody thought of his father. It hadn't worked all these months, but he tried anyway.

"Dad? Dad, where are you? I really need you now."

The reflection vanished; all was black. Many warriors gasped.

A face loomed into view. The face of an old man.

"Cody?"

"Dad?" but he couldn't believe it. For a split second he'd though it was the old man Zamma. It wasn't, but it couldn't be his dad either. *Could it?*

The old face, deep with age lines, confirmed, "It's me Cody."

CHAPTER NINETEEN

The Relics

John and Julien sat on the sofa, opposite the teens on a facing couch. John kept touching Julien's face – the body that contained his wife Unna.

"Rougher than I remember," said John, referring to Julien's stubble.

"The River gives us no choice." Julien held up his arms. "I haven't been a man in centuries. It's a lot less work. No menstruating, so that's nice."

Katie laughed. Ariana looked embarrassed, but finally said, "Umm, I know you two have a lot to catch up on, but could we...?"

"Of course. You are right, my dear." said Julien. "I promised answers. I owe that to you most, my Pentoss."

"Everyone deserves the truth." John squeezed Julien's hand. "Why didn't you come back to me?"

"I couldn't, my love. When I died, I thought only of you – getting back to you. I hoped to be re-birthed quickly, but I got this life only 38 years ago."

"We are the same age this time," smiled John.

"The River has a sense of humor."

John frowned. "A cruel one. To keep you from me since the 1850's."

Ariana couldn't help herself. "That still really freaks me out. You died in the 1850's – like, cowboy times?"

"Yes. My last death was 1859. Just a few miles from here."

"Here?" said John.

"Yes, Pentoss. Strange, no?"

John's brow furrowed. "Your last letter said you were headed for San Francisco. That's where I searched."

"I was. I did. Then I met a man..."

John's eyebrow raised.

"Calm down. I wanted information. The man was a useless drunkard, but his wife told me of a man who was headed to make his fortune near Santa Helena. He was travelling the Spanish Mission route, trading along the way."

Details of her mission flooded John's memories. He asked, "Did he have them?"

"Let me show you, my love." Julien motioned to the man in the corner of the room. "Jonah, will you unlock the safe room, please."

The large man who both gave them invitations and ushered them in was standing like a guard.

John's eyes lingered on Jonah. "Who is that man?"

"A good ally," Julien said. "He is Sect."

Jonah reached in his pocket for his keys.

"The Sect is openly helping you?" asked John.

Lucas eyed him suspiciously and added. "Why?"

Jonah answered for himself. "The balance has shifted too far. The center cannot hold as it is. The Sect has ordered a few agents to work with key players."

"The Sect knew my wife was alive?" asked John with too much heat.

Jonah soured at John's tone. "The Sect knows a lot of things. I'm supposed to ask you the whereabouts of David Nichols, by the way."

"He's safe," said John. "That's all you need to know. Did you tell Pete's family what really happened to him?"

Jonah nodded. "Peter McNulty was a good agent. His family was told about his death."

"They were told the brothers did it?" asked John. Something about this man bothered him.

Jonah didn't immediately answer. "The Sect doesn't answer to either side. We are referees..."

John shook his head. "Don't give me that old line of garbage."

"Pentoss," Julien touched John's arm, an old soothing signal.

John shook it off, gently. "Even Pete knew it was wrong. The Sect has been on the sidelines too long. They need to choose the right side, finally."

"Pentoss. Enough." This time the hand went to his shoulder, firmly. Julien said, "The Sect is going through their own troubles. There are more factions than ever. They have been very helpful. And this is my house. Control yourself, my love. Jonah, please unlock the door."

Jonah did, without a word. John noticed he had a limp. The room was empty except for a case in the center. It was lit with LED lights, but what the cases contained were anything but modern.

"You found this many?" John looked at the objects, in awe.

Ariana, Katie and Lucas crowded around the case, staring at the objects.

Lucas spoke as Elgisard in a low voice, "Beautiful."

Five objects sat in the case: a two bladed knife, called a haladie in ancient times; a small axe; a round ring with three spikes, or kakute; a madu: an animal horn with a long, twisting spike jutting from its center; and a book.

John stared. "How did you find them all – keep them together, unseen?"

"Easy," Julien smiled wanly. "They died with me."

John turned to Julien, placing a hand on his back, his own soothing signal. "My love. This is why they killed you?"

"Yes. I wasn't the only one searching. An Elder was on the same quest for the relics."

"Relics?" Ariana asked, then realized, "Wait these are all relics? But... one is a book."

John reminded, "Relics can be made from any object."

"But what's the use?" Katie asked. "You can't kill someone with a book. Aren't relics supposed to make warriors not come back? To cause a true death?"

Julien replied, "When they are weapons, yes. But making something a relic also means that object survives forever. This is a very important book."

"What's in it?" asked Katie.

"Knowledge, of course," Julien replied, eyes flashing.

"I think I get it," said Ariana. "You said that books of magic the Rageto use sometimes get destroyed – and that knowledge goes back into the River, then eventually comes back out in different ways."

"Smart girl," said John.

"She is," said Lucas, smiling at Ariana. She smiled back.

"Yes, they both are," agreed John. "And if this book can never be destroyed, its knowledge is eternal."

"I kept them safe." The vivid memory slashed in Julien/Unna's brain. "The Elder created a Simoom – a great wave of heat. The land itself seemed to burst into flame as I rode for safety."

"You died in the fire? How did..." John indicated the relics.

"No, my love, I didn't die in fire, though it was killing me. I fell. There was a crevasse. This area is rich in diatomaceous earth. It's valuable if you know what to do with it, which my company does. It's also very unstable in places, especially in the raw form back in 1859. The crevasse opened and I fell clutching the relics. I died in the earth." Julien paused, remembering finding the spot after searching so long.

Julien said wistfully, "You know, it's strange. You think death would freeze memories perfectly, like a movie. I should have known precisely where my body laid."

John laughed gently. "If only it worked that way. I could have recovered lots of valuable antiques where I fell."

Julien smiled, sadly. "I finally found my body, just recently. Mining is a good business. My company is good at it. But I've really been looking for my last body. It took so long, but this circle has completed."

"You fell here, in this otherwise ordinary place." John stroked his chin. "The very place a breakout of five powerful warriors takes place all these years later."

Lucas added, "A small city along a Ley line."

Julien crossed his arms. "The coincidences are piling up."

"There are no coincidences. Just patterns to uncover," said Jonah. "That's why we had agents here."

"Agents? Plural? You had someone other than Pete?" asked John.

"Pete was a station chief. We have deep cover agents everywhere. Well..." Jonah stopped.

"What were you going to say?" asked John. He threw a glance to Lucas. Lucas eyed Jonah carefully.

"Nothing. As Julien said, there are more factions." Jonah straightened, "It's an internal Sect matter."

John guessed. "Are Sect agents going rogue?"

Jonah didn't respond.

"Five relics. Five of us," said Ariana.

Katie pointed to the weapons. "Are we supposed to fight with these? Against who? When?" She looked around and saw there were clearly only three teens present.

Lucas asked, "And how are we going to find Cody?"

Ariana added, "Yeah, and has anyone even checked on Zacke?"

CHAPTER TWENTY

Rescues & Lies

Deep in the night, Zacke's lips were locked onto Victoria. They stayed that way for a long time, until Victoria rubbed her hand on Zacke's side.

"Oww, oww."

"Oh, sorry!" said Victoria and drew back.

"It's okay. Just take it easy there, cougar," Zacke smiled. "Don't want to paw this cub to death."

"Funny. Age difference jokes." Victoria withdrew to her own side. "That ends the kissing portion of the date."

"This is an official date. And I just blew it." Zacke held his side.

They both straightened in their seats and stared ahead. Miller Grade was an old road that connected Sea Valley to the next city over, Santa Nina. It was less travelled than the newer, safer road a few miles away. It was known for two things: dangerous, twisty curves over narrow roads that had few guardrails, and the best vista view of Sea Valley. The frisky teenagers were staring at the view, all the lights of the city, thinking of a third use for the secluded area.

Victoria poked Zacke in the side.

"Oww. Quit," he winced but smiled anyway.

She smiled back. "Gonna tell me again how you really got those?" Victoria looked at Zacke's hand, still resting on his sore side. "This cougar knows about mountain lion attacks. They rarely happen around here and they don't look like that." Victoria locked onto Zacke's eyes. "Truth time, please."

"You are persistent." He thought about telling Victoria the truth. He wanted to.

"Zacke. Maybe I should start..." before she could finish a car pulled up behind them. The turn-out from the curvy road was wide, big enough for several cars. Probably other tourists checking out the view. They didn't think much of it until Zacke's mom got out of the car.

He saw her in his side view mirror. "What the hell?" Zacke said. He winced as he opened his door. His mom closed her passenger side door and stood there. He walked to her but stopped before he got too close.

His mom said, "Zacke, I thought it best we speak alone."

"Why?" Zacke shouted. "You rejected me!" He hadn't expected it, but it tumbled out.

"I know, baby." She took a step closer. "That's because I didn't understand. How could I? Did you understand what was happening to you?"

"No, Mom, but you couldn't see... you couldn't just see *me*?" Zacke knew Victoria was listening. "I didn't ask for these, these things to happen. But I was still *me*."

"I know, baby." Tears sprang to her eyes, flowed down her cheek. She was still dressed up, her Sunday best. She drew a handkerchief from her sleeve and dabbed her eye. She took a step toward him, perhaps to hug.

Zacke couldn't and stepped back. Victoria jumped out of the car. She came around and stood behind Zacke.

"You okay?" she found his hand and squeezed.

His mother smiled, "Is this your girlfriend?" She seemed happy, perhaps only for a change of subject. "Does she know? Does she know what you..."

"No. Mom. You don't get to do that." Zacke felt a lump in his throat but swallowed hard. "You rejected me and then you left. You don't get to know my life now."

"That's because I didn't understand," she turned back to the car, grasping. "I... I understand now. I finally found the church that helped me understand."

Zacke fought the urge to roll his eyes. "What church, Mom?"

"The church of Ra. They are lovely people. They explained about children of God like you. This is Cimo."

A man stepped out of the car and came around to his mother. It was the Matrix wannabe man from the riverbed.

Zacke's rage flared. *They got to my mother.* "Mom, it's not Ra – it's Rageto."

"Yes, yes that's right." Mom looked to Cimo to elaborate. But he just stared at Zacke.

Mom continued, "They explained..."

"Lies, Mom." Zacke stared into Cimo's eyes. "Get away from that man."

"But he can show you, baby. You are not alone. That's what I wanted to tell you!" she turned to Janus. "Show Zacke the wind of God that will bring him back to me."

A breeze arose, but not over them all, just Zacke. A great pressure pushed him. Zacke groaned and the wind forced him toward her.

"Don't fight it, honey. Come back to me." Mom's arms were outstretched, for a tender embrace.

He fought the wind, but he stumbled forward. His back muscles tensed. Another step.

"Zacke, what's he doing to you?" yelled Victoria, going back to the driver side. She grabbed the taser.

Cimo added, "Don't fight it, Zacke. Come to mother."

Zacke realized the man was right, best not to fight it. Zacke pushed against the wind as hard as he could, holding his arms out in front of him, balling his fists. Then he stopped fighting it. The immense pressure made him leave the ground like a cannonball. He veered from his mom's path and aimed for Cimo's stomach, using the warrior's wind trick to add extra force. It worked. Zacke slammed into Cimo. They flew into the car.

Mom screamed, "Zacke!"

Cimo made a dent in his own door, then slumped to the ground. Zacke tumbled onto the gravel. Cimo laid groaning.

"Zacke! Zacke stop. He's here to help you!" Mom went to Cimo.

Zacke ignored his mom, pushed her aside. He stood, bent over, and grabbed Cimo's belt buckle. He lifted him straight up. Cimo yelped as the pants dug into his groin. Zacke threw the man over his own car into a small bush on the opposite side.

Screeching tires sounded as another car came to a halt next to Victoria's Toyota. Victoria and Zacke wheeled around. Two men rushed out. One was about Zacke's size. One was much larger. He wore no hoodie but was the same size as the man who attacked them in the night. He also had a limp.

"Damn it, Jonah!" shouted Victoria. "Zacke, time to go."

"Wait, you know him?"

"No time. Let's go!" Victoria jumped behind the wheel. Jonah lurched for her. He grabbed the door and opened it. He grabbed Victoria's arm. She laced her other arm through the steering wheel. She reached for the taser, but it fell to the floor of the car. The other man came around the back of the car to the passenger side. Zacke closed the distance and pushed the man into Victoria's car. The man slammed hard, the car rocked, and the smaller man flopped to the ground.

Zacke half leaped, half flew over the hood, landing on the driver's side. The door blocked him from grabbing the large man. He yanked the door hard, tearing it off its hinges. He shoved the door into Jonah. His giant shield slammed the man to the ground.

Victoria gunned the engine. "Get in!"

"Wait!" screamed Zacke's mom, getting Cimo to his feet. "Wait!"

Zacke struggled with the seatbelt as Victoria slammed the accelerator. She revved the engine and they took off. They sped past Cimo's car, headed away from Sea Valley, toward the top of the grade. She zipped the first steep turn too fast and overcorrected. Zacke still hadn't got his seatbelt on and slammed into his door. He felt it give a little. "Hey!"

"Sorry," said Victoria and sped on.

He looked to her seatbelt. It was on. Since she had no door, that was good. "I'm sorry about the door."

Victoria said, "Zacke, I..."

"Look out!" Zacke said and pointed. Around the next turn, Zacke saw the headlights of an oncoming car. The curve looked sharp. Victoria was going at least 45 miles per hour. The car missed them and honked as they passed. The curve was even sharper than Zacke thought. They touched the gravel shoulder. There was no guardrail here, just dark nothingness over the side.

She skidded to a halt. Before Zacke could see how close to the edge they were, they skidded out of the curve onto the road.

Zacke finally got his belt buckled as Victoria banked another curve. A horn blared ahead.

"Which ones are chasing us?" asked Victoria.

Zacke looked back. "Can't tell. All I see are headlights."

Victoria veered into the wrong lane to see around the next corner. A rusty old truck barreled toward them. Victoria swerved back and barely missed him. The trunk's honk was loud and angry.

"Sorry," she said, but Zacke didn't know if it was to him or the passing truck.

In his mirror, the car was closer and gaining, taking the curves even faster than Victoria. It was Cimo and his mother. His mother seemed genuinely terrified. She'd always been a terrible back seat driver to dad. Zacke didn't have time to worry what she was screaming at the Rageto driver. Victoria zagged again.

They'd reached the apex of the high, steep grade and the road toward the farms of Santa Nina. They began downhill. Victoria followed the road the best she could, tires squealing. Behind them, Cimo gained. Less than a car length now.

Cimo revved, threatening. Victoria couldn't go any faster and not lose control. Slam! Cimo bumped them. "Shit," screamed Victoria and swerved again, around a new curve.

Zacke heard a loud screeching of tires behind them. He glanced in the side mirror. Cimo was gone. No headlights. The car had vanished. He looked over his shoulder to make sure. Gone.

"Where did they go?" asked Victoria, checking the rearview mirror.

"I think they went over the edge. We need to go back."

Victoria looked straight ahead.

Zacke put his arm on hers. "Vic. She's my mom."

Victoria looked over and nodded. She slowed, pulled to the narrow bank and turned the car around.

Jonah and the other man were parked on the side of the road, staring down the ravine.

Victoria pulled up, barely enough room to park safely. Jonah, looking down the ravine, a steep drop off with no guard rail.

Zacke leaped out.

The small man made a move when Victoria jumped out then saw the taser in her hand.

Zacke said, "Don't touch her."

The small man didn't even look at Zacke, just kept staring with open rage at Victoria. "You did this."

"Screw you," she flashed the taser.

Zacke looked over the edge. He spotted faint light shining upwards. "Looks like they got stuck on the way down." He turned to Victoria. "I have to do something now, Vic. It's gonna seem crazy."

"I know Zacke," she nodded, almost embarrassed. "Do what you need to do."

Zacke's was confused but had no time. He said to the two men. "If you touch her, I will launch you both into the upper atmosphere."

Victoria said, "It's okay Zacke. They won't hurt me. They were just confused," she stared at both men in turn. She softened and said to Zacke, "Go get your mom."

Zacke didn't have time to be confused. He acted, taking flight and floating down the rough contour of the steep ravine. He followed the glow of headlights. About thirty feet down the car was wedged into a small tree growing out of the ravine wall. It swayed, like it was deciding if it could hold the car's weight.

The closer Zacke got, the louder the groans of the tree became.

He couldn't tell if the car was slipping farther, so he wasted no time. Dropping down just behind the car, he tried to get a foot hold. He saw through the back window that Cimo and his mom were moving. "Mom? Can you hear me?"

"Zacke?" came a muffled cry.

"Yeah, Mom. I'm gonna..." what was he going to do? He's never done anything like this before, with lives at stake. His foot slipped. There was no way to get any leverage against the ever swaying tree. He peered over the car, to the valley below. It was pitch black, but might be a hundred-foot drop, with nothing else to catch the car if it fell.

He couldn't lift the car back to the roadway. He couldn't carry the car all the way down. *Even if I could handle the weight, it's too awkward. Where would I grab it?* He felt the tree sway again. The groaning wood got louder.

Zacke had to get them out. "Okay, Mom. I'm going to reach through the branch and open the door. Find the handle from the inside, that would help."

"Oh, please help Cimo first. His head is bleeding."

Good, thought Zacke, then focused. "No, Mom. I'm going to get you out first." His mom protested, "But..."

"Not a discussion," said Zacke before she could object again, He reached through the branch, the sharp needles and bark digging into him. He could fly and lift heavy things, but his skin was just like everyone else's. He ignored the thought and pushed through. The tree swayed again.

He felt the bush scratch at him, but he found the door handle. It opened, then hit against a thick branch of the bush. "Stuck. Mom, can you push?"

"I... I think so," she pushed, but the branch held.

The tree swayed and something cracked. "Mom, push!"

She did. And he pulled. The door handle flexed in his hand, threatening to break off. Another crack. The whole tree swayed, but Zacke was committed now. He pulled hard and the branch broke. The door flung open.

Mom climbed out the best she could. The car door opened, it shifted the weight of the car. The tree swayed the other way.

Zacke said, "I'll put my arm around your waist, but you need to wrap your arms around my shoulders and hold on tight, okay?"

The tree swayed again. At the wheel, Cimo moaned, holding his bleeding head.

"Oh, Zacke, you need to help him. He's a Deacon in our church."

"No, he's not Mom. He's... never mind. I'll get you to safety then come back. Now grab on."

She looked down again, then grabbed hold. He didn't give her time to say anything else. He lifted into the air, her cry of surprise in his ear.

"It's okay, Mom. Are you hurt?"

She grew silent, staring down at the dark valley below. Zacke only kept them about ten feet off the slope, not wanting to frighten her too badly in midair.

They finally landed by the roadside. Zacke thought he heard sirens vaguely, but they were still far away. His mom couldn't stand, so she lay on her side, dust covering her outfit.

It was obvious that Victoria and the two men had been talking.

Zacke eyed the men, then Victoria. "Everything good?"

Victoria nodded.

"Good. I'll be right back," Zacke said. He lifted off again.

The car had slipped again. The tree swayed dangerously, wood groaning. Two cracks. The car had slid and turned. Now the driver side was parallel to the ground. The passenger door was still open. Zacke hovered down to the car and reached out an arm. Cimo had removed his seatbelt.

"No Zacke," Cimo said. "I don't need help." He opened his driver side door. Gravity nearly tore off the hinges. Zacke saw the two lines, neon blue against the blackness below.

"You will see us again." Cimo fell from the car. The blue lines expanded into a box just before he reached it. It swallowed him and winked out.

The after image burned into Zacke's vision.

The last groan sounded and the car fell like an anchor.

There was no sound for a long time. It was a deep ravine after all. The crash finally came, a series of sounds, like it tumbled and flipped as it fell. Zacke floated up, the sirens much closer now. He landed by his mom.

"Where is Cimo?"

"Gone, mom. I'm sorry."

"Oh no, oh no," she burst into tears, grabbing for her handkerchief.

Zacke had no idea how long she had known him, what lies he told her or how many Rageto she'd met, but her sobs made his stomach turn.

"I'm okay, though..." Zacke was tired, his side hurt again. "...if you were wondering."

She continued to sob, glancing over the side, then turning back. She didn't look at him.

Zacke looked at Victoria.

The sirens were getting close. Zacke looked at the two men, "What's going on?"

Jonah said, "Just following orders. Trying to bring her in." he pointed to Victoria.

"Zacke... I... I was going to tell you before."

"We're Sect," the small man said, "so is she."

"Hardly," said Victoria. "I'm with the true Sect, the one that gives a shit."

Jonah shook his head. "Cops are almost here. We better come up with a story fast."

Zacke looked to the ground. "I'm so stupid." He shook his head slowly.

"Zacke..."

His head shot up and he bore into her, his gaze afire.

Zacke wanted to know why these men wanted her, what she was hiding, all of it. He shut his eyes tight and breathed heavily.

He finally looked at her again. "You lied."

"I did." She looked at him and crossed her arms. "So did you."

He looked at his mom, blubbering on the ground. The sirens were only minutes away now. Zacke stared at Victoria. He was tired. So tired.

He took flight. Straight up.

Zacke wasn't sure he would ever come down again.

PART 3

"Darkness is our only ally."
-Rageto Proverb

CHAPTER TWENTY ONE

Two Sisters

The wind blew down the field and filtered through the trees lining Katie's ranch. They kept a lookout for drones while they figured out how to train with the new weapon.

"What do I do with this?" Katie asked aloud.

"At least you got a weapon." Ariana crossed her arms. "They want me to study that book."

Katie turned over the strange weapon in her hand, "How do you work this thing?"

Ariana got close and examined it. It looked like a small shield, about the size of Katie's hand. From either side sprung two twisted spikes each about five inches long. They were horns from some animal. *Did John say antelope horns?*

Katie asked, "So it's like a double edge sword? With horns?"

Ariana offered, "Umm, I think so."

"I use shields." Katie poked her fingers on one of the sharp horns. "Oww. Why do I need this? Do they really want me to stab someone?"

"The part you hold in your hands looks like a shield. Maybe they think you need an offensive weapon since your shields are defensive?" Ariana said this as question, because she wasn't sure. As usual, John had provided few details before he and Julien had gone off together and told them to train. "Just, I don't know, try it out, I guess."

Katie tried spinning it in her hand, stepping forward with a stabbing gesture. She tried spinning around, stabbing the air high and low, then finally she faced Ariana and stabbed the air, making what she though was a warrior grunt, "Hughh!"

Katie laughed. Ariana burst into laughter too. They laughed for a while. Then Katie noticed Megan over Ariana's shoulder. She'd appeared out of the copse of trees. "Hey," Megan shouted as she approached.

"Hey yourself." Katie said, and instinctively hid the weapon behind her back. The antelope horns made that impossible, which made Katie laugh. Ariana joined in. Katie ended up holding the thing in her hand. She said to Ariana, "I mean seriously, antelope horns?"

"Ooh, what is that?" asked Megan, coming to her stepsister.

"It's nothing. Just a crazy thing they gave me to train with."

"Can I hold it?" asked Megan with an impish smile.

"No," Katie held it up, "this is a very dangerous, apparently."

Megan jumped up and grabbed it from her.

"Hey!" Katie shouted and held out her hand. "Give it back, kid. I'm not playing."

Megan laughed and examined it. "Do you two know what this is?"

Ariana's brow furrowed. "Yes. It's called a madu, from India. Do you know what it is?"

"I do," said Megan as she smiled widely and slashed Ariana's arm.

"Oww! What the...?" said Ariana as she grabbed her arm and checked for blood.

Before Katie knew what was happening, Megan slashed at her, too. She pulled back her arm. Her stepsister had cut her elbow.

Megan laughed and ran for the trees to the right.

"That little... why did she do that?" Katie said. *That laugh. Something isn't right.*

"Wait, that's a relic," said Ariana, "did she just, like doom us to not be re-birthed?"

Katie was shocked. Holding her arm she looked after her fleeing sister.

Then Megan walked in from the left. They stared at her, then realized she wasn't holding anything.

Megan cocked her head to one side like a puppy.

Ariana pointed to Megan, then the opposite way Megan ran.

"Two Megans. Shit," said Katie and ran for the fleeing Megan.

Ariana followed Katie, telling the other Megan, "Stay here."

She replied, "Umm, no," and scrambled after the new mystery.

Both Ariana and Katie ran as fast as they could, forgetting their fresh wounds, searching for the Megan with the madu.

Katie spotted her, among the trees ahead. She shot shield balls, but they only hit trees. *Too far.* Ariana caught up and tried to freeze her, but with the same result.

"Stop!" shouted Katie.

"Jeez, okay," the real Megan came up behind them.

"Not you," said Katie. "Well, not exactly."

Ariana said, "I'll go look over there. You two should stay together."

Ariana disappeared behind the trees to their left.

"What's this?" Megan said.

Katie scanned around for the fake Megan. The trees were Eucalyptus, the bark constantly shedding in sheets, the ground a mess of natural debris. Every footfall crunched and echoed. She didn't call out for her sister again. She stopped, stood and watched for movement.

She looked back absently, "What?"

Megan was standing a few feet away, holding the madu like she'd never seen it. Just behind her, the other Megan stood there.

"Megan, give that to me and walk to me slowly," said Katie, too late.

Megan sensed someone behind her and turned. When she saw it was another Megan, she screamed and dropped the weapon. The other Megan screamed too.

Just then Ariana came back, "Did you find her?" she stopped dead.

Katie turned to Ariana. When she turned back around, both Megans were standing a few feet apart.

"What is happening?" left Megan whispered.

Right Megan said, "What is this? I am freaking out."

Katie looked from one to the other. "Crazy scary crap, kid."

"That's me. I'm scared," said right Megan.

"I'm me, you liar," accused left Megan.

"Katie," said right Megan. "What do I do?"

Left Megan said, "Oh, I see what you're doing. This never works." Megan picked up the madu and handed it to Katie. "Your favorite movie is Hocus Pocus."

Katie smiled and pushed left Megan, the real Megan, behind her. Ariana came behind Katie's right side.

In front of them, the imposter Megan grew a foot taller, a strange woman shedding the disguise like rice paper. The false Megan shredded and dropped to the ground. "Can't blame a girl for trying."

The woman was in her early twenties with deeply red hair, almost black. Her purple blouse flowed over her white pants.

Suddenly, Katie saw so much. It felt like she woke up after a long sleep, remembering the dream she just had. Zhanna smiled from within. She knew how to use the weapon in her hand. It felt like an old friend. She also knew exactly who stood before them. Zhanna said, "Azoria. I've missed you."

Azoria's smile faltered as the shield hit her like a plate glass window.

The woman flew off her feet, backwards until she slammed into a eucalyptus tree.

The warrior Zhanna ran for Azoria, madu held high.

She plunged the antelope horn at Azoria, but she ducked and the horn skidded off the shredded bark.

Azoria kicked Katie/Zhanna in the side and she went tumbling.

"This should be fun," said Azoria. "See you all again soon."

She ran a few steps when a blue gate opened up. Katie jumped up and ran after her, slashing. The gate winked out.

Zhanna growled and rubbed her side as the gate disappeared.

Ariana and Megan ran to her side and looked at her stepsister Katie. She didn't recognize her. Ariana didn't either.

"Are you..." began Ariana.

"Activated?" Katie asked. "Yes. I think so."

Ariana smiled sadly. *Will I ever learn what I am?*

Katie hugged her sister, who resisted at first, then finally hugged back. "Are you okay, little sis?"

"Are you?" asked Megan, still in the hug. "This is so crazy."

"I know." The hug broke. "Time to tell you everything."

"Finally," Megan nodded.

Katie looked to Ariana. "They're testing us, getting family involved. I'm done playing. Time to make a plan."

CHAPTER TWENTY TWO

Stolen

Back at Julien's house, Ariana and Katie relayed their experience.

John smiled. "Welcome back, Zhanna."

"Thank you Pentoss," said Zhanna through Katie. Katie said, "I take back all the crap I've been giving you, Lucas. Activating is freaky."

Lucas smiled and gave a nod.

Ariana said, "John, it's not safe out there. She knew how to trick us and she threatened Katie and her sister."

Julien said, "Agreed. He knew where you would be, and an Elder was monitoring the area to pull her to safety. Thank the River you defeated her."

"I didn't. She kicked me and ran," said Katie.

"Plus," added Ariana, "we saw a drone there a few days ago. Same spot."

"That was ours," admitted Julien. "Sorry, we needed to keep tabs on you all."

Katie crossed her arms. "Great. Everybody's watching and no one is helping."

"How did they watch without any of us feeling anything?" asked Lucas.

Zhanna offered, "Elder's eye?"

"That's Elder Yarro's trick. Maybe," said Julien.

"What's that?" Ariana looked around the room filled with ancient warriors, a room of strangers. "I'm just the dumb one with no past lives and useless abilities, remember?"

Lucas put a hand over Ariana's. "You're a lot more than that." She pulled away.

Lucas frowned and took a step back from Ariana. "Azoria worked for Elder Sorrento, didn't she?"

"Most of the time, yes." John stroked his chin. "And the blue gates are Or-dway."

"Three elders working together," Julien said soberly. "That hasn't happened since..."

"World War II?"

Elgisard nodded. "Yeah. That's bad. At least we have these." He indicated the glass case with the relics.

Jonah walked in, with the smaller Sect man and someone else.

"Victoria?" asked Lucas.

"What's going on?" said Katie.

Victoria said, "Zacke's in trouble."

Ariana stepped toward her. "Why?"

"What happened? Where is he?" John demanded.

"I'm not sure." Victoria's hands slid into her pockets. "Not answering my texts." He flew away very angry.

"Why are you here, anyway?" asked Ariana. "You work at a burger place."

"I'm a Sect agent," said Victoria.

"Not anymore," said Jonah.

"Not your decision," spat Victoria. "your group need to get your heads out of your asses."

"Okay," said Katie, raising her voice. "I don't even want to know what any of that is about. Focus. What about Zacke?"

Victoria sighed. "He found out his mother was working with the Rageto."

"What?" said Ariana, "The same mom that called him a demon and left for some church?"

"It wasn't a real church," explained Victoria, "It was the Rageto, apparently. They tricked her."

"Not the only one being fooled, looks like," said Katie.

"I wasn't trying to fool him. I was here on a mission. Zacke and me just... happened."

Katie said, "I thought the Sect just wrote books and stuff."

"Some do. Other actually try to help," Victoria aimed this at Jonah.

The small sect man spoke up, "The Sect don't get involved!"

"They killed Pete!" shouted Victoria.

"How did you know Pete?" asked John.

"He was like my uncle." Victoria elaborated, "Not by blood, but he trained me. We were very close. And the brothers killed three other Sect agents that day." She stared at Jonah. "There's no neutral for me."

"That's not the Sect's role," said Jonah.

"Really?" She pointed to Julien. "What are you doing here, then?"

"My duty. Documenting a breakout. Facilitating a discovery of a relics cache. Keeping the sides balanced."

"Bullshit. Things have changed. Five relics, five warriors in the same place? Wake up!"

"Balance," Jonah insisted.

Victoria yelled, "That motto was written on papyrus. Look around. There is no balance."

"There will be," Jonah spit the words at her.

"Quiet!" said Lucas.

"No!" shouted Victoria. But she felt something too.

Lucas pointed up. "Listen!"

They all heard nothing. That was the point. A large wave a silence was pushing in, oppressive, like sound fled the world and left only pressure. It grew oppressive on their eardrums, pushing in.

John yelled, "Get down!"

The pressure bore into them, no sound, just an invisible wall of pressure. John and Julien went down, pulling Katie to the corner of the room. Lucas grabbed Ariana and Victoria and laid flat on the ground.

Jonah and the small man stood and faced Victoria. They shouted the word, "Balance!"

The ceiling exploded upward. There was still no sound, just the dense pressure escaping the room as the roof and ceiling ripped away. The two Sect men were sucked into the night. No time for screaming, just gone. It was like the roof and the men left out an air lock in space.

The pressure abruptly ceased. Bits of asphalt roofing fell back in, debris and dust from the drywall filled the air, coated everything. Sound returned. More debris rained down. Julien looked up to the night sky, the entire roof gone, only splinters floating in the night. He was the first one to see the blue lines form.

Blue lines formed into a small rectangle. It elongated and pushed toward the ground. It reached for the display case. Julien leapt for the relics. His right hand almost to the case, he shouted, "No!"

The Blue lines sliced down to the ground, surrounding the case. Three of Julien's fingers disappeared into the lines. He screamed. John pulled his hand back.

The glowing blue box rushed back into the sky, gone. The display case was gone, as though it never existed.

Julien shouted. He shoved his hand under his armpit. The blood poured from the open wounds and down his shirt, the red circle getting bigger.

John tore his own shirt, making a bandage around Julien's ruined hand. They all rose, tiny debris still falling all around.

The relics were gone.

They rose to their feet, covered in drywall dust and spotted with debris. No one spoke.

Julien held his bandaged hand and stared at the loss. The relics that had been safe in the hills nearby since 1859, they were now in the hands of Rageto elders.

CHAPTER TWENTY THREE
Poison

David's breathing was ragged and hard, like he was Cody's grandfather instead of his father.

"Dad, what happened?"

Cody had been with his father for nearly an hour, but David couldn't or wouldn't speak. He seemed very sick, but Cody had no idea what to do.

They were in a cave somewhere. It was well stocked with provisions and modern camping gear. The cave was warm, with a steady electric heater going. The natural space was large and spotting the two cots, Cody knew his dad hadn't been alone. *John.*

The warmth made him feel strange. He looked at his dad, who was clearly struggling. Cody realized with horror that he'd finally found his dad and his bladder was screaming at him. "Really?" he said out loud but aimed it at his inconvenient bladder. Then he remembered all the beer he'd been drinking. *This never happens in the movies.*

He didn't want to leave his dad, but he had to pee, so he asked his dad where to go. His dad pointed and Cody followed his directions. It led to the mouth of the cave. As he got closer, the warmth left him and by the time he reached the mouth of the cave, Cody was shivering.

Outside, the cold air hit his lungs and made him cough. The view was gorgeous. Trees everywhere he looked. They were on a hill or mountain, not too far up, maybe a few hundred feet. Snow covered distant hills and dusted all the treetops. Cody peed off the edge. Seemed the only practical thing to do.

He zipped and turned back. Carvings on the cave mouth caught his attention. They were old, but the symbols were nothing he recognized. He traced his fingers along the shapes, but the cold rock just made him shiver. He went back to his dad.

As he turned the corner, his father was over the heater. There was a small camp stove with a pot. David took it and poured the liquid in two metal cups, using a mitten to keep from scalding his skin.

"John... He only got tea. No coffee, sorry."

"Dad?" Cody rushed to hug him, but David stopped him with a hand, firmly outstretched. It crackled once with a spark, as David warned, "It's not safe."

Cody stopped, trying to ignore the rejection. He just wanted to understand, "Dad, are you okay?"

"No," answered David.

He offered sugar packets to Cody, who took two and poured them into his tea. He swirled the tea and drank.

"The last attack has passed," David wheezed. "John brought me here to be away from people. You shouldn't be here."

"Dad," he tried to keep his voice steady, "I haven't seen you in months. You promised to come back. Tell me what happened."

His father sighed, ran his hands through his long hair. His full beard showed flecks of silver reflecting off the firelight. David sucked in air, then released heavily. "I have Zamma in me. Sazzo, too."

"What? Dad, no. They're both dead. You used John's relic sword, remember. They're gone forever. John said..."

"John didn't know. Or he was wrong. Doesn't matter." David stared into the fire, his mind unfocused.

He couldn't take it. Cody shouted, "It does matter! I have so many questions and every time you give me half answers. Stop being John!"

Cody thought he wasn't going to answer. Cody was about to explode. His dad noticed and held up a hand.

"He had the only cell phone. No other way to contact me in here." David put down his tea and turned fully to his son. "Cody, what happened in that room – when Sazzo killed Zamma and took his power?"

"He – Sazzo, Derek – he took a knife from somewhere. I can't remember exactly. Derek was talking a lot, on and on. He said if he killed an elder and said the right spell that he would get his powers. Then he stabbed Zamma over and over."

"Did he say the spell three times?"

"I think so. Yeah. I'm sure it was three times. He always said his spells three times – at the mission, at the beach. The weird words sounded kind of stupid, but they were still scary."

"That's it," David sighed, "it's permanent then."

"What does that mean? I want to help you. What can I do?"

"Nothing. Sazzo killed Zamma and took his power, his knowledge, everything. I try to block them out, but his memories are ancient, foul. Poisonous. I killed Sazzo with a relic."

Cody realized where this was going. "Wait, you didn't say any spell. You couldn't have their powers."

David shook his head. "Sazzo said the spell three times. Many Rageto do this. But they don't have to. A magic spell works when it is said only once. The brothers said it three times to deepen the spell, to lengthen the effect. That's why Sazzo's conjurings were so powerful."

Cody remembered the horde of spiders, the giant squid, and of course that dragon.

Cody tried to remember the intricacies. "John explained the rules. If you get killed by a relic, true death. No do-overs. If you get cut with a relic weapon, no more re-births. Your ancient dies with the body you are in. Right?"

David nodded, "Yes. Relic injury will prevent re-birth unless the person giving that injury is killed with true death themselves. It is a habit to assume a relic injury means this instantly, but also is impetus to end that person, thus breaking the 'spell.' "

"So, when Derek/Sazzo slashed John at the tower, John was stopped from re-birthing again," David elaborated. "But then I killed Derek with a relic, he got a true death, and the spell broke for John. That's also why Zamma kept trying to find John, so Zamma would be free to re-birth."

Cody said, "But after the battle, John said he couldn't re-birth after he got slashed."

"Chalk it up to the craziness of that night. Or wishful thinking," said David, "but when John realized he was still in the struggle forever, he didn't take it well."

Cody shook his head. "What about you? That's not what happened to you."

"No. Must have been the power of that spell. I lived among them for years, learned more than I ever wanted to about magic. I think when Sazzo killed Zamma the same night, less than an hour before he died..."

"The spell was still active, so it like, overflowed and melded inside you?" Cody asked. "But, Dad, that's great. You must be a super badass now!"

David shook his head, tried to smile. "I'm a lot of things, kiddo. But I'm not that." David clutched his chest. "It's... it's like poison." David rolled to his side, rocking again, but not gently. He seemed racked with pain.

David winced and tried to find a happier subject, "Enough about me. How are you. How's Caroline?"

"Mom? Oh crap. She must be out of her mind right now. I've been gone for... I don't even know how long."

David stared deep into the fire. "She is so beautiful." David took notice of the cave. "Do you remember our camping trips? Oh, of course not. You were so young when I left. So young." His eyes filled with tears. "I didn't mean to leave. Not really. Do you know that?"

"I know, Dad. The brothers took you, made you a prisoner."

"Yes. So long. So long." He looked up. "Then I saw you. On that beach. That was a bad night, mostly, but... but I got to see you. I got to see my boy." He sobbed, rocking, the tears a flood down his cheeks.

Cody reached to hug him.

Suddenly, the air jumped to life, a current of electricity. "Dad?"

A lightning storm erupted from David, leapt across the cave and attacked one of the cots. It jumped and burst into flame.

The storm died as fast as it came. Cody jumped to his feet, eyeing a sleeping bag that might put out the fire. Before he could act, ice crystals formed all over the ruined cot. The fire died instantly, even the smoke whizzed out of existence. David lowered his weary arm. Cody noticed his fingertips were blue for a moment before they turned back to pink.

David sipped his tea and stared at the cot. "That's Zamma."

Cody followed his dad's gaze. "Wow. That's pretty cool." Cody shook his head and tried to focus. "Dad, where are we?"

"Canada." His dad kept staring at the cot, sipping his tea.

"Random," said Cody.

The full-length mirror in the corner caught his eye. He'd come through it just a short time ago. He wasn't sure how long. The traveling messed with his internal clock. "Why the mirror, Dad?" He didn't want to say, *Because you look really bad.*

"I've been watching you." David cocked an eyebrow, "You're too young to drink, Cody."

Cody blushed, then it flashed into anger. "Wait. If you can watch me like Zamma, why didn't you leave? Contact me?"

"I can't travel through them, just look." He looked into his son's eyes, "I'm sorry Cody. It was too dangerous to leave. John agreed."

"John." The old anger at John returned. He knew it was unfair to blame everything on John, but he couldn't help it. *I need to be mad at someone,* he thought. "Why didn't he contact us? Something?"

"He wouldn't leave me." David sipped. The tea seemed to calm him.

"Where is he now, then?"

"Not sure. He felt the Ley line activate. He disappeared. Could be anywhere."

Cody remembered his unexpected trip to Manila. "Yeah, I get that." Cody looked at the mirror. *How do I help? Mom? No, that wouldn't work. She might kill Dad on the spot. John? No, John's already been here. He obviously couldn't help him.*

He thought of the book. *The scholar had a book. Didn't he say that some of the warriors back there were Rageto and Amartus? Someone must have a power that can help.*

Cody said, "Dad, we have to go."

"No, son, too... too dangerous to be around others."

Cody hooked his arm under his dad and lifted. It wasn't hard. Whatever John had been feeding him wasn't much. Cody walked his dad toward the mirror. Cody didn't know if he could do this. Mirror walking freaked him the hell out. Last time he tried to get home he'd ended up in that crazy place of stone corridors. Now he was trying to get back to that prison willingly. *I have to do it. I hope this works.*

Cody closed his eyes. He thought only of there, stone and gray and warriors. He tried to remember every detail, not just of the architecture, but the way the stone felt against his fingers. He thought of the warriors' faces, their clothes, the smell of so many people together.

David wheezed but didn't fight him. Cody opened his eyes. The stone room appeared in the mirror. He concentrated and then pushed his dad through the mirror. David disappeared from the cave in Canada.

And instantly came flying out of the shield in the stone prison. David's head popped up, surprised by the water. He crawled out awkwardly and stumbled to the stone floor, a stranger helping him up. "Where's..." David sputtered, "Where's Cody? Help him! Help my son, please!" David pleaded to the room of strangers.

An older man rushed over and filled the shield with water again. "Everyone stay put. Let the water still." They all stood and waited. A moment passed. Then another. Everyone stayed perfectly still. A few stopped breathing. The water in the shield was still, calm. Like glass.

A head rose from the shield, then shoulders. Cody tried to be fast, not knowing if he would be stuck — half in and half out. He yelled in surprise and his eyes darted open. "Cold!" He used his arms on either side of the shield and pushed up, but the shield wasn't flat, it was like a shallow bowl. He wobbled. Two warriors rushed over and yanked him out. Cody's foot caught the edge of the shield and it tipped end over end, the last of the water spilling out as it clattered on stone.

"So cold," Cody said again, the warriors put him down on shaky legs.

David rushed to his son. He checked over his son, top to bottom, spinning him around.

Cody said. "I forgot about the water."

David hugged his son and the room erupted in cheers.

His dad was struggling to stay up, making what Cody first thought was a rasp. The rasp deepened and then slowly turned into a wild laugh. "Damn son. That was some ride!" The room laughed with them.

David realized there were a lot of strangers around them.

A warrior stepped forward and sniffed the air. "Why does it smell like Zamma?"

Cody spotted the scholar, book in hand. "This is my dad. We need your help."

CHAPTER TWENTY FOUR

Aftermath

Katie stared at the gaping hole where Julien's ceiling used to be. "How could they attack your house?" asked Katie. "John said our houses were off limits."

"That's true much of the time, but it is not an absolute." Julien unwrapped the second layer of his bandage. "Pentoss. I hope you have told these people the whole truth."

"I have, I told them."

"You told them the thing we tell all the young ones, right?" Julien said, another layer of bloody bandage unwrapped around his hand. "That while the ancient is being rebirthed, their homes are filled with inherent protection. That's true. But I have lived in this house less than a year. I am a fully activated adult warrior. There is no inherent protection built up here. Unless I want to put Rageto magic charms on my house, which I would never do."

Julien said this as he was unwrapping his – her, hand. Ariana imagined a woman as she watched Julien unwrap his hand. He was clearly a man, but Ariana thought that she was taking on more and more of a woman's mannerisms, like becoming Unna as he spoke. The bloody towel was soaked red. Ariana didn't want to look at the ruined fingers again. When the towel was taken away, the stubs of his fingers were fully healed.

Katie began, "What the hell?"

"Language," Ariana said. Katie pursed her lips, but Ariana reminded, "You asked me to help you with that." She looked at Julien's hand again, the stubs that used to be fingers healed over as though a wound from childhood. Ariana couldn't help herself, "But seriously, what the F?"

"Unna's talent is healing," said John.

"That's convenient," said Ariana, "and really cool." She kept staring at the hand.

"You can't just grow new fingers?" Katie blurted, not sure if she was kidding. "No, I think I'm serious. Can some warriors do that?"

Julien smiled at her, no answer.

Katie looked at his hand. "Oh crap. Awkward? Too soon?"

"Not at all. It was funny. But I'm not a lizard." Julien examined his hand. "I will miss these fingers. But we must be serious, now. We lost good people tonight."

Victoria didn't respond to that.

"And five relics," Lucas said.

"And the elders will pay for that," said John. Caressing Julien's healed hand.

"Why didn't they just attack us?" Katie pointed to the enormous hole where the roof had been. "If they could do that?"

Julien answered, "Because now they have five relics, enough to come back and finish us all."

John added, "Forever."

* * *

Zacke waited until dark. He made his way off the rooftop in a shadow, floating down where he was sure no one could see. Sea Valley didn't have a lot of high buildings. The four-story hotel he descended was the tallest in town, not counting the seven-story fire tower at the edge of the city. On firm ground, he walked home. The old shame of flying his mother had caused was gone, but not the danger. Even in this small city, people were everywhere. He could be spotted any time, day or night. It was only luck so far that he hadn't been caught. But now that he had flown without guilt, he couldn't imagine not doing it. It was a part of him, and it also drained his energy less and less. He imagined a world where he could fly anywhere, no secrets.

He arrived home and heard soft jazz playing on his dad's old ihome. He'd never been into it, but it gave him comfort when his dad put on a jazz classic from the 50's. Ella, Getz, Gillespie. He smiled as he entered, then stopped smiling when he saw the beer in his dad's hand.

His dad heard him enter. Sitting in his chair, he faced the music. He didn't turn around when he said, "I thought of hiding it, to make you feel better."

Zacke collapsed into the love seat facing his dad. "Dad, it's okay. I'm too tired to lecture you."

"I see it. You look weary, Zacke," said his dad. "Care to tell you old dad your troubles. Is it just about your mom?"

"No. I mean, yes, it's partially about her," he knew he couldn't tell him everything. "You wouldn't believe me anyway, dad."

"Try me."

Zacke looked at his dad. He looked to the beer in his hand. He thought of all that happened; his mom leaving, his guilt, the ancient struggle he was involved in without his consent. Zacke closed his eyes. When he opened them, he said, "Okay, here it is."

Zacke told his dad everything. From the first moment he felt different as a kid, to quitting sports when he found out he could fly, to what really happened at the fire tower and all the way into the day's events. It took just under two hours.

His dad hadn't moved, though his face had been a roil of emotions. Zacke ended up looking past his dad, telling him the story almost like a shaman telling a tale. He'd even gotten up and acted out a few parts of the story. He glanced back at his dad's face only for emphasis or to make a point. Dad's face was like watching someone see a great film for the first time. He was so invested he'd let his beer go flat and had to set it down so he wouldn't spill it.

Zacke sat on the loveseat, spent. He finally said, "Sorry that took so long. I forgot a lot of those details."

His dad burst into tears.

"What? What is it?" Zacke leaned forward.

"I'm so sorry," Dad sobbed, covered his face. His sniffed back the last sob and looked into his son's eyes. "You've been through so much. I'm so sorry I wasn't there for you."

"Wait? You believe me?"

Dad spread his hands out, "Of course."

Zacke leaned back into the loveseat. "Wow. Thank you. I really needed to talk to someone."

"I'm honored it was me. Deke hasn't had a real conversation with me since he was twelve."

Zacke laughed.

"Besides, I have to believe you, Zacke. You're smart, but even you couldn't have made up all that stuff."

They both laughed at that.

Dad noticed his warm beer. "I'd say you can grab a beer after that story, but I already feel like the world's worst dad."

"Dad, you aren't."

"I wasn't fishing for that but thank you. Tonight isn't a pity party, not exactly."

"Yeah, otherwise there'd be beer cans everywhere." Zacke raised an eyebrow.

His dad laughed. "I'm glad we can joke about my recovery. Even if it's on pause tonight."

Zacke put his feet up on the coffee table. Zacke realized it wasn't just Jazz playing. Right now, it was Howlin' Wolf, 1959. *It's the blues he's drinking to,* thought Zacke.

"I keep thinking about you, Zacke. I mean, I get Deke. He's mad I let your mom walk out. He's mad I started drinking. We push each other's buttons, too."

"Ya think?" Zacke smiled.

"Okay, understatement. I won't judge him for the stuff I suspect he's doing. I can't father him anymore. I can only try to help. I can sure as hell worry. But you, Zacke. Different kid altogether. I love you both equally, but Deke demands to walk his own path. You, I think you've been trying to find a path for a while. Maybe this is it."

"I don't know. I'm still confused as hell."

"I bet. But, to no one's surprise, least of all me, you turn out to be a true hero."

"Dad, stop."

"And the sad thing is I had nothing to do with that," said Zacke's dad.

"Hey. That's not true. You think I got any of what I am from Mom?"

"Hey. She's still your mother."

"I know, I know." Zacke struggled for the words. "I got a lot from you, dad. You're not perfect."

"Hmm. Thanks?"

"No, I mean, that's what I like about you. You're a man. Just a good man. You don't go shooting up your workplace, you didn't sleep around on mom, when you fell into the bottle you found your way back again and I know how hard that must be for you."

"That's a pretty low bar, is it?" Dad smiled.

"Stop it." Zacke held his side, "Don't make me laugh right now. And you listened to my story. When I told you everything, you really listened."

"Least I can do, son."

"And you believe me."

"Of course I do, son." Dad thought for a long moment. "Actually, it explains a lot. With your mom, but also how you've been for that last few months. I just..." his dad choked up. He took a swig of beer, and winced at the hours old taste. "I just know I can't help you." He put his can down and looked at Zacke, "And that scares the hell out of me."

"It's okay Pops. I got this." He gave his dad a wide smile and thought of Victoria. The last betrayal. *Who else do I have?* He smiled again at his dad.

Right on cue, the song "No place to go" came on.

"Goodnight Dad."

"'Night Zacke."

Zacke went to his room, passing Deke's quiet room on the way, meaning he was probably out for the night. He thought of texting Victoria. He pulled up her number, a picture of them together popped up with her contact.

He hit delete and threw it on his nightstand. He'd noticed the dozens of texts from the others. He rolled over and finally fell asleep.

* * *

"Holy River, what is he?" said a warrior woman, coming from the back of the room and getting her first look at David.

"He's my dad, so watch it." He turned to David, who could barely stand again. "Help me get him to a bed."

What ended up passing for a bed was a raised stone bench, long enough for a man and draped with cushions to resemble a mattress. Being stuck in this magical realm didn't offer much comfort, Cody realized.

David moaned, clutching his chest.

"Okay, what do we do?" asked Cody, addressing the scholar Bevan.

The scholar wasn't sure Cody was speaking to him.

"The book," Cody pointed, "what does the book say?"

He looked puzzled, the scholar, then he realized what Cody meant. He held it up, "This? It's just an old novel I had with me when I was dumped here. H.G. Wells, 'War of the Worlds.' "

"What? You said you were a scholar – a Sect scholar!"

"I am," answered Bevan.

"Then help him," said Cody.

He put down the book. "What's wrong with him?"

Cody recounted the string of events, from Sazzo killing the elder and taking his powers, to all the events that led to his father killing Sazzo, he even threw in John and David's theories about what was happening to him.

"That's tricky." Then the scholar pontificated, "I figured one of those brothers would kill an Elder one day. Nothing but trouble. There's an old tale about them around 1440..."

David groaned and seem to pass out.

"What about a partition spell?" said one of the Rageto warriors.

"You got that spell handy, do you?" Bevan shook his head.

An arc of electricity sparked around David. It wreathed his face.

"Never seen that before," chimed in an Amartus warrior.

"What's his ancient's name?" asked Bevan.

Cody answered, "I don't think he has one. John – umm, Pentoss, thinks he's a new birth."

"Really? So, from an act of betrayal and murder by disciple to elder – all that power poured into a new birth. And an Amartus one at that. Hmm." Bevan stroked his chin but didn't say anything else.

"Does it mean something?" Cody asked hopefully.

The scholar scratched his chin. "Not sure."

"Not helpful!" yelled Cody.

"Hey. I have a lot of knowledge in here," Bevan tapped his head. "But I've been here a long time. Memory's fuzzy. Do you know when he manifested his abilities? Age 15? 16?"

"No. They came late." Cody tried to remember what his dad told him. "He was grown, maybe in his twenties? I'm not sure."

"Isn't he your father?" asked Bevan.

"He was gone a lot. Long story."

"I'm so sorry, Cody," David muttered. "I was 27."

"Wait. Maybe?" Bevan scratched his head. "Yes! That might explain it." he looked around. "Nestor, come here. And..." he scanned the room. "Amina, I need you too."

A broad-shouldered man around forty and a woman in her twenties came over.

"You've heard what was said?" asked Bevan.

"Of course. Nothing ever happens to us here. We've all been listening." Nestor waved his arm, and many applauded like they agreed.

"Good. Then you see our problem. Amina, you are a body healer. You once pulled energy from an entire stadium of people, correct?"

Amina nodded. "Yes. My elder needed an emergency source of energy."

"Right," Nestor laughed, "Because Pentoss was sent to kill the old bastard."

"We got away," said Amina. "Didn't see his ass again for thirty years."

"My point is, you can diagnose this man if his body needs healing. Nestor uses his best ability and help order and heal his mind."

Nestor clarified, "I can bring his mind into focus, help him see memories clearer. The healing is up to him." He hooked his thumb at Amina, "But I'm not working with her."

The scholar rose and slammed his palm into the man's forehead. "Focus your own mind. Have you been listening as well as gawping? This man has Sazzo and Zamma's powers."

"So?" said Amina, "Zamma and my elder hated each other."

"Zamma killed your elder, I'm afraid," said Bevan.

"You lie!" screamed Amina.

"Not helpful," Cody muttered.

"Sometimes I do lie, but not now." said Bevan. "The Sect is certain. So, think. If he got Zamma's powers, he also got his memories. Who trapped us all here?"

Nestor's voice was broken glass, "Zamma."

Bevan finished his thought, "And who may be the only one to get us out?"

Amina glared at Nestor, who nodded back. They both knew what to do.

They stood on either side of David, who was still breathing in short, shallow breaths.

They began.

CHAPTER TWENTY FIVE

Focus

Chet the Uber driver stopped. "Umm, are you sure this is it?" said Zacke.

"Yeah. I dropped off some people here last night." The driver pointed to the roof, which showed massive damage. "I wonder what happened?"

"Are we good?" asked Zacke as he stood at the car door.

"Yeah. Paid through the app." Chet backed out and drove away, too fast.

Zacke sighed and steeled himself for whatever he was walking into. He'd finally checked all his texts, but they didn't make a lot of sense. John has a wife? More trouble with relics? Something about healed fingers as the texts got more intense.

He walked up to the house, where someone that seemed like security met him. "You Zacke?"

"Yeah. Where do I go?"

"This way," said the sect man sent to replace Jonah.

He was led into a very expensive home. In the next room were his friends, John, and a strange man. They were arguing. One of thin man's hands was missing fingers. Zacke overheard, "Pentoss, no. There aren't enough of us and we don't know where they are."

John answered, "We can't let them have five relics."

"Umm, hey everyone," said Zacke.

Katie and Ariana jumped up and ran to him, pulling him into a hug.

Katie patted him on the arm. "More crazy shit happening, bro."

He hugged back. "What else is new?"

"Oh. Quite a lot," said Ariana.

Lucas smiled across the room at him. Zacke could see the warrior within him more every day. He wasn't sure if it was Lucas maturing or the ancient taking over. Maybe both.

The strange man was moving toward Zacke, extending his hand. "Oh, better shake this one." They awkwardly repositioned their shake as Julien had almost offered his damaged hand.

The awkward left-hand shake done, John spoke. "Zacke, this is my wife Unna."

"Wait, you're gay?" asked Zacke.

John smiled. "No, this is just the body she got this time."

"You've missed a lot," said Katie.

"I'll bet," said Zacke.

Lucas added, "We also had five relics — but lost them when an Elder attacked."

Zacke said, "Yeah, well some stuff has happened to me too."

"We need you to help get the relics back," John said to Zacke.

"Pentoss," said Lucas, or more likely his ancient, "he just got here. Give him time to catch up."

John didn't seem to hear and headed straight to Zacke, clamping his shoulder. "Zacke, we can't let an Elder possess so many relics. They could wipe us out, for good. We must..."

"Must what?" Zacke threw off John's hand. "So, you're back. Great. You have a guy-wife, old ancient or whatever. We supposed to just jump back in your crazy adventure and take your word? How much truth do we get this time John? Want to start with where you've been?" Zacke realized he was not just mad at John. If felt good to aim it all at someone.

No one tried to calm Zacke. They all wanted to say some version of that stuff to John. Lucas stood motionless with his ancient smiling through, enjoying the new drama. Katie stood by Zacke's side.

"You are right." John's face changed. The defiant leader and warrior dissolved, and lines showed that Zacke had never noticed before. He appeared ten years older, weary. "Of course. Unna, can we all sit at the table? I need to sit, and I don't think I've eaten for a few days."

Julien rushed to John, taking his arm and leading him into the next room. The dining room was a formal one, with a large round table in the center. The chairs were surprisingly sturdy for their thin, sleek Norwegian style.

"Sit here, love. I'll get us all something." Julien left for the kitchen.

"I'm sorry Zacke," John said. "It is time for answers. I don't know where to start. Ask anything."

Katie jumped in. "First, where have you been? Why haven't you contacted us? It's been months."

"I know. I'm sorry. I was with David. He needed me."

"Why? What happed to David?" asked Lucas.

"We left and planned to come back. But only hours after we left, David changed. It started with a throbbing pain, then got worse quickly," said John.

"Was it the fight on the tower?" asked Ariana. "Was he hurt because of my linking?"

"Not hurt, cursed. He got Zamma's and Sazzo's abilities. I fear he got their memories, too." John was still frustrated that he hadn't figured it out. "Something about the spell Sazzo used."

"How?" asked Lucas. "I thought a spell had to accompany the taking of that kind of power. How did David end up with it?"

John shrugged, "How are you alive, old friend?"

"That's right," Kate pointed. "That's why the German brother was so scared of you. He kept saying you got a true death."

"The truth is..." said Elgisard, "I did."

Julien came back in with sandwiches, a whole array of different meats and cheeses, and fruit on a large platter. The guard from outside brought in pitchers of tea and water.

John turned to Lucas. "Explain, Elgisard. No one comes back from a true death."

"Is that on topic?" asked Katie.

"I know, this seems unrelated," said John. "But the River has been throwing new curveballs at us. This might help put more pieces together."

Julien smiled. "Curveballs? Using analogies from the current century? That's new."

John smiled and grabbed a sandwich, then another. "Elgisard, please. It may help. Then I will elaborate about David."

Lucas' mind sunk into Elgisard's memory. "If you think it will help." He closed his eyes and took Lucas back to the memory.

Cold. Bitter, but different from home. The Nordic winds of his childhood drove into the bone and could kill in seconds in deepest winter, like it had a wicked will. Alaskan cold tucked in like a friend and clung to you. Or maybe it was his fur lined jacket that made the difference. He shrugged and thanked the River for modern science. Easter was nearly here. It was Good Friday and he was looking forward to eating meat again in a few days. He didn't pray to any God anymore, but tried to follow local customs to fit in.

Then Elgisard spotted him. One of the brothers. Caron. Here. How? Didn't matter. Of course, he could be wrong. It was something about the walk. Then he caught the man's stare. Cold hatred poured from Caron's eyes. He smiled, not hiding it at all now.

Elgisard only had a bowie knife. He'd been hunting for weeks, though no one knew he was hunting for relics, not wild game. It was after five p.m., the streets of the small Alaskan town bustled, families everywhere getting ready for supper. No place for an open fight.

Caron was openly stalking him now. Ducking into a coffee shop, he announced the neighborly, "Evening," to all. Some murmured back. He asked the waitress, "Bathroom, darlin'?"

"In the back, sweetie."

"Thanks." He gave her a smile as he watched for Caron's approach. Did he get lucky? Would it be that easy? He turned his attention to the back door. As he left the building, Caron kicked his knee with all his weight.

Elgisard had been moving forward, but the kick came from his side, bending his knee the wrong way. He screeched, but before he could maneuver, Caron was on him, sticking something in his mouth. He instinctively bit down, but he only tasted wood. He couldn't bite his tongue for the blood rage.

"The berserker won't be out today, Viking," Caron spoke in a French accent this time. He felt pressure in his stomach, which bloomed quickly into intense pain. Caron had a knife of his own. He'd hit something vital. Elgisard knew no doctor could help him.

"I found the relic knife first. Goodbye forever, Viking."

He tried to rise again but couldn't. Killed for good by that particular monster. Stupid end.

A woman screamed, perhaps the waitress. "It's okay," whispered Elgisard. She screamed again. That worried him. Caron didn't like witnesses. Her screaming stopped. He heard the body fall.

"Merde!" was all Caron said as he stalked off, not even trying to hide the knife.

Elgisard lay dying. A few men came out the back, probably investigating the woman's scream.

That's when he felt the shaking. The ground beneath him made a terrible sound, then seemed to turn to water.

Elgisard relayed all this to the group at the round table. Coming out of a fifteen-year-old boy's mouth, it sounded even more surreal. He had never told anyone of his last death. Ariana sat with him. She didn't speak, just laid her head on his shoulder and squeezed his arm.

"I looked it up," said Lucas, "he covered up my death with the 1964 earthquake in Alaska. Just to cover his tracks."

"I've never heard of that one," said Julien.

Lucas said, "Big one. 9.5 magnitude. Killed lots of people and even moved the shoreline. Caused tsunamis up to 200 feet high. It must have been awful. But I was already dead. Didn't feel any of that."

Katie stared at Lucas. "Do you have a lot of memories like that?"

"Yeah. It's been kinda overwhelming," Lucas said. "I've learned so much from him. Everything hasn't come through yet, not all the memories of his lives. But I'm already not sure where he ends and I begin."

Julien asked. "How did you come back?"

"Maybe Caron lied about killing you with a relic," said John, still eating.

"From the German's face when he saw me come back, he believed it," said Lucas.

"And now, you are here." said John. "In the same place five new and old warriors reveal themselves? It's too much coincidence, even for the River."

"Maybe the River is changing." said Ariana, pulling away from Lucas. Lucas noticed, but said nothing.

"How?" asked Julien.

Katie looked to the sky and hit the table. "You're supposed to tell us!"

Ariana stood next to Katie. "Exactly. You're the adults. You're also super old ancient warrior people that are supposed to tell us what is happening. And you ask us? No, enough. What did that guy at the riverbed say? The Elders want us to Dissemble. Was that it?"

"You can't!" said John.

"The hell I can't," Ariana stood.

"Ari! Language," said Katie.

"Oh shut up," Ariana said. "I don't want this. I never did. I can barely control it. The voices are coming back. I'm starting to feel other people's thoughts again. Anybody else?"

"Me too," confirmed Katie.

"Yeah," said Lucas.

Zacke didn't acknowledge their response. "It's worse now. You..." he pointed to Lucas, "You're thinking about old battles as the Viking. And a lot about sex."

"Hey!" shouted Lucas, but the Viking gave a wry smile. Lucas shot a glance to Ariana, who looked uncomfortable.

Zacke turned to Ariana. "And you like Lucas but are freaked out by the Viking. You guys should talk to each other about that."

Ariana didn't respond. She looked to Lucas. He looked away.

"You are worried about your sister, but more about crazy ancient thoughts like Lucas." He looked at Katie closer, "And, yes I do know about Victoria. Were any of you going to tell me she'd been here? That she is Sect?"

"Hey! Stay out of my head, fly boy," said Katie, standing.

"I think we should all..." began Julien, but Zacke cut him off.

Zacke pointed at Julien, "You are trying to figure out how to get the relics back." He looked around at all of them. "And not one of you is thinking about Cody right now. Where is he?"

"Zacke. Enough," said John.

Zacke pointed to John. "And you! All you're thinking about is your wife. You need to focus. Be the leader, John."

John slumped.

Zacke shouted, "You left us! I have enough of that in my life." He sat down.

John just looked at them all. "I know. I'm sorry. I... I didn't know how to help David and get back here to help you too. David needed me."

"So did we, John," Ariana said.

"I know. I know," said John.

Julien took John's arm. "We are not the enemy. It seems my Pentoss can still make mistakes. But he is trying." He touched Zacke's arm. Zacke flinched, but then immediately relaxed.

Zacke looked at Julien. "Did you do that?"

"One of my talents, Zacke. Healing and soothing are the same talent."

"Nice to meet you, Unna," Zacke said, smiling despite himself. He wanted to hold onto his anger at John, but it slipped away. "Are you drugging me?"

Julien laughed, "No. Just soothing."

"Nice trick," Zacke smiled.

"I know," John said. "Try to win an argument when your wife can do that."

Julien smiled, "I was always right anyway."

John shook his head, neither confirming nor denying.

Julien said, "We need everyone calm, if we are to get the relics back."

"How?" asked Ariana.

"They are still close. They may use them as bait." answered Julien.

"But we saw them go," said Katie. "That blue Elder gate thing. They could be anywhere in the world."

"Yet they are still here. I feel them close."

"Okay, we're listening. Please don't do that John thing where you only tell us a few things now, promising to tell us everything later," said Ariana, folding her arms, staring at John.

"Does he still do that?" Julien chided John. "I've always told you to tell the team everything."

John began, "I didn't think..."

"That's the problem, dear." Julien shut him down. "We called it Pentoss-ing, by the way. Giving just enough information so we were more confused before a fight than before."

"I..." John gave up, "yes dear."

"See, that's all you had to say," Julien smiled. "It makes everything better."

John stayed silent.

Julien explained, "Relics are strange things. They have the power to destroy a warrior and bar them from the River, but they are also a connection to the River."

Ariana asked, "What does that mean?"

Julien said, "I died with these relics. My essence flowed back into the River, but I wasn't reborn into a new body for many decades. It is said that my healing ability is tied to the River's current."

Ariana arched a brow. "It's not a real River, so how does that work?"

"It is called the River because it flows. It's a flow of energy where we are born and where we rest. It's also a flow through all human consciousness. Some can tap into its power."

"Power? John said that power was only for the Rageto."

"I did, and it is. Natural power is one thing – the power of nature. They corrupt nature using magic," John elaborated. "Everything in nature has two sides. When one side uses power for their own ends, that is power used badly. It will corrupt."

"Is that true?" Zacke asked, Unna's soothing beginning to fade. "I have the power of flight, as crazy as that is to say out loud, but it is power. When I use it, it drains me."

"Me too. Overusing my shields sucks me dry," said Katie.

"True. The word power, too, is just a concept. An idea, a way to understand. The power of the River is where we come from. I can use it to heal."

John agreed. "You used it, too Ariana. When you linked us, that was the power of the River tying us together, making our abilities as one."

"Pentoss uses it in his muscles to fight well, even uses the River to help find other warriors. Of course, he was never the best at that," Julien smiled.

"No, thanks for reminding me. My ability, which is a gift from the River brought me to this city but finding you all wasn't easy. I used more practical means."

"David found us," said Zacke.

Katie said, "But, he didn't see that Cody was his son."

"The River has her mysterious ways," said Julien.

"The River is a bitch," said Katie.

Ariana shot her a look.

Katie shrugged. "Why would they keep the relics close for us to find?"

The teens said together, "It's a trap."

John laughed, "Yes, it surely is."

"But you want us to help, anyway, right?" Zacke asked, sighing.

"I do," John announced. "And I can't guarantee your safety."

"Well, that was honest," said Ariana.

Kate asked, "How do we find the relics?"

John said, "Ordway is very businesslike, compared to Zamma, who liked to hide and do things in the dark. But all Elders are megalomaniacal monsters, at heart."

Julien said. "She will make it obvious. Ordway wants us to find her henchmen."

"Are we ready for that?" Ariana asked the table.

John said, "Ordway fled last time."

"Last time we were all together," said Zacke, "seven against three."

"Now we have Unna. She has more than the ability to heal."

"Ariana, you're the local history expert," said John.

Ariana asked, "What kind of place are we looking for?"

John asked, "Are there any abandoned warehouses, or storage places that could be easily guarded, but still out of sight to the public?"

"Hmm." Ariana mentally scanned their city. "There are self-storage places and warehouse all over town."

"Those kinds of modern storage places have cameras everywhere." reminded Julien.

"Where are there no cameras these days?" asked Zacke. He scanned his brain for all the places he flies to around town.

Ariana said to herself, "Wait, would they be that...? What about a giant, abandoned theatre that has been boarded up for decades?"

John asked, "Where is this theatre?"

"Downtown, right on the corner of Ocean and Sequoia street."

John looked quizzical. "I didn't get to know the town that well. Where is that?"

Katie said, "Old town. Where the two main streets meet."

Zacke added, "Not many cameras in old town. Public building, but no one's been inside for years. Totally private."

Lucas got out his phone and pulled up a map.

Julien said, "Giant abandoned building..."

John finished, "Yet, In the heart of the city."

"And dramatic," said Julien. "a literal stage."

CHAPTER TWENTY SIX

Truth and Family

"Another crazy plan," Katie muttered under her breath as she came through her front door.

"Hey Katie," said Jason, her stepfather.

"Hey Jason. Where's mom?"

"She has to pull another double. Won't be home until late. Can I help?"

"No," Katie said, trying to keep the frustration out of her voice. She smiled. "Thanks anyway. Girl stuff."

"Got it." Jason hurried away.

"Maybe I can help," said Megan.

"You always just pop up, don't you little monster?"

"Grrr," Megan held up claws but kept a dead-pan expression. A bored, post-millennial mock of a monster.

Katie burst with laughter. "I needed that kid." Katie thought of tousling her hair, which Megan hated, but refrained. "Yeah, I could actually use your help."

"Really?" Megan did a double take. "I didn't see that coming. What's up?"

They headed to Katie's room. She hesitated. Megan had been dragged into her craziness earlier in the school year and ended up in the hospital. There was no scar, but Katie looked to where the bandage on her forehead had been, reluctant to put her near danger again. But now that Megan knew everything, she might be helpful. A voice still nagged inside, *You shouldn't get her more involved.*

Megan stepped back. "Okay, you're looking at me funny. What's going on?"

"I was going to ask you for help, but..."

"Ooh, is it dangerous?" Megan brightened. "Your super friends going to a battle?"

"We're not super... stop that. I wish you didn't know what you know, but you do, so..."

"So, I can help." Megan grabbed a pad of paper and a pen from her table. "What do you need?"

"Sometimes you freak me out. I was not this together at 11."

Megan wrote "Super To-do stuff" on the top of the pad and underlined it. She wagged her pen at Katie. "Almost 12."

"Yeah, right," Katie scoffed, "almost 12 in like seven months."

Megan swirled her pen upward. "You always round up."

"You are a kick, kid."

"What's the mission, sis?" asked Megan, on topic.

Katie paused. "That's the first time I did not have the urge to correct you with 'step-sis'."

"Good. Your powers are making you less of a jerk."

Katie laughed. "If only that was true. Okay, you can help. But only if you promise to be super safe."

"Got it. What's the plan?"

Katie asked, "Do you still hang out with your friends at the SouthWest coffee place?"

"Yeah. Every Saturday morning. I got a coffee drink last week. Like real coffee in it."

"Bold for 11." Katie felt a pang. Megan might go boy crazy soon, or worse. She said hopefully, "No more hot chocolate?"

"It was basically hot chocolate with a little coffee," Megan admitted. "But it was good!"

Katie smiled. "Okay, you know that old theatre across the street from South-West?"

"Of course. The haunted theatre."

"That's right. They did have a haunted house in that theatre when I was a kid. Forgot about that."

"No!" said Megan with the deep knowledge of local history. "Agnes lives there. She's still looking for her baby..."

"Agnes lives on the hill outside town. But she isn't living because she's a ghost," Katie corrected, "plus she isn't real."

Megan said seriously. "Umm. Yes she is. Chloe told me. Her brother had a friend who broke in one night and saw her. Swear to God."

"Kid, Chloe's brother and his friends are total douches, trust me." Knowing exactly the boys that kid ran with, all in Katie's grade. "Don't believe anything they say."

"I still think she's real." Megan let her nerves show. "Wait. I don't have to go in the theatre, do I?"

"No! That's the last thing I want. I just need eyes on the building. Can you convince your friends to walk close to, but not too close to the building? I need to know if anyone's been in it lately and how they got in."

"Yeah, I can do that."

"I mean it, Megan. You need to be safe. Don't go too close to the building and text me pics of what you find. Stay together, all of you. And if you see anyone, just run."

"It's downtown, in the morning. There will be lots of people around."

"Good. That's what I want to hear."

Megan stopped writing. "How much?"

"What?"

"How much are you paying me?" Megan said without a hint of kidding.

"What do you want?" Katie sighed.

Megan cocked a brow. "You know."

Katie did. "No. You are not watching that show. It will give you nightmares."

"I can handle it."

"I doubt it. Sorry kid, the whole thing's off. Price is too high. It probably would have gone south anyway."

"Aren't you using mom's Netflix password, anyway? Does she know you're watching *Hill House*?"

Caught. Katie nearly sputtered, but her eyes narrowed instead. "That was actually pretty slick. Okay, I will restart the show with you and we can watch two episodes tonight. Little black mailer."

Megan shrugged. "But, it worked."

"Our planet is doomed."

* * *

"Is that you Mija?" asked Josie, Ariana's mom.

"Yes, Mami," replied Ariana.

"Hungry?"

"Starved," admitted Ariana.

"Come here and help me."

"With what?" Ariana nearly raced into the kitchen. She'd been too worried to eat at Julien's house.

Ariana rounded the corner, her mouth watering. "Tamales? Really?"

"Yes, and I could use your help."

Ariana jumped in and started spreading the masa on the corn husks. "What's the occasion? Did I miss a holiday?"

"No." Josie rolled her eyes. "We have a girl coming for dinner."

Ariana chuckled. Her older brother Jorge had brought a few girls home for dinner, always a disaster. Then she remembered. "Wait. I thought Jorge was with Jaqueline now."

"He is." Josie placed the bowl of seasoned beef next to her daughter. "Move over. Let's get this assembly line going." Ariana handed her the corn husk spread with masa for the beef filling. "This girl is with Lalo."

"Lalo?" Ariana sputtered, thinking of her younger brother. "But he's like twelve. Who is this girl?"

Josie laughed. "Lalo is fourteen. His Quinceañero is coming up."

"Oh my God. Really?" a pang of guilt hit her, realizing how little time she'd spent with her family lately. She did the math in her head. Lalo really was 14 years old, nearly 15.

"Keep them coming, mija. Jorge will eat 12 of these if I let him. Lalo won't be far behind."

Ariana kept up the pace, handing off the tamales to Josie, who expertly filled them with beef and wrapped the end of the husk. They had made a few dozen.

"What's wrong, mija?" asked Josie.

Ariana flushed, realizing how deep she was in her own thoughts. "Nothing. Everything. I don't know."

"You have been distracted lately. Is it Lucas?"

Ariana shrugged. "Partially. I guess." She handed off another tamale. "What do you call it when you like someone, but you don't like a very particular thing about them."

"You call it a man."

Ariana chuckled.

"I'm serious. You think your Papi is perfect?" asked Josie.

"Of course. He's Papi."

"You and me, mija, are surrounded by men. You can't really think that."

"Of course not. I know my brothers are gross. But this boy." She wished she could just tell her, but how do you explain an ancient Viking is living in Lucas, *is* Lucas. "I want the boy Lucas is. That part I like. But it's like there is a man there too. Tough, dumb... sometimes completely inappropriate. I don't want that part of him."

Josie chuckled now. "Wouldn't that be nice? To pick and choose what parts we get of them. I would take your father's kindness and slap the abs of Drake on to his belly."

"Mami!" Ariana laughed. "Now that's all I'm going to see that when Papi walks in."

"It's only fair..." She motioned down to her own 300 pound body. "...since Papi gets this perfect goddess."

They both laughed. Just then Papi walked into the kitchen, his beer belly protruding. "What's so funny?" he asked.

Ariana stared at her dad's belly imagining the singer Drake's perfect abs superimposed. She howled with laughter. Josie joined her. Papi looked confused, shook his head and wandered out of the kitchen. As he left, Ariana offered a weak, "I love you Papi."

They kept the assembly line going, dozens of tamales done. The laughter died away.

Ariana said, "I guess mostly I want to find out who I am first. I still don't know where I fit." The masa nearly gone now, the assembly line slowed. "I just... just don't want to follow what a guy wants. I'm afraid if I don't find out where I fit, his stronger personality will, I don't know, lessen who I am. Does that make any sense?"

"It makes perfect sense, mija." Josie nudged her daughter gently, shoulder to shoulder. "You find yourself first. Boys can wait."

* * *

Lucas heard a knock at the door, the gateway between his garage bedroom and the house.

"Come." Lucas had been thinking of the next battle by going over Elgisard's experiences. He came out of his deep thoughts.

His mom and dad came in, both awash with worry. Mom said. "Lucas. We need to talk."

Lucas thought, *That doesn't sound good.* Elgisard rolled his eyes.

"He rolled his eyes," Dad pointed out.

"I saw," said Mom.

Lucas sat on the edge of his bed, putting his phone down on his rumpled bedspread. "Sorry. What's up?"

"You finished your sessions up a while ago," said Mom, "but I've called Dr. Mason. I think he can help. He's agreed to see you again."

Lucas shot onto his feet. "What? Why? I don't need a psychologist again." *I never did, actually.*

His father took a step back, but his mother stood firm.

"For things like that," Mom gestured to Lucas, "over aggressiveness, your grades are slipping, and you're wearing those blue contacts all the time now."

Not contacts, thought Lucas.

Dad added, "We think it's great that you have new friends, but random grown men traipsing through your bedroom is a bit..."

"Weird, dad? I got enough of that at school. I'm done with that, thanks."

"Hey!" said Mom, "That kind of thing. That's what I mean. You've never snapped at your father like that. If you won't talk to us, you need to talk to someone."

"It's like you're a different person, Lucas," said Dad.

More rage was coursing through Lucas than he liked. He'd noticed the spikes lately. He forced them under control. "I'm sorry. I know I've been... moody lately."

"Since the fire tower," Mom agreed. "We think you have PTSD."

"Mom, no!" another flare. "Sorry. Sorry. Mom, Dad, yes. I have been going through lots of changes lately, since even before that night."

"And you should talk to someone about them. You never talk to us anymore." A quaver in her voice betrayed her real fear.

Lucas didn't know what to say. *Giving any truth would ensure I'd be talking to a psychologist, or worse.*

"Your scaring us, son," said Dad gently.

Elgisard stretched through Lucas' mind, like milk through clear water. He put a hand gently on those of Lucas' parents. Lucas knew what Elgisard was thinking. He took over and said, "My transformation, this journey to becoming a man was sudden. True, recent events sped it up. I still love you both. You are great parents. My body still hasn't caught up to the changes inside." He stared into both of his parent's eyes, soft but firm. "But there is no going back."

Both parents drew in a sigh. Lucas wanted to hug them. He wanted to tell them that he was still their little boy. But what Elgisard said was true. The words to his parents were his own.

Mom said, "Will you see Dr. Mason?"

"No, Mom. I'm sorry."

She nodded, sadly. "We're here if you need us."

"For anything," added Dad.

Elgisard and Lucas smiled, but stood firm. Mom and Dad realized this conversation would not end in a hug and they left the room.

Lucas thought of rushing to them, hugging them, but the moment was lost. The door closed. He stared at the door, then noticed his old eyeglasses sitting on a table. The ones he'd never need again. They could never understand the ancient warrior inside, but either way growing up is a one-way road.

* * *

Cody paced back and forth.

The two warriors over his father were stood on either side, eyes closed.

The woman chanted the same phrase over and over. It was in a mix of languages, a spell. The man moved his hands over David's body up and down, hovering above as though scanning for something.

"Any luck?" asked Cody.

Nestor said, "Not yet. This is difficult..."

"It's more difficult when you talk," Amina replied, ending the spell. "Spells need concentration."

Nestor scoffed, "You'd never make it in the Amartus, if that's all it takes to distract you."

The scholar Bevan broke in. "Even trapped together, we Sect must referee. Concentrate, both of you. This man has the powers of two Rageto ancients in his Amartus body and mind. And he's probably a new birth."

"That's the problem," said Amina. "He can't take it. Not his body, but his psyche. A weak Amartus."

"We are the strongest," Nestor reasoned. "We don't need foul magic to fight or heal... wait. Here it is." Nestor moved his hands to David's side, less than an inch above his body.

Cody stopped pacing to see closer.

"It's behind his heart," said Nestor.

"Yes," Amina agreed, "I feel it now." Her hands made a triangle shape. "You are correct, Amartus, behind the heart. It is not of the body."

"What is?" asked Cody.

"Not sure," Nestor said. "I'm a healer, but my talent is intuitive. I can't see inside your father like an x-ray. It's more..."

"Like an allegory?" asked Amina.

"Yes." Nestor said, surprised. "Is that how it is for you?"

"What does that mean?" Cody held up his hands, frustrated.

"It's like tarot cards," said Amina. "In most people's hands it's rubbish..."

"It is rubbish," said Bevan.

"Yes, but in the hands of someone attuned to the River anything can be revealed." The woman elaborated, "A set of pictures tell a story, of what may be."

Nestor added, "Like visualizing an idea. Yes. For me as well," he nodded. "Something is wrong with his heart. But it is not clear what."

"Does he need surgery?" Cody looked at his dad, his face twisted in pain. "What is it?"

"It's not the physical organ," Nestor stared at David. "It's at the back of his heart. Might be a regret, self-loathing, something getting in the way of his talents."

"A blockage," said Amina, nodding.

Nestor looked to Cody. "Not physical. This is a block in his mind or spirit, possibly self-imposed."

David gasped. His eyes grew wild and made Cody jump back. His breathing grew shallow again, then fell back into uneasy sleep.

"There is nothing either of us can do." Nestor looked into Cody's eyes. "If you don't unlock what is blocking him, the strain will kill him."

Cody looked down on his father and had no idea what to do.

* * *

Zacke was back at home, alone in his room. His mind wouldn't shut off. He wanted to relax, block out reality. He also wanted to think about the next day, the sure trap they were walking into, but his thoughts kept going back to Victoria. As if he conjured her, a knock came at his bedroom door.

Victoria said, "Zacke? It's me. Can we talk?"

He rose and stood but paused at the door. His hands rested on either side of the doorframe; eyes closed. He finally grabbed the doorknob and opened it.

Victoria stood there. "I'm sorry."

"That it?" Zacke asked with a cold stare.

"No. There's more." Victoria gestured to his room, "Can we please talk?"

"Fine." Zacke closed his door, "But not here. I need some fresh air. If we take a walk, will we be jumped by your Sect buddies?"

"No." Victoria thought about Jonah and his partner sacrificing themselves for their faction's version of duty. "Things have changed. There's a cease fire, for now."

"Can't wait to find out what that means." He motioned for her to go first. They headed out of the hall, past the living room.

Dad offered, "Oh, hey Zacke, I hope it was okay to let her in."

"Yeah. Fine, dad. Going out." He glanced over to see what beer his dad was on. Just one can. He hoped that was a good sign. They walked out the front door, Zacke snagging a light coat against the cold night air.

Victoria said, "Okay, you are walking really fast."

He continued down the residential sidewalk, passing under streetlights. "That's because I'm really pissed. So, talk. I'll think about listening."

"I hope so. First, I'm very, very sorry I didn't tell you everything."

"You didn't tell me *anything*," said Zacke. "I went back over everything. From the day I met you. I know nothing about you. Zero. I don't know why I never questioned that, almost like I didn't notice. Do you have powers, too? Some spell or something?"

"No. Sect don't do that. I have told you things," offered Victoria, "How I feel about you is true."

They turned a corner on the dark street, only illuminated by intermittent streetlights on each corner. The darker streets were fine with Zacke.

Zacke threw his list at her. "For a fact I only know is what kind of car you drive, that you have a strange love of that Cranberries band from the '90's and that you work at Ocean Burgers. That's it. Are you really eighteen?"

"Yes," she said, knowing some interrogation needed to happen.

"Have tons of roommates?"

Victoria answered, "No. I live alone, but Sect business happens there, so I lied."

"First day we met, first day at Ocean Burgers," asked Zacke, "I couldn't hear your thoughts. Was I hired so you could watch me?"

"No, actually," said Victoria, "we didn't know who the players were yet. Another 'not-coincidence.' The River just placed you there, I think."

"Did you accidentally save me that first time with The Brothers, like, weeks later?"

"No. Not an accident," she admitted. "By then we knew it was a breakout and that agents from both sides were headed here. We didn't know it was the brothers until that night."

Zacke's pace quickened with all his questions. "And who is we, exactly? Why were Sect people chasing you when you are Sect. In fact, what is the Sect a sect of? It's kind of a stupid name."

"Will you slow down?!" Victoria grabbed Zacke's arm and stopped him. "I'll tell you everything, right here and now. But my legs are shorter than yours!"

Zacke slowed his pace. They spotted a low brick wall in front of a house and sat down.

Victoria panted a moment. "You were doing that on purpose, right?"

"Yep. You deserved it."

"I know. I know." She caught her breath.

"Talk."

"The Sect are like the first scientists. We didn't believe in the hero complex of the Amartus, or the magic power grabbers of the Rageto. We chose to chronicle the River and the fight between the two groups."

"So what are you a Sect of, exactly?" asked Zacke.

"The name started as kind of a joke, then stuck. Most Sects in history are heretics that break off from the main religion. We are outside the struggle between the Amartus and the Rageto as they battle across the world and history."

"I know that part," said Zacke.

Victoria said, "Just throwing in some context. We have always been chroniclers of this true history, but we also get involved when the balance shifts too far in any direction."

"But that's crazy. Anyone can see the Rageto are monsters. They kill, do whatever they want. Why would you ever help them?"

"We don't help either side. And the Amartus are no angels. They've done really bad things. Killed lots of innocents, whether by accident or not. Many disasters aren't natural at all. It's not always the Rageto," Victoria said.

"Yeah, Cody told us about the trophies on the Brother's walls. All those disasters they caused. But, come on, it's clear who the good guys are."

"I agree."

"You do? You just said..."

"I was giving context, overview," Victoria said. "But what I'm saying is that everything has changed. You changed all of it."

"Me?" Zacke stood, stepping away. "How?"

"Look at what's happening." Victoria stood too, counting off on her fingers. "Lucas is a re-birthed warrior that got a true death more than sixty years ago. They don't ever come back. He did. In this place. Five warriors, a mix of new births and re-births in the same place? That doesn't happen. Zamma's book being here as this all started? A Sect station in the same town?" She was running out of fingers. "And.. and..."

"What's wrong?"

"Pete," she wiped her eyes. "Pete was the station chief here. He was my mentor. I called him Uncle Pete. They killed him."

"I know. The brothers." Zacke said, "I didn't know you were close."

"I'm an orphan. I stumbled onto the Sect when I witnessed a battle in an alley. A Rageto warrior won. A man saw I was in danger and got me out before the warrior spotted me. It was Pete. I've been with the Sect ever since."

Zacke put his arm on Victoria's. "I didn't know."

She wiped her tears. "No. Because I had to lie to you. I hated that. But all these coincidences, they just don't happen. The Sect has been around as long as The Amartus and Rageto. Nostradamus was Sect. He was a man, but could tap into the River, see future things. He wrote about Rivers and Warriors, all of it."

Zacke furrowed his brow. "Are you saying we're living some kind of, what, prophecy?"

"No!" Victoria yelled. She looked around the quiet street and lowered her voice. "The exact opposite. No one saw this coming."

"No one?"

"No one. Nostradamus is, well, let's be frank – is hard to pin down. A lot of his stuff sounds like madness. Some probably was. But there are lots of Sect scholars in history that have made predictions and prophesies. Many have come true. But this? What's happening now? This is new. It's shaken up all of the Sect, spilt us into more factions than ever."

"That's why those guys were after you?"

"Yes. My job used to be reporting on day to day activities, basic stuff." Victoria said. "Since Pete, I've taken on more. The Sect is fighting now. I'm with a faction that is done with the Rageto. Those guys were ordered to bring me back in, so their faction could convince me I was wrong."

"Is this just revenge for Pete?"

"Justice, hopefully. But it's more than that. Pete was building a private file. When I read about all the atrocities by the Rageto, it was bad. Then I saw the brothers up close. No side gets to hurt so many innocents."

They saw a shadow move across the street.

Zacke said, "Let's keep moving."

"Those aren't Sect." Victoria walked next him, keeping pace this time. "I know all the players now. It might just be someone out for a stroll."

"I don't believe in coincidences anymore," said Zacke.

They heard the shadow keeping pace across the street. Zacke suddenly ducked into an alley, cut off from all light. He hugged Victoria close.

"Umm. Okay," she hugged back.

"Shh. Hold on tight."

She laced her arms around him.

He whispered, "Don't be scared."

Victoria squeezed tighter.

Zacke left the earth. As they rose in the darkness, the feeling of nothing under her feet was disorienting. So was hugging Zacke again, for other reasons. She wrapped her legs around him. She thought, *You know, for safety.*

Zacke kept to the shadows, avoiding streetlights until he saw a safe place to land. The historic town square was the old heart of the city, where most of the buildings at least 100 years. There were some old three-story buildings facing each other where the two main streets met. He landed on one of them. Since the shiny new parts of town were more than a mile away, old town was quiet, no cameras. Plus, old town businesses were all closed early. No one should hear them on the roof.

He landed. Reluctantly, Victoria unfurled her legs from Zacke. She stepped onto the roof. The roof was flat. There were short walls all around at the edges, so no one could see the ugly metal ductwork from street level. Or them.

Zacke asked the question he'd held back. "Were we a part of Sect's plan?"

"No! My falling for you was not in the plan," she admitted. "And I did, Zacke. Pretty hard."

"How can I believe that?" Zacke shrugged. "Anything you say?"

"I don't know." she shrugged. "I probably wouldn't if I were you. Especially after how your mom treated you."

"Leave her out of it." The heat was instant and sharp. He softened, a little. "She had nothing to do with us, this."

"Doesn't she? Trust issues and women?" Victoria said softly. "I didn't want to lie to you."

"I don't either. I wanted to tell you everything, too, but..." he trailed off.

"What is it?" asked Victoria.

Zacke spotted some graffiti. It was painted on a place on the old theatre only visible from another roof. It was in bright white spray paint, which got his attention. What it said kept him staring.

Victoria stared too. "How did they know? Have you landed around here before?"

"I used to come her a lot. I've been trying to avoid flying altogether, lately."

Victoria said the obvious, "They've definitely been watching you."

"Yeah." They stared at the message. It was written in big letters, but it could only be seen from this height.

It read: "Fly boy. See you soon"

Backlit from streetlights behind it, the dark towering building stood silent except for the message meant just for Zacke.

"We guessed right." Zacke stared at the building. "And it's definitely a trap."

Victoria stood next to Zacke and took his hand. She squeezed as they stared at the towering old theatre. He squeezed back. The next battle was coming and they knew exactly where to go.

CHAPTER TWENTY SEVEN

Ticket To The Theatre

Megan came out laughing with her friends, breezing through the door. South-West Coffee was the hub of old town. Sitting at the corner of the new main drag and Ocean Avenue, it was the local's hangout, even with three Starbucks in town.

Currently, SouthWest coffee was, of course, on the southwest corner of old town; across the street was an antique shop, and real estate office, and various other shops. The last corner was an empty lot turned pocket park spruced up by a local committee until someone built something there again. Next to that was the derelict Sea Valley Movie Theatre.

As the girls walked towards it, they chatted about everything and nothing. Clothes, boys, school, teachers, TV shows they were binge watching.

"It's so ugly," Symone said as the theatre loomed. "Why did you want to go this way?"

They were half a block away, the large 1950's style marquee jutting out in a V shape. On either side, the old and broken neon shouted "SEA VALLEY." The marquee read "Save This Theatre" and gave a .org website.

"It's haunted, you know," said Jenn.

Symone rolled her eyes. "Everyone knows that."

"I don't want to get too close," said Megan, "I just wanted to check it out."

"It's just an old building," moaned Jenn. "I think my uncle is helping restore it. It was built in the 1920's."

"Old," said Symone.

"Classic. I think it's cool," Megan said. "Let's walk around." then she remembered her sister's warning. "Not too close."

Symone cocked her head. "Scared?"

Megan began, "No, I just don't want to..."

"I'm going," Jenn ran toward the theatre.

"No. Stop!" Megan said and ran after her.

They arrived and it wasn't scary at all. The asymmetrical building had four retail doors and windows that had been closed for years. Thick dust covered three of them, black painted plywood the other. In roughly the middle was the marquee above the main entrance. It was recessed, creating a small waiting area. To the right was an empty poster frame creaking in the wind. To the left was the old box office window. The glass had sizable cracks through the length of it. The front doors were glass, one covered in plywood. Two of the art deco door handles had a heavy chain around them with a combination padlock. From the cobwebs, Megan didn't think anyone had gone through those doors recently.

They all peered through the dusty glass front doors. The lobby was shallow and dominated by the concession stand. It was also a triangle shape, like the marquee. At its apex was a giant old machine labeled POPCORN in 1950's font.

Symone tugged on the chain. "I wonder what the combo is?"

"6969?"

The girls giggled. Megan wasn't sure why that was funny. She pretended she did.

"Let's walk around," said Megan.

They walked around the side to the old parking lot. It was overgrown with tufts of weeds, some knee high. Remnants of an old arm-like barrier to let cars in was half broken off, all solid orange with rust. Megan looked up at the closest window, a second story above one of the storefronts.

Did that curtain move? She looked back but couldn't be sure.

They walked to the back of the building, behind the long storefront, where they spotted a dirty homeless man sleeping on a mattress. He was tucked behind the building, next to an older wood structure attached to the building.

"My uncle said that used to be dressing rooms. It was just an old wooden building sitting down the block, so they attached it."

They walked past, toward the back of the building, a long way from the homeless guy. Megan kept one eye on the homeless man, making sure he wasn't watching or following.

The back of the building towered over them. It was easily four stories high. "Why is that part so tall?"

"Umm..." Jenn remembered, "oh yeah, my uncle said..."

"My uncle, my uncle," mimicked Symone.

"Stop. My uncle's cool. He knows stuff. My uncle..." she said to quiet the mocking chant, "says it's where the scenery is flown and the movie screen is stored. It's on these old ropes and pulleys and sandbags."

They kept walking, rounding the back side of the building, the alley. The back wall of the theatre was all concrete wall except for one red stage door. It didn't look used, elaborate cobwebs all over the corners and handle.

"Wish we could see inside," Symone said.

Jenn added, "I bet its cool in there."

I'll bet it's creepy and scary, thought Megan.

They completed the walk around by heading up the other long side of the building, towards the front again. They passed three more red painted doors, heavily adorned with graffiti. The first was an arched set of loading doors, the other two double doors, perhaps exits. The sconces over them were busted and glass and weeds covered the bottom of the long wall.

Megan scanned for anything strange. *Not much to see. I don't think anyone's here, sis.* As they rounded the last corner, nearly back to where they started, Megan scanned the two second story windows on this side. One had a heavy curtain, no movement. The other was blank, an open black triangle. She kept thinking someone would suddenly appear, but no one did.

By now, all girls were on their phones. "Gotta go. My mom will just pick me up here," said Symone.

"I need to walk back to SouthWest," Jenn said as she texted, "my Dad's picking me up there."

"Okay," Megan said, "I'll hang here with Symone until her mom comes."

"Ok. Bye-ey."

"Bye-ey," their signature sing-song goodbye echoed around.

They chatted and texted in front of the theatre. Megan texted her report to her sister, while Symone was probably texting something mean about her to Jenn, who just left. *I need new friends*, thought Megan.

Symone's mom pulled up, and they said their goodbyes. Her mom asked Megan if she needed a ride. She said no, but thanks anyway. They left. Megan looked back toward the theatre. The lobby was dark. A shadow moved. Megan squeaked. A bird hit the inside of the glass and flapped to the floor.

Megan took a step closer. "A pigeon?"

It was. A pigeon was inside the lobby. Just bobbing along on the deep red, heavily stained carpet. It pecked at the glass door. Once. Twice.

"Sorry little guy. Or girl. I can't get you out." Megan looked at the heavy chain again.

I wonder how it got in? Megan got a text back from Katie.

DON'T go near the theatre. Stay across the street. I'll come get you.

Megan: It's fine. I was with friends.

Katie: Was? Are you alone now???

Megan continued texting as she walked. She wanted to know how the bird got in there. None of the second story windows were broken, or open as far as she could see. *Did I miss something?*

She walked a wide berth around the theatre again, making sure not to walk around a blind corner. Walking to the middle of the parking lot, she made sure no one was around. Nope. Deserted. She looked up to a set of windows on the second story at the back of the building. She hadn't noticed those.

Aha! Two windows were broken on the second story. Either the bird crashed through, or a person broke in. *Person.* She glanced down. The homeless man was gone. The mattress was still there, but no man.

Crap. A text popped up. She looked at her phone.

Katie: Megan. Get out of there. I'll pick you up at the coffee place.

Yes, that was a good idea. Standing in the middle of the parking lot, she saw the two paths. Walk back by the front, where that deep recessed entrance was, or go around the back of the building. She looked up. *It's daytime.* More cars whizzed by down the main drag. *Plenty of people around.* Megan remembered the heavily cobwebbed door at the back of the theatre. She headed down that path. She stayed far away from the building, reaching the alley, giving it a wide berth. To her right was the long back wall, one door. To the left of the alley was another open field, overgrown, but nowhere for someone to hide and pounce. She looked all around. No one.

Megan walked down the alley. She stared at the approaching door. Confirmed just one door. But it wasn't red. She stopped and stared. The door had changed colors. It was black.

It's open, she thought. She started to run. Her phone rang. She stopped. It was Katie. Before she could swipe to answer, Megan heard a voice.

"Hi Megan."

A man stood at the door. She tried to run again, but someone had her arm. He wheeled her around. He was directly behind her. It was the homeless man.

She glanced back to the door. The same man stood there that had her. Twins? The man swung his arm over her mouth before she could scream. She bucked hard, but he was so strong. She tried to scream anyway as he pushed her toward his twin. She bit into his arm.

The man yowled but didn't release. He pushed her inside. The rusty red door shut tight and she was lost.

* * *

"Oh my God. Megan, answer!"

What do I do? Call the cops? No, how would I tell them what's wrong? Maybe nothing is wrong. No, something is wrong. Stupid. Why did I send her there?

She dialed Zacke, "Zacke. You need to fly me to the theatre right now. My sister might be in trouble."

"What happened?"

She told him.

"Katie, you shouldn't have sent her."

"I know, I know. I'm stupid. Just please help me."

"I mean, it's daytime. I can't just fly down the middle of town."

"It's my sister!" screamed Katie.

Zacke said, "Hold up. I'll call John. His wife guy has a car."

"Please hurry," said Katie.

John called back immediately, "Katie. On the way. We'll pick you up. Everyone is coming to help."

"Okay, okay." Katie fought back the panic. "Just hurry, please."

"On the way," said John and hung up.

Katie had sent what seemed like hundreds of texts to Megan. No response. She called, but it just rang and rang until it finally went to voicemail, which wasn't even set up.

She bounded out of the door, waiting for John. She paced up and down her driveway, furious at her parents for living so far out of town. *My parents! How will I ever... no. No.* She told herself that everything would be fine. Then she got a text.

Megan: She's very pretty.

Katie's blood tingled, then froze.

Megan: Poor thing is very scared.

Katie's hand shook, but she managed to text. She typed slower than usual.

Katie: If you hurt her.

She hit send by accident before she finished her text. A reply came immediately.

Megan: Oh, we will.

Julien's car screeched to a halt.

Megan: See you soon.

Katie got in the car and closed her eyes. She shook badly.

John said, "We'll get her back."

Katie answered, "You don't understand. I sent her there. She wanted to help..."

"This is not your fault. It is theirs," said Julien. "Only monsters take children as bait."

"Oh my God. At the riverbed, before you showed up, one of them said we had to... shit." Katie's mind swam. "What was the word? Like give up our abilities or they would kill our families."

"Dissemble?" offered Julien.

"Yes! Dissemble. They're going to kill her John!"

John answered, "Not if we kill them first."

Katie was near hysterics. Julien was driving very fast.

* * *

Very soon, they were all in the car and headed to the theatre. Ariana consoled Katie the best she could, Zacke looked determined. Lucas was calm, but his ancient seethed. He held his twin fighting batons. His fingers pulsed over them, knuckles white.

They parked in the theatre parking lot, as far from the building as possible, the car aimed at the building.

John said, "This is a trap. They will be ready for us and we have no idea what we're walking into. Our first priority is Megan, her safety. We will get her and get out as fast as possible. Use everything you've learned. Don't hold back."

Katie took deep breaths and focused. She felt her talents inside and remembered how hard she'd been training. *Megan is all that matters. Zhanna,* she thought, *help me.*

Julien pulled two LED flashlights from the glove box. "We might need these."

They all got out of the car. It was broad daylight, but John drew his sword, keeping it to his left side, where passing traffic wouldn't notice it. It was the hub of the old town area, part of an old highway system, so cars passed frequently. John was grateful that it was Saturday morning before the town got moving. They walked toward the building.

"The front?" asked Julien.

"Of course. They are expecting us. They chose an old theatre, a grand entrance. It's all Rageto hubris today." John spat on the ground.

Ariana made herself seem strong. But the fear still sat on her chest. She still didn't know any more about her own abilities. Ariana breathed in and hoped she would make it through this day.

Zacke looked over the building. He worried his talent would be stilted. Inside battles were not made for flying. Maybe that's why they chose this place. *Come on Zacke, focus. Megan needs us.*

Lucas felt his ancient, mind and body. They were nearly one person. The weapons in his hands were ready.

Katie prayed. She wasn't religious. She still had little idea what The River really was. She prayed anyway. *Take me if you need to, but let Megan be okay. Please.*

They got to the recessed entrance under the marquee. The chain that Megan had seen was gone. It appeared they were to enter at the front, just as John thought. A pigeon was perched on the ledge to the box office, bobbing and staring. Just then, a hawk swooped in and grabbed the pigeon. It sheared off the head and then screeched at the group. It grabbed the pigeon's body and flew away with the prey.

"Jesus!" said Zacke.

"Foreshadowing?" asked Julien.

"Omen," said Lucas/Elgisard.

"Yes to both" said John through clenched teeth, "but we are the hawk."

They made no further comment and John grabbed the door handle.

Julien clicked on the flashlights and they entered. Some light penetrated the lobby through the glass doors now behind them, but not much. John and Julien split at the V of the POPCORN machine counter. To the left, Julien discovered the ladies' room. She checked all the stalls. John did the same to the right, the men's room. A pigeon flew at his head. He cut it in half. It didn't have time to squawk. Nothing else. Room cleared.

The teens waited for them in the lobby, noticing all the broken plaster and debris. There was also pigeon poop everywhere. Streaked down the concession stand, in the corners. Loose feathers strewn around the lobby. It smelled really, really bad.

On either side of the concession stand were a set of double doors. They appeared to be covered in old leather, studded with brass tacks. Decorative art deco handles adorned them.

John beckoned for them all to enter through the right door. The doors opened toward them, so Julien and John each grabbed a door handle and swung slowly. It was pitch black in the theatre.

They shined their lights. The room was huge, the light wouldn't penetrate the length of it. The LED beams found the turquoise, scalloped art deco end chairs, illuminated scalloped sconces made of plaster, the walls a crumbling peach color. Bird dung was on most of the seats, as was fallen plaster. Large chunks of the ceiling had come down in patches.

They all entered a few more feet down the aisle. The doors swung shut on automatic door closers. Just then, clicks resounded through the cavernous space. There was no balcony, just hundreds of neat rows of chairs, so the sounds bounced around the ruined room like a cavernous cathedral. The clicking was accompanied by light after light popping to life on the stage.

On the stage, people were tied to chairs.

"Megan!" shouted Katie.

Her sister was tied to a chair in the middle of the stage. No other warriors were in sight. Megan was gagged. Even from the distance of the long room, it was clear she was terrified.

Two other people were tied up. A woman John didn't recognize and...

"Deke!" shouted Zacke. His brother was slumped in the chair, blood on his forehead. Zacke rushed forward, but Lucas stopped him.

"No Zacke," John said. "Remember, this is a trap. They want you to lose control. Don't give them that."

Julien asked, "Does anyone know who the woman is?"

Lucas said, "I think that's Cody's mom. I'm not sure. Only met her once at Cody's door."

"So, they expected Cody to be here, too," said John.

"That means they don't know everything," said Julien.

"Where are the Rageto?" asked Ariana.

They formed a rough circle. John and Julien used their flashlights to scan the gloom. Only the stage was lit. The rest of the gloomy space held nothing but dust, cobwebs, plaster, and pigeon poop. A few pigeons flapped in and out of the broken ceiling plaster.

Zacke stared at his brother. He moved, so he was alive. They couldn't see who was in the darkness. Deke was gagged too, as was Cody's mom. A man appeared, stood behind Katie.

Katie yelled at the sudden man appearing. He held a weapon in each hand. On the left, the madu with the two sharp horns, in his right was the relic axe.

As through splitting like an amoeba, the one man stretched into two. They stood side by side now, both wearing the same face, like evil twins. Now each held a weapon.

"Janus," said John.

They split into two groups. John led Lucas and Ariana left, while Julien led Katie and Zacke down the right-side aisle. They each moved down the two aisles slowly, flashing lights around. John and Julien scanned continually, making sure they wouldn't get ambushed from warriors hiding among the seats. Each Janus stalked a group, slowly, in no hurry.

Julien spoke, "You're still creepy, Janus. But we don't fear you."

The first Janus asked, "And who are you?" The other Janus spoke, "Your ancient, we mean."

"Figure it out yourself." said Julien.

John pointed at the stage, "Let the innocents go. We know they are just bait. And a child at that. It's beneath even you."

Both Janus' announced in unison, "Under orders. Servus Crea Gabraa."

That sparked a memory and Julien whipped around. Shapes were now moving between the seats. Roughly the shape of men, they moved silently, but quickly.

"What are those?" yelled Ariana.

John growled, "Gollums."

"Like Lord of the Rings?" Ariana screamed as one grabbed her. She instinctively froze it and Lucas shook both hands. The small black handles slid out to become batons. They locked into place and Lucas swung at the creature. It crumbled back to the dust it was made from.

"Gollums," Julien repeated, "monsters from the Torah, old testament. Man shaped monsters that do Janus' bidding. Nasty things."

The flashlights swung about. There were eight Gollums. The creatures were in the form of men and looked solid. One shambled to Katie, moving its arms around her neck. She nearly choked when she realized what it was made from. She made a shield around her body and pushed out. The shape exploded and showered all of her group.

"Gross. That's not clay. What is that?"

"Yeah. Oooh." Katie spit to make sure none had gotten in her mouth. "That one was made of plaster and pigeon poop."

Both groups were surrounded. The others were bigger, resembling giants, looming over them and reaching down for them.

First Janus said, "I have a lot of material in here." Janus two added, "we could do this all day."

John used his sword, Lucas his batons. Gollums crumbled into piles of dust and dung. Ariana froze another behind Lucas, and he pivoted and smashed the creature. Katie made a small shield ball and threw it at a Gollum. It stuck in the belly and Katie pushed her hands out. The ball grew in size and the creature exploded outward, like a bomb in the belly of the Gollum. Unfortunately, it covered her in pigeon poop. "Oh, come on!" she shouted.

One grabbed for Julien's leg and swung her off her feet. She pivoted in mid-air and slammed her other foot into the creature's head. It came off in one giant clump, smashing to the ground and crumbled like a dirt clod.

"This is a distraction," Julien yelled.

"Agreed," John said as he cut the last one down. They looked around, Both Janus' were gone. All that remained were the three hostages. They were all trying to shout something through their gags.

Cimo appeared in front of the stage, where an orchestra pit might have been. He held a relic, the bladed haladie in his hand. The two curvy blades protruded from the central handle on either side and the spike on top of the handle glistened in the stage light. Julien and Lucas scanned around. A woman appeared at the back of the theatre, no weapon as far as anyone could see. Janus one appeared again, axe in hand, standing behind Deke. The other Janus held his relic madu and stood near Megan.

John and Julien's groups huddled the best they could in each aisle, trying to keep a rough circle, to see all their attackers.

Cimo announced, "Indoire Mens Embrouiller." Katie felt her mind twist. Her feet became unsteady as though recovering from a dizzying twirl.

"It's a psychic attack. Fight it." John tried to run for Cimo, but he stumbled, not sure why the concrete floor was shifting under his feat. *Dammit, he's got me too.* John tried to fight the attack in his mind but had to grab a filthy seat to steady himself. John focused on pushing Cimo out of his mind.

Julien shook his head. Even as she felt her equilibrium turn her in knots, she saw that Cimo was close to her, the relic ready to kill. She shoved the flashlight in her pocket and found her old metal zippo lighter. She flipped open the lid and slid her finger on the strike. It lit a tiny flame. Cimo cocked his head to one side, curious if this was the last pitiful act of this stranger. Julien saw the look on his face. He smiled. "Forgotten that soon?"

Cimo did remember Unna's talent. His eyes grew wide and he shouted, "Everyone down!"

"Huh?" asked Katie.

Flame erupted at Cimo. The jet sprayed out from the tiny flame like a flamethrower. Lucas and John dove for the floor. Katie got the idea and ducked behind a nearby seat.

Cimo had ducked behind a chair but was already engulfed. His screams quickly faded as he fell between the seats. The relic blade fell to the floor. The seats around him quickly ablaze, Julien leapt over the next row and searched for the relic.

"Die!" shouted both Janus's in unison as they jumped off the stage and ran for Julien.

"Come and get me, twin boy." He found the relic blade, just cool enough to touch.

The second Janus yelled, changed direction and ran at Zacke.

Zacke glanced to his brother and ran at Janus Two. The man sliced at Zacke, but he ducked, his fist coming up and connecting with the man's chin. Janus' head snapped back and his feet came off the floor.

Zacke grabbed Janus' arm and flew straight up. Janus dropped his weapon. The ceiling plaster crushed upward, Janus disappearing into the ruined ceiling.

Zacke left him there, thirty feet up. Zacke came down to earth, looking for a relic to cut his brother loose.

That's when Ariana felt the first drip. She looked up and got a face full of rain. Light drops. She looked for the source.

"The storm maker!" shouted John, looking for the Rageto woman. "It's Azoria."

Lucas whipped around to the back of the theatre. The woman wore a flowing white blouse. Her long red hair draped over her shoulders. Her twisted grin was the same as always. "I see you Azoria." Lucas ran for her.

Azoria saw him. "The scrawny one. Which one are you again?"

He growled at her and ran up the aisle. She recognized the growl. "The Viking. So it is true."

Elgisard growled again, running straight for her. "Here I am."

Azoria chanted "Chuva Vanta Durum" and spread her hands upward. Ariana followed her gaze, blinking hard in the rain. She couldn't believe what she saw. A dark cloud hung above them, forming out of nothing. It loomed over the giant space. Within seconds it was a torrent, water cutting at her face. Then the wind hit her and she stumbled to the ground.

Julien toppled over onto the soggy thin carpet and tumbled down the slant. Since the entire floor sloped toward the stage, the thin red carpet now acted like a waterslide, the wind pushing them down the slope. Julien tried to get to her feet, with little effect. Rain pelted at them sideways, slashing at their eyes, faces.

Lucas struggled to stay on his feet. The wind and rain filled the whole space. Splotches of wet dirt and bird poop were like wet shrapnel. Lucas cried out and squeezed his eyes shut, fighting the onslaught.

Katie looked to the stage. The three in the chairs were trying to dodge the wet debris, squirming in their chairs. Random pigeons beat their wings and fell victim to the wind, falling out of the ceiling holes. One flapped wildly but failed to fight the wind and splatted against the back concrete wall. It just missed Deke.

John helped Julien, scanning for the last Janus.

Zacke saw that no one could reach the woman. He ran against the wind. His feet left the ground and he flew at her. He cut through the wind and slammed into her with both fists. The wind stopped. Azoria slammed to the back wall of the theatre. Zacke put her over his shoulder and flew up.

The woman was a wild animal. She screamed and clawed at Zacke. "Have it your way," he said. Zacke let her go. She fell thirty feet to the wet carpet. A sharp thud sounded and Azoria was quiet.

Katie and Ariana wasted no time. They rushed the stage, jumping over the footlights onto the stage.

"Wait!" John shouted. "They want us on that stage."

"It's still a trap!" Julien screamed. He ran to try and stop the girls.

Katie didn't care. On stage, she ripped off her sister's gag, fumbling with the duct tape around her wrists. Ariana helped Cody's mom, who kept looking out, not sure what was going on.

Both Janus' and Azoria limped toward the stage, down the aisle. One Janus looked in bad shape. Zacke wondered how he got down from the wrecked ceiling. They stopped at the end of the aisles, just staring.

John and Julien were just below the stage and they watched the Rageto stand motionless. They stood not ten feet apart. Both Janus' smiled. It wasn't good. Then the answer came. Deke was still tied and gagged, Zacke unable to cut the duct tape fast enough. Deke's chair began to lift. Zacke jumped back, into the wings of the stage. Katie felt the pull too. Ariana stood off stage left. She looked up. In the fly space, some forty feet up, abyss stared back. A gaping rectangle sat above them, roughly the size of the stage. It was black on black, the absence of all light. Bordering it were glowing blue lines. Cody's mom felt herself being pulled upward, feeling the sense of sudden weightlessness.

At the side of the building, a metal exit door exploded outward. Victoria and three men ran in through the broken doors. The next set of red doors swung open, more men running in.

Everyone on stage was floating up, toward the gate. Victoria shouted, "Out. There are vehicles waiting."

Katie stood on stage left, in a trance as her sister floated up. Katie stood just outside the trap, feet still on the wood floor.

"Grab her!" shouted Julien.

The spell broken, Katie jumped. Megan and the chair floated six feet up now. Katie's hand just reached the leg of the chair and clamped on. But now she was floating too. Katie felt someone grab her leg. She looked down. A man held her leg firm, outside the lifting spell. Another man grabbed him and they slowly walked backwards, a human chain. Katie clasped the chair leg tightly. The lifting stopped, and they were pulled out of the zone, the human chain working. The sudden return of gravity was instant on stage left. Katie fell, but a Sect man broke her fall. Another Sect man caught Megan's chair and set her down carefully.

Deke and Cody's mom floated ever upward.

John and Julien had leapt onto the very edge of the stage, but could go no further or they would be stuck in the trap. They both scanned everywhere for rope to throw them. They glanced back into the theatre seats and saw the Rageto just standing there. John ignored them and scanned for any way he could help. Nothing.

Zacke jumped into the trap and pushed off the ground like a swimmer pushing off a wall, straight for Deke. Deke was staring up, still trying to shake loose his bonds. Zacke got close and grabbed for his leg but missed and pushed his brother instead. The chair started to spin and rose faster. Deke was now spinning faster toward the open gate.

Julien looked back to the Rageto. They were gone. Julien looked around one more time for any way to help. He suddenly kissed John. "They will need help." Julien leapt to the center of the stage, jumping into the rising field.

"No!" yelled John, but it was too late. Julien rose quickly, following Zacke and the others up.

Deke, Zacke, and Cody's mom disappeared into the black. Julien followed close behind and vanished into the void. Suddenly the ceiling reappeared. The gate had vanished.

Ariana comforted Katie and Megan.

John stormed around the stage. He had no idea where they'd gone. He ran to the dressing rooms, searched all of backstage. Nothing. No Rageto. When he got back, Victoria and several Sect men gathered around Ariana. They heard sirens not far off.

"Better go," said Victoria flatly.

John looked up again, then over to where Cimo fell, a charred mess and the theatre full of water and debris of all kinds. He simply said, "Yes."

They left out the exit door. A car and a truck were waiting for the Sect who took Katie and Megan, who was still shaken up. Ariana went with them, to help if she could.

John said to Victoria, "You come with me." She did and the two ran to their car just in time. A block away, they saw the two police cruisers round the corner to the theatre.

In the vehicle Victoria asked John, "What do you need?"

"I have an idea how we can contact the Rageto," said John. "I need your help."

CHAPTER TWENTY EIGHT

Prisoners

Zacke landed on a dusty stone floor. He looked to his right. There was a strange gray light where daylight should have been.

He looked to his left and saw Deke, lying on his side. He was still tied to the chair. He rushed to his brother. Zacke set the chair up, which woke Deke. The head wound he'd gotten from the Rageto had re-opened but didn't look serious. He carefully removed the gag and started in on his hands. They had used a lot of duct tape.

Deke said, "What the... Oww!" Zacke had removed duct tape from Deke's wrist along with a chunk of arm hair. "What is going on, bro? I saw you fly."

"Yeah. Now you know why I don't play hoops anymore."

Deke thought for a second as the last of the duct tape came off. "That's why mom freaked out."

"Yeah," said Zacke, undoing the last of the duct tape from his legs. "They taped you up good."

"That's because I fought those guys. Who were they, anyway?"

"It's a long story." Zacke corrected, "Actually, several long stories. Basically, they are the bad guys."

"I know! They gave me this." Deke touched his head. He sucked in breath at the pain. "Is it still bleeding?"

"Yeah, a little. But I think it'll stop soon."

Deke asked, "Where are we?"

Zacke looked around. "I have no idea. Let's go find out."

The others were not far off. Julien had already untied Cody's mom. She was sitting on a stone step, rubbing her wrists and ankles, trying to get her bearings.

They'd found each other and Zacke asked Julien. "Do you know where we are?"

"No," said Julien, indicating Cody's mom. "This is Caroline."

"I'd shake your hands, but I'm too freaked," said Deke. "Can someone tell me what is going on?"

Before anyone could explain anything, they had a visitor. "New arrivals," said a large man from the doorway. He'd aimed the comment behind him, to someone out of sight.

Julien stepped up the stone step to a man. "I am Julien. Can you tell us where we are?"

"King's Road," he answered.

Julien looked around. "Not a prisoner of a Rageto elder?"

"Pretty much the same thing. If you were dumped here, you must have made one of them angry. Amartus?"

"Yes," said Julien, deep in thought. "I thought the Kings' Road was a myth. A tale to frighten those that misbehaved."

The man mockingly knocked on a stone wall. "Very real. Are you thirsty? The others are this way."

"Others?" asked Julien. "How many?"

"Come this way and see," he said and walked out of the room, leading them.

Zacke paused. Julien said, "We're already in the trap. Might as well go." He put out his hand, indicating it was safe to follow.

Deke touched his head, winced, but followed with Zacke. Julien hung behind and accompanied Caroline. "How much do you want to know?"

"Just enough that my head doesn't explode. I think that kid knows my kid. I saw him fly, like superhero fly," said Caroline. "The other woman made it rain, inside."

"For now, just know that there are two sides, fighting each other with extraordinary talents. Lately, the epicenter has been your little city. How long were you captive?"

"Half a day, I think." Caroline shivered. "That old theatre gets dark, it's hard to tell."

"Sorry you got dragged into this," said Julien. "Their side, The Rageto, know no boundaries."

Caroline asked, "Why did they take me?" She stared at Zacke's back, who was trying to explain to the other boy what was happening. She knew.

"It's Cody. I've missed him at home the last couple days, but..." Caroline trailed off. She thought of all the incidents she'd both carefully stowed away and purposefully tried to ignore. Cody's unfortunate luck with electronics. He couldn't even carry a cell phone. The strange early stories he would tell about seeing things in mirrors. Then all the broken mirrors. The abrupt way he quit the football team. The strange story he and his friends told about that night on the tower. She knew it hadn't added up, but he was safe and that's all she cared about. Caroline called ahead. "It's Zacke, right?"

Zacke stopped and turned. He looked back with a mix of shame and guilt. Caroline thought, *This kid should not play poker.*

Zacke asked, "Yes, Mrs. Nichols?"

"Do you know where Cody is?"

Zacke answered honestly, "No." But he knew something, obviously.

Caroline focused her mom truth detector. "You sure about that?"

"Listen, I really don't," Zacke admitted. "But there's a lot you don't know. I mean, I don't even know where to start."

Caroline got beside Zacke. "I'll walk next to you. You can start from the beginning."

"Man," said Deke, "she's got the mom face on. Watch out."

They rounded a corner at the end of the long corridor. It was a large room. People lounged, collected in groups, talked freely. All turned when they entered. The nearest to the doorway said, "New blood! Amartus or Rageto?"

"Amartus," said Julien absentmindedly as he scanned the room. He sensed at least a dozen people, some old friends. Also, a few old enemies.

"Me too," answered the man. "We got Rageto here, too. Be warned."

Boos and calls whipped around the room.

"How did you all get here?" asked Julien.

"Same way as you." Another man lifted his cup. "We displeased an Elder. This has become their dumping ground."

A voice called from the far side of the room, "Mom?"

"Cody? Oh my God, Cody!" Caroline rushed to her son. "Are you okay, baby?"

Cody grabbed his mom and they hugged fiercely. He pulled away reluctantly. "Mom, what happened? Why are you all here?"

"Same question, kiddo. Someone better explain what's going on and quick."

"Hey Zacke," Cody said with an absent nod. He glanced behind himself and back to his mom. "Umm. There is a lot to explain. I'm glad I can finally tell you everything. But, Mom... there is one big surprise before I tell you what's happening." he glanced back to the corner of the room. "Don't freak out."

* * *

John and Victoria arrived at Zacke's door. Zacke's dad answered and welcomed them in.

Since Victoria knew his dad, she took the lead as agreed. "Sir, we need to know where to find Zacke's mom."

"Oliver. I keep telling you."

"Sorry, Oliver," Victoria smiled, "I keep forgetting. Do you know where she is?"

Oliver Penna looked John in the eyes. "I don't know if I should shake your hand or punch you in the jaw."

John looked puzzled.

"Zacke told me everything. You're John, right? On one hand, you've protected my boy through some truly scary stuff. On the other hand, you also got him into a lot of trouble."

"Oliver..." John began.

"Mr. Penna."

John tread carefully. "Mr. Penna. I'm glad Zacke told you everything. It's all true, as crazy as it sounds."

Victoria put her hand on Oliver's arm. "Oliver, Zacke's in trouble. We need to talk to his mom to find him. They took Deke, too."

Oliver's eyes darted between them. "My God. Then we should call... no. Of course, we can't call the police." A mix of emotions swirled across Oliver's face. He let the anger pass and settled on action. "Can she really help? I'll write down the address. She's at a nearby hotel."

John nodded and turned to leave. Oliver's hand shot out and grabbed John's arm. "You find my boys and bring them back."

John nodded again, feeling a new wave of guilt. They left for the hotel.

They found Amelia, Zacke's mom, at the hotel. A few minutes into the conversation and John was losing his patience. "Ma'am, you don't understand. They have taken your sons."

"That's a lie! No one in my church would do anything like that," said Amelia.

"I don't know what church you mean," John said firmly, "but the men you are dealing with are not telling you the truth."

Amelia shook her head and laughed softly. "They told me you would say that. I see your tricks, devil, but you will not get my sons."

John closed his eyes. Victoria took over. "Ma'am..."

"Don't ma'am me. They told me what you were, too, that sect of the true faith meddling in our Rageto church." Amelia shot a finger at Victoria. "You stay away from my boy, tramp."

Victoria felt like she'd been slapped. She opened her mouth, but nothing came out.

John tried again. "What exactly does your church believe?"

"You should know. The Rageto are the true faith, the one all other faiths were born from, the original." Amelia flung her hand as if shooing a fly. "You Amartus have been the demons trying to spoil the true path. Go back to your hell, devil."

John had seen zealotry before. It was hard to penetrate. "Why don't you try calling your sons. Then you'll see that something is wrong."

"I don't use cell phones. They give you brain cancer. I've already tried calling by land line," she indicated the hotel phone by her bed. "Besides, they won't talk to me. You've turned my sons against me."

"You did that, lady." It slipped out before Victoria could help it.

"You need to leave now. Go on, get out."

John said, "Please, Amelia. Even if you don't believe us, your sons are in trouble. At least call them again."

"I will call! And you'll be sorry," she grabbed the phone and dialed.

Victoria whispered to John, "That's what we wanted her to do in the first place."

Amelia spoke into the phone, "Hello, Cimo? This is Amelia."

John grabbed the phone out of her hand. "Cimo. Palaver. Now."

Amelia tried to get the phone from John, but Victoria pulled her away.

"How dare you!" she slapped Victoria.

Victoria whipped out a zip tie and tied Amelia's hands quickly, then forced her to a sitting position on the bed. She looked around for something appropriate and reached to the small table. Victoria stuffed tissues into Amelia's mouth. She yelled through her gag, but Victoria put her hand over the mouth so she couldn't spit it out. Victoria gave her a warning. "Shhh, Amelia. John's on the phone."

"No palaver," said Cimo with a soft chuckle. "It was smart to use the mother."

John looked to the phone quickly. There was a speakerphone button. John pressed it.

Cimo's voice continued, "She is a useful pawn in our little game. You will never see those boys or the others again. They have been taken off the board... permanently."

John stared at Amelia, who's eyes grew wide with the words.

"You've killed them, then?" asked John, as calmly as he could.

"They are as good as dead. Lost. In a prison with no door," said Cimo.

John closed his eyed. Zacke's mother yelled through her gag.

"What was that? Am I on speaker?" asked Cimo.

"Yep," said Victoria.

"You never were very bright," said John.

"I see," Cimo spoke through the speaker. "Amelia, don't listen to these Amartus scum. I only meant that your boys are safe. We are protecting them in a safe location. No one, and I mean no one can get at them now."

Amelia looked confused. John knew Cimo was giving a message to him as well as the mother.

John said, "Why don't you come here and tell me that, coward?"

Cimo chuckled. "We will all see you soon enough. But we choose the time and place. You'll be informed."

The phone clicked off. John replaced the receiver.

Victoria produced a small knife and sliced the zip tie. Victoria was off her and Amelia spit out her mess of wet tissues, shaking her head to get rid of the taste. Victoria got within an inch of her face.

"If Zacke gets hurt, it won't be that demon that comes after you. It will be me." Before Amelia could say anything, Victoria had breezed out the door. Amelia sputtered as John let the hotel door close.

John said, "That went well."

"That woman!" yelled Victoria.

"I know. But she did help us."

"How?" asked Victoria.

"We know they are alive. And that thing Cimo said about the prison with no door. I'm sure that is important. Can the Sect help?"

"The main part of the Sect won't. They still want to stay out of this. But I'll help."

"Have you broken away from the sect?" John smirked. "A sect of the Sect?"

"We need a better name, but basically," Victoria said. "Until the Sect leadership see our point of view. Uncle Pete was right. The time to choose sides is now."

"Good. Do you have access to the Sect's knowledge?"

They'd reached the car. Victoria said, "Not exactly. I've been barred from the database, for now. I'm working on some key players to change things. I have some hard copy Sect histories, though."

"Let's hope they will help."

* * *

Cody didn't think he could stall anymore.

"Just tell me, Cody," said his mom, Caroline. She'd crossed her arms. Cody knew that was it, her patience done. The Mom stare began.

Cody rushed, "There's a lot to tell. I better show you. This way." Cody led her around a few half walls, across the large space. People lounged and gathered all around. They all looked at the new arrivals.

Some concerned people were gathered around a man laid out, damp cloth on his forehead. As they approached, Caroline could only see his graying hair. The man was groaning softly. Cody led her around the make-shift bed. She rounded and saw the old man laid out. Her breath caught.

"David?" she searched his face, looked him up and down, trying to visually peel away the years. She stepped closer. His face was so pained, so weary. She put a hand over her mouth.

"Mom," said Cody, "we found each other a few months ago. A lot of crazy stuff happened. I'll explain, but Dad was taken prisoner and kept captive for years. He didn't leave us, not really."

This was too much, too confusing. Caroline's emotions had their own will. Tears sprouted from her eyes. She kneeled beside her husband. She'd imagined seeing him again so many times. Those thoughts were always drenched in anger. She touched his face and he opened his eyes. "What's wrong with him?"

Pain carved his face. He slowly opened his eyes, trying to focus. He blinked. Then saw her. Tears leaked from both eyes, spilling off both of his cheeks. He didn't speak. A sob rocked him, and he wheezed, shutting his eyes again. She touched his face, first time in over a decade.

David whispered, "I'm sorry. Sorry. So sorry..." the whisper turned into a sharper wheeze, then a hack. A rumble came through him. David bucked in pain, then calmed down again.

Caroline looked to Cody. "Is there a doctor?"

"No. No healers here. Mostly warriors," said Bevan.

Caroline looked around. She sniffed, then stood. Wiping her tears, she spoke sharply. "Okay, you," she pointed to Bevan. "Yes you. Get more wet cloth. Cody, put your hand under his neck. Does anyone have a flashlight?"

They all stood around, no response.

"Flashlight!" Caroline shouted. The circle around her started, then sprung to action.

"Flashlight? Flashlight?" the word pinged around the great room.

Then a distant voice. "Yeah, I do. On my keychain. LED. Not sure if the battery... hey, it works!"

Caroline broke into nurse mode. The small LED flashlight was placed in her hand and she looked in his throat for obstructions. "Okay Cody, let his head down again. Is he on anything? Pain meds, prescription, over the counter?" she looked Bevan, but he looked back to Cody.

Cody said, "We don't know. I don't think so."

Caroline opened each eye of David's eyes and inspected. "He's on something. Is he a drug addict?"

"What? Mom, no. He's..."

"He's high on Elder magic," said the scholar.

"Is that a synthetic drug? Something new? I need specifics!"

David came around again. "Car... Caroline. So glad, so glad you're... I want to tell you everything. So sorry... just let me rest a while and I'll tell you every-thing." David trailed off again. His breathing was regular, but ragged. Caroline put a hand to David's chest and stood up.

"Okay, Cody. Tell me everything and don't leave anything out."

* * *

"You want us to read a bunch of books?" asked Lucas as he welcomed everyone into the lair. The room now contained John, Victoria, Ariana, Katie, Megan and a few Sect guys. They were handed three books each.

"Yes. These are Sect histories provided by Victoria. It may not seem important," said John, "but this could lead us to find them."

Megan asked, "You're sure they aren't..."

"Yes. We're sure." Victoria said, "They are alive. If they were killed, Cimo would have boasted about it."

Katie whispered to Megan, "You should be a t home resting after what happened."

"No way," said Megan, steel in her young voice. "We need to find our friends. Then you guys can end those monsters."

Katie was still feeling guilty over Megan getting involved, but she was glad she could watch over her. She didn't want to leave her side ever again. Katie cracked open her own assigned books.

"What are we looking for?" asked Ariana.

John said, "We're looking for anything that sounds like a prison, or jail, camp. Anywhere they might be held. Cimo said the prison has no door."

"How can any room have no door?" asked Lucas.

"They got sucked into a magic gateway. Maybe their cell has no roof. They could have been dropped into a cell with no door." Megan shrugged. "Magic, right?"

"The open roof would act as a door," John pointed out.

"Then how would they feed them? Like, open a gate and drop food to them."

"Or not feed them at all and let them starve," offered Katie.

"Really, Katie?" said Ariana. "First they're dead and now they are starving?"

"Starving someone would kill them. I think this place is too keep them separated, out of the struggle. If they were killed, the River would bring them back." John let the thought go. "The good news is that Unna is on the other side, trying to figure out the same problem."

"If they're still together," said Katie.

Ariana stared at Katie, eye daggers flying.

Victoria said, "Guys, let's try to find some answers."

They all dug into their books, reading as fast as they could. Katie felt like she was in school. Whenever someone came to a possibility, they shouted it out loud.

"How about this?" Katie announced. "This says Paxix was imprisoned in The Tower of England for over a year, executed, then re-birthed into a girl in the Ottoman empire 15 years later. That's a famous prison, right?"

"Yes, but it has many doors." said John absently, "I had an unpleasant stay there before I got pardoned by the king. Can't be there. It's a place for tourists now."

"Maybe something here," said Ariana. "How about an island prison. I just googled Alcatraz and Devil's Island. Islands don't have doors."

John came over to look over her shoulder. "Hmm. Maybe. I'm not sure that's what Cimo meant. He made it sound like there was no escape. Every room or cell in those prisons has a door."

Katie slammed her book and grabbed another. "This is so frustrating. They could be torturing them right now and we're sitting around reading books."

"They have my wife," said John, "I understand your frustration."

"I know John, I'm sorry. It's just... how are we supposed to find them?" asked Katie.

John paced around the room, thinking. "I'm missing something. I've felt it from the beginning. I still think you are the key, Ariana."

"Me? Umm, I don't think so. My abilities are weird. I can't fly, I can't throw shield bubbles that break people's faces."

"Break faces?" asked Megan.

Katie winced. "I forgot to tell you that part."

"I mean... what am I good for?" Ariana tried to concentrate on her book. "When a battle happens, I just stand there, scared and mad that I can't help more. I don't feel like a key to anything. John."

"I don't think you are a re-birth, since I've never heard of your abilities before now. That means there is a lot to discover."

"I guess." Ariana shrugged.

"Let's try your mind, and where it can go." John instructed. "Put down those books and sit on the bed. Legs crossed please."

"Okay," Ariana crossed her legs. She closed her eyes when John asked her to.

Katie quipped, "She's not going to start chanting a chakra, is she?"

John said, "That doesn't help, Katie."

"I thought it was funny," whispered Megan.

"Quiet please," said John. "Ariana, I want you to stretch out your mind."

"Feel the Force flowing through you," said Lucas.

Ariana smiled at that. "Okay, that was funny. But I really want to find out, like, what I am. Can you guys help, please?"

"Sorry," said Lucas. They all kept quiet.

John continued, "Go to that quiet mental place. We all have one. You looked into all of our inner minds when you linked us. I'd like you to go to the core of your mind, then reach out from there."

She remembered. Ariana imagined her inner mind as an ornate silver jewelry box.

"Whose mind do you want me to try to find? Zacke?"

John almost agreed, but said, "No. Don't search for anyone specific. Let's see where the River takes you."

She nodded. Her breathing slowed. *Let the River guide you.* A visual popped into her mind – A box also, but like a pirate treasure box with a giant metal lock.

"I have it," said Ariana. "I think it's Cody."

"Good. He's been missing the longest." John urged. "Now reach your mind out to his. You once said that when you get flashes, you feel like you *are* that person."

"Yes. Like I'm inside them, or at least in the room with them."

John said, "Good. Go there. See if you can see through Cody."

She did. Since the night on the fire tower, when they linked through her, she had warm memories of how it felt. Ariana hadn't tried to do anything like that again. Not only was it scary, but she didn't want to invade anyone else's mind by accident.

Back here now, closer to another mind, her body warmed, and she imagined reaching out hands to touch the wooden chest. She actually felt the cold metal of the clasp.

Ariana felt a tug. She found herself in a new place. It was cold and gray. Stone corridors seem to stretch on forever. Her mind was there, in the corridors, traveling. She looked to her right. The sky was a dull gray fog. It reminded her of Sea Valley when the marine layer came in off the ocean, but knew she was clearly elsewhere. She abruptly stopped at a statue. The stone figure was hooded, sword between his leg, pointed down. She looked at the base. It read Lord Joland. It moved. It came to life and swung its blade at her.

Ariana's eyed jolted open. Back in Lucas' room, she bucked back on the bed as though the blade was in the room. "Oh my God," she looked at her body, checking for injury.

"What happened?" asked John.

"A statue," Ariana breathed heavily. "It came to life and tried to kill me."

"Where were you? Did you see Cody?" said Katie.

"No." She described the scene, how if looked and felt.

"Lord Joland?" said John, recognizing the name. He rubbed his chin. John asked the group, "Did anyone come across a reference to the King's Road? Or Lord Joland?"

Megan said, "I think I saw something."

Lucas moved to John. "I thought that was a myth."

"Me too."

"Here it is," said Megan. "Something about Lord Joland's principles, but it doesn't say what they are."

"I don't remember them all offhand," muttered John.

Elgisard said, "One of them was that there are many unseen ways to travel."

"That's kind of vague," Katie remarked.

"Many of his principles are, but a legend says he discovered the King's Road. A way to travel unseen by most. Very difficult to access and even harder to navigate."

Elgisard asked, "Wasn't it also an endless maze that no one could escape?"

John nodded. "A prison with no door."

"How did Cody get there?" asked Megan "If it is the right place, I mean."

"He disappeared when John appeared by that ley line thingy," noted Katie.

"One thing is clear," said John, "the legend I knew said when you enter the King's Road, you never escape."

"Umm, John?" Katie said, pointing to Ariana. Her eyes were closed again.

"Ariana, don't go back there. It's too dangerous."

"I'm not. I feel something... else." Ariana opened her eyes. She jumped up. "Something big is coming. We need to go now."

* * *

Cody finished telling his mom everything that had happened. He tried not to leave anything out. Caroline sat, growing more disturbed as the tale unfolded. By the end, she was tired, as though she'd been through all of it herself. She tried to focus on one aspect at a time so she wouldn't feel insane.

Caroline asked carefully, "Your dad was a prisoner all those years."

"Yes. The brothers got him."

Caroline looked at David, how he'd aged. "They sound like monsters."

"They were. They're both dead now," Cody clarified, "well one will come back eventually..."

Caroline put her hand up. "I'm not sure I can process any more. I believe you, baby, although a lot of that is beyond crazy."

"I know."

Caroline asked, "So they think David has something wrong with his heart?"

"He does," Cody said, "but it's not physical, exactly. They say it's like a metaphor, like..."

"Like a spiritual problem?" Caroline struggled with all the new information.

"Like a blockage, I guess." Cody rubbed the back of his neck. "I don't really get it either."

"Let's see if I can figure it out." Caroline knelt by David. She had no equipment, not even a stethoscope or a blood pressure monitor. She put her ear to David's chest. It was a strong beat, though definitely troubled. She sat back up by his side, letting her hand linger on his labored breathing. Old memories flooded back. "I thought... I thought I hated you for a long time. Then it was resignation. Now... now I don't know how to feel."

Caroline continued to talk to David. "You've changed so much. Older. Well, so am I. I can't imagine what you've been through. Sounds like you saved lives. Thank you for coming back to our son."

Cody teared up. He felt helpless, no idea how he could help his dad. He never thought he'd see his parents in the same room again.

Bevan spoke up. "I don't know what else can be done. This blockage may not be physical, but that doesn't give us any more answers."

Caroline thought about that. Blockage. Not physical. "I've had to read a lot of psychological cases in my training. It talks about the body shutting down even when everything is alright physically."

"You think it's something like that?" asked Cody.

She looked to Cody. "How did you leave things with you dad?"

"I was kinda mad he left again after the fire tower, but I understood."

"Did you talk things out before that? I really wish you'd told me all of this sooner, Cody."

"How could I?"

"I know. I get it. Even I'm surprised I believe you. I guess what I mean is that David must have been racked with guilt. For abandoning us, then not being able to make it right."

"He was. He told me that. When I found out how he lived all those years, I forgave him." said Cody.

"Did you?" Caroline looked at David. She took his hands. He came around and blinked his eyes open.

"Caroline?" he looked down at his hands, saw hers and squeezed. Tears came to his eyes. "I thought I dreamed you. But you're real." David's gaze narrowed, as if she was fading in front of him. "You are real, aren't you?"

"Yes David," said Caroline.

"Thank God. I need to tell you..." David arched his back, moaning again.

Caroline said, "Cody told me everything."

"Everything?" David's eyes unfocused, staring past her.

Caroline feared he would pass out again.

David wheezed, "Everything..."

Caroline squeezed his hand again. "David, I don't know how to help you. There's no equipment here, no meds. But one thing I can do is tell you..." she swallowed hard. Years of fear when he disappeared, then anger, outright rage when things got tough. Now this broken man before her. Her David. "I need to tell you that I forgive you."

David stared at her, his face crinkling up in despair. Tears gushed. He squeezed her hand and brought them to his lips, more hot tears streaming. "I wanted to come back."

"I know," she hugged him. "It's not your fault. You came back and protected our son."

"Thank you, thank you." David sucked in a breath. He curled in on himself. Caroline let go, alarmed. She tried to stretch David flat again. He breathed in again, clearly in pain, in full fetal position. Then he stiffened, squeezing his eyes shut. David breathed in, out, then seemed to pass out.

David's body suddenly straightened. He lay on his back, chest pushed out. He opened his mouth. Caroline thought he might scream. Cody grabbed his mom's arm for support. They stared, helpless.

A black mist poured from David's mouth. The rest stood back at the intense smell of rot. Then the vile mist poured from his ears, his nose, his fingertips. The dark tendrils spiraled upward like a rare, foul gas. After a few moments, it faded as if never there.

David closed his mouth. His eyes slowly opened, as from a long sleep. His eyes fluttered and David seemed to be looking at nothing, just staring up. They all though he was wheezing again, but it soon turned not to laughter. David rose off his makeshift bed.

"You saved me." David hugged Caroline and Cody at the same time. They hugged back and eventually the hug broke. David examined his own body, like he'd been through a car accident and realized he had no injuries.

"I don't understand what just happened." said Caroline. "I didn't do anything."

"But you did," said David. "You allowed me to release my guilt." David put his hand on his forehead. "How do I explain? You see... I got Zamma and Sazzo's abilities and much of Zamma's memory. I also got their rage and hate and a whole swirl of emotions from both."

"That's what was making you sick?" asked Cody.

David tapped his head and searched Zamma's knowledge and a way to explain. "Partly. But it got mixed with my guilt. My strongest emotion — my old fears and regrets got locked together with their bile filled hate and rage. It made a blockage. Like a kidney stone in my heart." He looked to Caroline. "Your forgiveness saved me."

David went to Caroline again, hugging fiercely. He felt twenty years younger. The hug broke and David looked around, taking in his surroundings. He said, "The King's Road. Of course."

David looked around at all the others, recognition coming through his combined memories. "Zamma trapped many of you here. I have his knowledge, and now I can put it to use. What do you say we get out of here?"

CHAPTER TWENTY NINE

The Final Piece

Ordway leaned over her electronic display. Two 40-inch computer screens looked at her like giant rectangular eyes. She swiped her finger on the touch screen to the right and swished her finger until the images floated onto the left screen.

Ordway announced, "You can't sneak up on me that easily. I have spells all over this ballroom." She didn't bother swiveling her chair around to look at Elder Yarro.

"Wouldn't dream of it." Yarro indicated the room, "Do all your work in this ballroom? This looks more like one of your war rooms. I remember that large map table you had, where was it back then? In Burgundy, right? Always the planner."

"I hadn't planned for the black death," Ordway sniffed. "Dropped me flat in three days. That's the only reason you ever saw my war room."

"True. Bad luck for you. I had fun stealing your spell books and burning that place to the ground," laughed Yarro.

"That's where they went," she cocked a brow. "Do you still have them?"

"No," Yarro said. "Ironically, the black death took my body not two months later. I was re-birthed about ten years after that."

"That's right, you became Queen of Bavaria, didn't you? Ruled through your husband." Ordway asked. "Did he ever know the truth?"

"No." Yarro leaned on her desk. "Enough reminiscing. I've come for my relics and an update. How is the plan going?"

"Well, though not perfect," she indicated the computer screens. "All the players are where they belong, for now. We are quickly headed toward the climax."

Yarro asked, "Have you worked out the final stuff. Explosives or magic?"

"Still working on that," replied Ordway.

"And my relics?" asked Yarro.

"They are to be yours when I say so." She felt his eyes dart around the room. "They are not here. I won't turn over those weapons to a former enemy in person. It might tempt you." she picked up her cell phone, tapped, and said. "I just texted the coordinates. They are in a storage locker. Here is the key."

Yarro produced his ancient flip phone. "I don't have a texting plan. I keep a phone from before they were 'smart.' New devices are too easy to track."

Ordway shook her head gently, writing the coordinates down on paper and handing Yarro both the key and the paper.

"Your idea was a good one," Yarro said smiling. "You and I will both get two relics. As you suggested, Sorrento will get one relic…" he chuckled, "the book."

Ordway stood; her work done. "My idea? Why, whatever do you mean?" she said, innocently.

Yarro chuckled again. "Have it your way. Sorrento will be very displeased we broke the pact and met without him."

She smiled. "That's ridiculous." Ordway got louder, "I wouldn't dream of breaking our pact or double crossing him."

"Oh, wouldn't you?" Sorrento came from behind a pillar and stalked over on his small legs. "I agreed to one relic, but not the book! What use is that to me?"

"You could bash them over the head with it, I suppose," Yarro suggested.

Ordway added, "Take a page out and give them paper cuts until they die?"

"Outrage!" huffed Sorrento.

"Calm down," said Ordway, "you won't need a relic weapon. When we spring the last trap, all the Amartus will die, along with any trace of whatever nonsense the River had planned for that little town."

"Oh?" Sorrento smirked. "Have you worked out the last detail? How will we accomplish it in time?"

"I'm still working on that," said Ordway, taking a step closer. "Yarro, you sure your power couldn't do it."

"No. Concrete is too thick for that," said Yarro.

"Too bad," said Ordway. "The timing has to be right, we won't have much time."

"So explosives, then?" Yarro suggested again.

"I've thought of that, but it sits near too many people. Someone might alert the authorities. Plus, this must look like a natural disaster, as always."

"The Sect will know it was us," said Sorrento. "They've been pestering me with questions for months. I don't like their tone."

"Agreed," said Ordway. "Until the conclusion, we still need the cover of shadows. We will deal with the Sect after. Their factions will tear each other apart, then we can clean up the pieces."

Sorrento smiled. It made Yarro scowl.

Ordway crinkled her nose at his unpleasant face. "Sorrento, smiling doesn't agree with you. Please stop it."

Sorrento ignored the insult. "But, I have the solution." He snapped his fingers, "Come here, boy."

A shape came out of the gloomy ballroom. From behind Sorrento's pillar, the thin shape hobbled and slid one foot across the floor. His wheezing grew in volume as the thing approached. The young teenage boy stood before them, loping to one side. His foot was bent away from his body by degrees that looked painful. His face and arms were bruised and scratched. He was no higher than five foot.

"This is Kurt," Sorrento smiled again. Ordway winced at the unpleasant boy.

Yarro wrinkled his nose at the unfortunate before him. "What does this crippled, broken boy have that we possibly need?"

Sorrento smiled. "He was found beaten and bloody by the side of the road. My finder isn't very good to be honest. All the best ones are gone forever. He often finds vagrant teens that end up having no powers at all. He kills them or lets them go if they can do no harm."

The boy hadn't looked away from Ordway. He was clearly burning with rage. The boy stared, but Ordway didn't think it was for her.

"Who are you really, boy?" she asked, keeping the unease out of her voice.

His voice was a whisper, broken and cracked. His eyes were clear and brimming with hatred. "I... am... Caron."

CHAPTER THIRTY

Come Together

David realized they were in trouble. Now that the flow of memories felt calmer, those around him were not calm at all. Everyone had a grudge with Zamma. As he looked at each angry face, the method by which Zamma had betrayed each one popped into his mind.

There were nearly thirty warriors throughout their area of the King's Road. Before they were scattered in different rooms, lounging, sleeping, talking in small groups. Now, everyone was gathered in the great room, shouting. Some looked murderous. David understood why. He was flanked by Bevan and a few others. The room was white hot with anger.

"Let's end it here. Zamma was a monster," shouted one Amartus, Creel, a large man in a brown shirt that needed washing. "We can't let any of his power survive."

Bevan bellowed, "Stay calm. This man didn't ask for Zamma's power."

"But he has it, Amartus. Be afraid!" said a Rageto man, Etton, as he took another drink.

The room had divided pretty evenly. Cody wasn't sure who was on what side, but he sensed the growing danger.

Bevan took a step forward. "Most of us were dumped here by Zamma. I understand your anger." Cody didn't think that would help.

Bevan shouted louder, "But this man is not Zamma!"

"This is our chance for vengeance. I won't let it pass." This Amartus man swung his large knife over his head.

Another shouted, "This is the River's gift to us!"

The man with the knife lunged for David. From behind, the man felt himself lifting. "Hey, what the...?" before he could finish, he was thrown across the stone room. He hit a far wall and went down, sputtering. His knife clanked away.

Zacke dusted himself off and stood in front of David. He said, "No one is gonna hurt this man." Deke stood next to his brother.

The crowd swelled toward him, but Zacke held firm. "What is wrong with you? You were all trapped here." He pointed to the scholar, "And you're wrong. A blue gate dropped us here. That's the other Elder. Ordway, right? Zamma's dead. We have a bigger fight now."

Another man yelled, "Let us pass, boy..."

"Don't call him boy," said Deke.

The man put up his hand. "Apologies. But the grudge must be answered."

"We're all prisoners here, right?" reasoned Zacke. "Some of you are on one side, some the other. And this guy is Sect, I gather?"

"A few of us are," a woman said.

Zacke said, "Exactly. There is a common enemy and it's not David."

The crowd had no answer for that.

Zacke continued, "Go ahead and kill each other when we get out." He turned to David, "You can get us out, right?"

David thought. If felt like he had access to a great library of memories that were not his. But they were strange, crooked. Nothing was in a straight line. He felt the worse parts of Zamma leave him, but his knowledge was in dark boxes buried in ancient ground. He concentrated, but it would take some time. He answered Zacke, "I'm working on it."

Cody suggested, "Zamma could mirror walk, right?"

David delved into memory. "No. He could pull things through only one way, no sending. The mirror walking was all you, Cody."

"Is there a mirror here, like a really big one?" asked Zacke.

"No," said Cody. "I tried that. Almost got stuck in a shield,"

Zacke looked confused.

"Long story. Tell you later."

Bevan said, "This is a stone prison. Except for food and drink, we have nothing else but what we came with."

"The boy walked through water and returned," a woman pointed at Cody.

Caroline asked, "You did what?"

Cody said, "I was thinking of dad. We made a calm, reflective surface on the shield and that's how I found him."

Zacke said, "Just do that again."

"But that was just to get myself through, and Dad. I couldn't get all these people through that tiny round shield."

"So you will escape with your family and leave us here to rot? I don't think so." A warrior woman said. She stared at Zacke, "You won't stop me."

"You'd be surprised," Zacke shot back. Deke smiled.

David looked around. He started to recognize people around him. He scanned around his mind, then the faces, then put faces with abilities. David called, "Amina, Nestor."

They looked at David, then one another.

David beckoned them forward. "Your talents combined might work."

They reluctantly went to David.

"Everyone!" David announces to the room. "Find the smoothest wall, one taller than a man and very wide."

They complied slowly, but everyone eventually helped.

One shouted, "How about this one?" David rushed to the spot.

"Good, good," David said.

Nestor was behind him. He asked, "What? I can't make glass."

"No," said David, "but glass is a surprisingly poor reflector by itself."

"Plus," said Bevan, "You'd have to coat the back with silver oxide and a binding agent to the glass."

"Think back," said David. "The first mirrors were made of polished bronze, silver, or..."

"Copper," said Nestor. "Got it. you want me to do the whole thing?"

"Please, Nestor. As thick as you can manage," said David.

Cody asked, "Wait, are you going to turn that wall into copper?"

"Yep," said Nestor. "Both my talents are awesome."

"Can you turn, like, lead into gold?" asked Deke.

"No, that was Midas. Long dead," Nestor said. "The Amartus gave him a true death a long time ago so the Rageto couldn't use him anymore."

Bevan added, "The gold prices all over the world shot up after that."

"Please focus," said David.

Nestor touched the stone wall. He reached up as far as he could, then methodically ran his hand back and forth. "This wall is not smooth. Don't think it's gonna work."

"That's why we work together." David nodded to Amina, a warrior woman dressed in earth tones and a beautiful skin tone to match. She was as tall as Zacke.

The formerly stone wall was now bright, pure copper. It glowed brilliantly. The wall was wide enough for three grown men to walk through side-by-side. It still was as rough as stone.

Nestor nearly stumbled over. Zacke caught him and led him to a stone step close by.

Nestor whispered, "I haven't done anything that big in a long time."

Deke said, "That was amazing. Is it real copper?"

"Yeah," Nestor chuckled weakly. "A few years ago, I was living off making copper and selling it, 'til I ended up in here."

"Cool power," said Deke. Nestor was Amartus, but too tired to correct him about the "power" thing. He laid back on the step, exhausted.

"Amina, is it too big?" asked David.

Nestor perked up. "Heh. Another coincidence? We make quite the team."

Amina sniffed and ignored Nestor. "Zamma should remember when I made the roof on the Thean Hou Temple go completely flat. Carrew, that shape shifter was a panther in that moment. That cat slid right off like the roof was made of ice. This is nothing."

David did remember. But he had to focus. Zamma's many lifetimes worth of memories threatened to flood his mind if he let them. "Smoother than glass, please."

"Of course," said Amina.

They all watched the wall. It wasn't gradual like Nestor's work. Amina waved her hands and snap — the wall was perfectly smooth, shining copper.

Cody walked up. He saw both himself and his father reflected in the supernaturally smooth surface. Zacke and Deke stood side by side, Cody's parents together for the first time since he was a small boy. The whole room of warriors stood at their backs.

David said, "I want you to close your eyes, son. That night, Zamma used a spell to strengthen the mirror gate that you opened. I have that knowledge in my head. For so many to pass through, we must do this together."

Cody asked, "Where should we go?"

"Think of a space you know well, that is wide enough for us all."

Cody closed his eyes, "Okay, got it. I know where to take us."

"You lead them through, and I'll go through last to keep it open." David called to the room, "Is everyone ready to leave this place forever?"

A cheer rose up into the room. They were ready.

Cody concentrated and the huge copper wall showed a different scene, a room full of sports equipment. Caroline was startled and squeezed Cody's hand.

Cody sent his mental flash to Ariana. He hoped she got it. He opened his eyes and led them out.

CHAPTER THIRTY ONE

Warriors Return

The football stadium at the high school was a maze of construction equipment. Pallets of building materials were everywhere. Most of the track was dug up and piled in large mounds of earth.

John said, "Did you all feel that flash?"

"Hard to miss. Where's it coming from?" asked Katie, looking around the field.

Lucas said, "Ariana, I thought you said they would be on the field."

"Somewhere on campus. I felt..." she searched her mind. The flash had been so huge in her mind. The feeling came again. "This way," Ariana ran toward the auditorium.

They all followed her, arriving at the building. Just then, the steel door opened from the inside.

A strange woman stood there, surprised to see them. She clearly wasn't an employee or security guard. John saw the sword hanging on her belt.

John smiled. "How many others?"

"Many," she said and pointed inside, "that way." They all ran inside the room, just off the hall in the auditorium. Sports equipment lay in neat stacks, the multi-purpose room closed for the holiday break. There were many people there, many doubled over in pain. John spotted Cody and rushed to him. "What happened?"

Cody spoke to the room, holding his own stomach. "Sorry guys. I forgot about the bars." he pointed to the mirrored walls lined with ballet bars. They were mounted in the walls about the height of the stomach. Another man came through the mirror gate, and flipped over the bar with a yelp.

"Bar!" Cody yelled. Just then, David came through with Caroline. They saw the bar in time and helped each other over.

Everyone ran to embrace friends. John hugged Julien. "You made it back."

"We did, thanks to these two." Indicating Cody and David.

Katie hugged Cody, John hugged David and was introduced to Caroline. David made the briefest report he could, catching John up on all that had happened. He finished with, "...And all these warriors are a mix of Rageto and Amartus, and a Sect member."

John answered, "That's a lot to process. Let's get everyone outside. I have much to share, as well."

The group made their way out of the building, onto the football field.

David addressed the group. "There is a lot to discuss. For now, let's figure out the basics: food and a place to sleep."

"I can help you all figure that out," said John.

"Who are you, warrior?" a woman asked.

"I am Pentoss." said John loudly. "Many of us have surely fought in the past. Let's not start new battles tonight. You must all be tired. Let's make a plan..."

From behind the crowd, John saw the thin blue line appear, then another until a blue gate was outlined under the goal post. They all turned, many knowing exactly what it meant.

They all turned to face the gate.

"Ordway," said David.

Many warriors fanned out, not knowing what to expect. Few had seen Ordway in her current body, but they all recognized that electric blue.

The middle-aged Ordway walked out of the gate in a tailored white pant suit. Many warriors drew what weapons instinctively. Others took a fighting stance. Several peeled off the group and quietly fled.

"More than I thought," Ordway said. "Once there, no one can see into the King's Road, not even me. I imaged less than twenty."

"No," David said, "we are an army."

Ordway scoffed, "Hilarious." she ignored David and spoke to the crowd. "Rageto warriors. Any that come with me now will get a full pardon and be restored. Decide now."

To Cody's horror, seven warriors left and walked toward Ordway, including a woman that had helped his dad. Cody said, "Really?"

She shrugged. "Hey kid, I know I can't beat Ordway. Better to be on the winning side."

A shower of lighting came down if front of Ordway. She noticeably flinched and reassessed David.

"I didn't come to fight," Ordway said lightly. "Not here, not now. In two days, a terrible thing will happen. You cannot stop it. Stay here, leave, it won't matter. You will die here, or we will hunt you down after."

David felt the urge. It came on suddenly, ferociously. He wanted to kill the prattling woman, this rival. Just before he let a storm of lighting down on her head, he stopped. It felt like Zamma wanted her dead. The old rivalry. He faltered, not sure of where his feeling began and ended.

Ordway sauntered away, back to her gate. John's sword was in hand, but it was too late. She'd gone under the goalpost with her warriors. The blue gate winked out of existence.

Julien looked around. Only a few warriors straggled. The rest had slipped away.

John assessed the scene. All around were vignettes of people hugging, talking, explaining – Lucas and Ariana, Cody with his parents, Katie with Zacke and his brother. Two warriors came up to John and Julien.

The tall man said, "That sword looks familiar."

"Sorry, I don't know that face," replied John.

The man tapped his own chest three times.

John's eyes went wide. John hugged the man. "Nestor!"

"Old Friend!" returned Nestor.

John said, "I've been looking for you a long time."

Nestor admitted, "It was hard to keep track of time there. Years were lost to us. Oh, this is Amina."

Julien said, "Amina. You are Rageto, as I recall?"

"It's true," said Amina, "I served Zamma. But he imprisoned me on the King's Road."

"And he got a true death," said John.

She glanced back to Julien. "It took me many lives and betrayals to see the Rageto faults. I've gotten to know many Amartus now. Maybe it's time for a change."

"You'll get a chance to prove it soon," said John, "Will you willingly fight the Rageto?"

"With all my might," said Amina.

"I never fought you," said Julien. "but I remember stories. You were a fierce acolyte for the Rageto. Elders don't forgive defectors."

"Prison changes people," said Amina.

Julien replied, "We shall see."

Nestor said, "Pentoss, the least you can do is buy us a drink. Where are we, anyway?"

"California," answered John.

"There is booze in California, as I remember," Nestor smiled.

"Yes, of course," John smiled.

Julien remarked, "Now is a good time to plan for the coming battle."

John and Julien talked to the remaining group.

John said, "Go home, everyone. Get some rest. We will meet tomorrow and plan. We all need some time to catch up and regroup."

"You sure we'll be safe? No more attacks on our families?" said Ariana, Lucas a shadow behind her.

"No. They are done testing us." John explained. "Ordway is gearing for a final battle. She will need all her resources ready for that."

Ariana looked as worried as ever.

Lucas offered, "I'll walk you home."

They all agreed and split into groups, leaving the field.

* * *

Ariana walked in silence for a few blocks. Lucas didn't break the silence. Ariana finally did. "I'm worried."

"I can tell." said Lucas.

"Is that you talking," Ariana's voice grew icy, "or the Viking?"

"Both. We are the same. That's how it works." said Lucas.

"You aren't the same. I mean, sometimes you seem like you, Lucas – skinny kid, kinda cool, that knows tons of stuff. Other times, if feels like this grownup is, I don't know..." Ariana shivered. "...leering at me."

"I'm always leering at you," Lucas smiled.

Ariana stopped and crossed her arms. "I'm trying to be real."

Lucas stopped smiling. "I know. I'm sorry. I don't know how to explain."

She waited for a good answer.

"Sometimes a joke or smart-ass thing comes out. It's not always him, or me. Not exactly. It's like..." Lucas scratched his head. "...it's like I got this new program downloaded into my brain. I'm still me, but new words, new memories, even new food cravings flood through me. It's still my brain, my denser, fuller..."

Ariana stopped walking. "Richer?"

"Richer, yes! It's like I thought that fifteen years of life was a lot. So many birthdays and family trips, and tests and movies, all of it. Then I suddenly have tons of lives and memories to sort through."

Ariana couldn't imagine that, so overwhelming. She focused on something smaller. "And the leering?"

"Wrong word," Lucas said. "I mean, I like you. I've liked you for a long time. I hope you know that."

She hesitated, then looked deeply into his blue eyes. "I do know."

"I'm also a teenage boy. You are super pretty. I can't not look sometimes." Lucas smiled. "I will try not to leer."

"Okay. That's fair." she considered, then shrugged and walked on. "I leer at you too."

"You do?" he followed.

"Of course. I'm a teenage girl. Boys and girls look at each other. Nothing wrong with that. It's natural. My parents were..." Ariana blushed and realized she was now older than her parents when they got married and started having babies. "... were young when they dated. This is getting confusing. Anyway, I like you too."

They walked side by side and Lucas basked in the confirmation.

Ariana sighed. "But this is a horrible time. People are trying to kill us. I'm just worried all the time."

"I know you are," Lucas replied.

Ariana caught the confidence in his voice, the surety. She pursed her lips. "See? You know who you are. That's kinda frustrating. Your answers are there for you. I still don't know what I am. What's my purpose?"

Lucas chuckled. "Even with all these memories of past lives and bodies, I don't know *that*. I don't think anyone does. What is anyone's purpose?"

"I don't mean 'why are we in the universe?' I mean, if the River does have a plan, what does it want with me? How can I help you guys, myself? Are we just going to be fighting for the rest of our lives?"

Lucas nodded. "That's the way it has been. Always. Rageto and Amartus battling through time."

"Sounds exhausting," sighed Ariana. "There must be a way to stop it."

Lucas shrugged, "Yeah. We win."

Ariana replied, "Sure. Piece of cake, right? We are finally the lucky group that will end all of this forever."

They both chuckled at that.

"New births are tricky." Lucas rubbed his head. "From what Elgisard has seen, new births are just a mystery until they aren't."

Ariana threw up her hands, "That doesn't help me."

Lucas said, "I mean when a re-birth gets activated, they get memories and abilities added to the person they are. New births definitely have it harder. You start from scratch."

"Yeah. I've noticed."

"You, Zacke, Cody – your abilities are new." Lucas slid into geek mode. "No one has dealt with them before. I, Elgisard, um, we once knew this guy – Guan Yu. He'd been around a while. I don't know what body he was on, but he was the first one to train me."

"I thought your father did. Your Viking dad," she laughed. "See? Who has conversations like this?"

"I know. I know. My 'Viking' father did train me. He was my first father, of course. I was a new birth then. We all start that way. Guan Yu was a big deal in China. When his abilities started to rise, he said it felt like 'fate had claimed me and filled me with destiny.' "

Ariana's brow knit. "Umm. Sounds kind of silly."

"Yeah. He was a little too poetic. He told me that when I started training with him. Then, one day it happened. It felt exactly like that. I felt clearly that I was on the right path."

"Just like that?" Ariana asked, dubious.

"Yes." said Lucas.

Ariana asked, "What happened next?"

"A few weeks later we were slaughtered by Norwegians. I went into my next body a few years later. Grew up in France that time."

"That was your first re-birth?" Ariana realized no one had talked about the details of the process. Certainly not John. "How many years had passed?"

"I got my full memories back at sixteen." Lucas smiled. "My whole village thought I'd gone crazy. I was speaking a different language. There was no one there to explain what was happening."

Fully invested, Ariana asked, "What did you do?"

"I ran away. I had to get back to my family. My first family."

Ariana couldn't imagine traveling across whole countries that long ago. "Where were they?"

"I was a Dane. I somehow made it from France to what now is the country of Denmark. The what you would call 'Viking' calendar is, to be generous, not very specific. The French were using a different calendar system. By the time I figured that out, I'd guessed that about twenty years had passed from my first birth to my leaving France."

Ariana's head swum. "This is getting complicated."

"Yes! Imagine a small French, totally clueless sixteen-year-old trying to fig-ure this out. All the time, I was doing anything to get to Denmark. Visions of two lives bounced around my brain. I thought I was crazy most of the time. Maybe I was."

"Did you ever make it?"

"I did. My second talent is tolerance of pain. It's not showy like the blood rage, but it helped," said Lucas, face animated. "It took me over two years to get there. There were raids, bad food, disease, a shipwreck. One of the Sect wrote a book about my adventures a long time ago. *Boy's Journey To Yesterday.*" Lucas stopped walking, deep in himself. "I made it, but it was too late."

"Why?" Ariana stopped too.

"I found my father's grave. The rest of my family had been killed as far as I could find out. It was hard for a French teen to get any information from Vikings. I'd learned French first, then the memories of my native tongue came later. I would never fit in again." Lucas walked again. "Then I was a slave until I died."

She started to speak but had no idea what to say. She began walking next to him.

Lucas let the silence prevail. They were only a few blocks from her house. He finally said, "Not all lives have a happy ending."

Ariana looked forward, keeping step with Lucas. "That's what I'm afraid of."

She abruptly stopped a block from her house. Lucas didn't know how to help her. He'd just unloaded a lot of ugly history. She uncrossed her arms and stepped to him.

Her lips pressed to his. She opened her eyes for a second, a look of surprise. She smiled and took another kiss. He kissed back. She closed her eyes and it lasted what felt like forever.

She stepped back and smiled. Ariana walked the rest of the way to her house. Lucas felt cemented to the spot as he watched her go. A flash of first kisses blinked through his mind like lightbulbs exploding. A list appeared in his mind, the one his ancient had built of first kisses. He smiled and put Ariana at the top.

CHAPTER THIRTY TWO

This Will Be Awkward

David walked through the door of a house he didn't know.

Caroline sat in the same clothes she had on when she was taken by the Rageto. David watched her. Her long brown hair was mussed, but the same beautiful tawny brown he remembered. She was nearly as tall as David, and as she spoke on the phone, her smooth complexion made David think she hadn't aged since he'd left.

Caroline was busy calling her two jobs explaining why she had missed work. She surprised herself with convincing lies. "Yes, huge family emergency. You wouldn't believe it if I told you. Yes, just a few days to sort it all out. Thanks so much." The real, crazy story Cody had told her was still flooding her brain. She got off the phone with her two quite different bosses. She clicked off her phone, exhausted.

David stood there awkwardly, looking around. Cody was on the couch, clearly exhausted.

Caroline looked from David to Cody. "Wow. This will be awkward."

David agreed, "It is. I don't feel like I have any right to be here."

"You don't. I left the place in Tarzana years ago." Caroline let the bitter memory rest. "Cody explained a lot to me, even though it was hard to believe. I'm exhausted, but I really need to hear your side."

David nodded, "It's the least I can do." Caroline invited him to sit at the small kitchen table stacked with schoolbooks and her homework. They gathered at the table, all three.

David began, "I came into my abilities late, causing the lightning storm that nearly burned our rental house down."

"Wait. That was you?" Caroline looked at Cody.

Cody threw up his hands, "I couldn't remember everything, mom."

"Yes. It was an accident." David continued, "I had a bad dream and I woke up. I knew it was me. It wasn't a dream."

Caroline remembered. "We nearly lost everything. Thank God for good neighbors and the fire department."

"Yes," said David.

"I don't remember that," said Cody.

"Good," said Caroline. "You were so young, baby. Scared the hell out of me."

"You acted strange for weeks after that." David asked, "Do you remember?"

"Of course," said Caroline. "I was just freaked out by the fire. I couldn't know that was you."

David said, "I didn't know what to do. I took time off of work without you knowing it. I tried to go to secluded places and master it."

"You went off and practiced your powers?" asked Cody.

"Abilities, please, Cody," said David. "It was a new curse. I couldn't control it. It was hard enough finding anywhere private in the Los Angeles area, even in the desert a few hours away. It didn't work. I started two brush fires."

"Oh my God. Really?" asked Caroline.

"Yes. The first one blew itself out. The second got out of control. I was sure the authorities would be after me. Thank god no one got hurt. They had it contained in a few days, no structures lost. I watched all the news reports."

"That's when you left," Caroline said, nodding.

"Yes. I wrote the note and left. I didn't want to take too much money from you and Cody, so I took the train east. I had no idea where I was going. I just knew it wasn't safe to be around you."

"That wasn't your decision to make." Caroline's gaze bore into David. "We were a team. There was nothing we couldn't figure out together."

"Not even crazy lightning powers?" asked Cody.

"You're not helping, baby," said Caroline in her mom voice. Cody stopped talking.

"I know." David looked at the floor. "It was the worst mistake of my life. I realized I couldn't live without you both, so I was headed home."

"That's when those men took you?" She looked to Cody, "The brothers, did you call them?"

"Yes. Monsters," said Cody.

"Yes. Yes, they were," David said, blinking away the memories. "But they are both gone now."

"Cody told me... okay, help me out with the details here — that you stabbed one of them on a fire tower with a special sword?" asked Caroline.

David said, "Yes. We were all flying over the tower. It was John's relic sword. We were linked and..."

Caroline rubbed her head and stood up. "I need some coffee."

"Good idea. Can I help?" David started to get up. Caroline pushed him gently back down with her gaze. David wanted to touch her but knew he couldn't. She made the coffee. Drinks all around, David continued.

He told her of his years of slavery, being forced to find teens with abilities. If he didn't, how he was punished. He told her about the tsunami in 2004. The he explained how he came back to the city, being freed by John, the struggle between the Amartus and Rageto. He finished with all the details of the battle over the fire tower and what had happened since. By the time he was done, Caroline had her hand over her mouth, tears in her eyes.

"I know," said Cody, "it's a lot."

She abruptly stood up, her chair screeching on the floor. She turned her back to them.

David froze, not knowing what came next.

"Mom?" asked Cody.

She turned back around and went around to the back of David's chair. She wove her arms around him until she encircled him. She whispered through her tears, "I'm sorry that happened to you."

David began to cry. They became silent sobs after a while and Caroline didn't let go.

When he was better, Caroline switched to Cody and hugged him fiercely. She let go.

Cody said, "Mom. Thank you for forgiving him. I'm so sorry you got..."

She stood up straight and punched Cody on the shoulder.

"I didn't say I forgive him. This will take time," said Caroline.

"Oww!" he said.

"You both should have told me. Everything." She walked around the table to face them again. "I could have helped. Doing this alone was stupid. Stupid men! Always thinking you have to protect your poor little women folk from the truth."

"Mom, I'm sorry, I..."

David stammered, "Caroline, I..."

"No. I get it. I think. It is a lot. David, when you were able, you took care of our son. Thank you for that." She took a step closer. "But you left us. I took care of Cody, alone, moved to new city and work two jobs. I even go to college online, you know, in my 'spare time'. I had a natural childbirth. I have periods every damned month and I still look this hot. I'm tougher than both you shitheads put together!"

David stifled his smile. It didn't seem appropriate. *God, I love her.*

Caroline grabbed each of their hands, one by one. "We should have been a team! This is a lot of crazy stuff to process. I will need time. But never again with the secrets."

They both nodded their assent.

Caroline composed herself. "Okay. I can't let you out in the wild. Not with crazy magical people after you. You sleep on the couch." Caroline whiffed, "And you both need a few showers each. I'm going to sleep now for about sixteen hours. We will figure the rest out together. Got it?" She pointed to both in turn.

They both nodded again. She left for her waiting bed.

"What a woman." David watched her go. "I was such an idiot."

"Yeah, you were." Cody put a hand on David's shoulder.

Cody gathered the cups, headed to the sink to wash them. He leaned over his dad. "Hey. Glad you're home, Dad."

* * *

Safe at home, Katie's mom cornered her.

"Is everything okay?" Katie's mom, Judith, said as she came in.

"Yeah," Katie quickly checked over herself for anything she couldn't explain. "Yes. Why?"

"Oh, no reason," her mom stared at her. It was an old trick, which worked on Katie every time. The silence would eventually make her spill her guts over whatever misdeed Katie had done. She couldn't let it work this time. *Did Megan say something?*

"Oh. Hi," Megan popped from around the corner.

Katie jumped. "Hey! Hey, little monster. You scared me."

Mom's radar picked up on whatever Katie was hiding. "There's some pizza in the fridge if you want," she kept eye contact with Katie. "You sure you're alright?"

Katie was about to lie, but Megan saved her. "Wanna watch a movie?"

"Umm. Sure," Katie said. "Pizza and a movie sounds great. Your room?"

Instead of answering, Megan marched to her room. Katie didn't even heat the pizza, grabbing a slice and a soda then rushing to Megan's room before her mom could corner her again.

In younger sister sanctuary, safe behind the closed door, she sat on the bed next to Megan. "Hey. You okay? Did you tell them anything?"

"Of course not, dummy," said Megan, working the remote.

Katie asked, "Okay. So why did you go in the theatre, anyway? I told you not to..."

"They grabbed me! My friends left and they got me."

Katie looked at her sister carefully. "Did they hurt you?"

"No. Just scared me," Megan said.

"I'll bet. If they had hurt you..." Katie didn't finish her thought.

Megan asked quietly, "Would you have killed them?"

That stopped Katie. "I... I don't know." But she did know.

"You were different there. It's like it wasn't you," Katie remarked.

"I know." How could Katie explain this part, when she didn't understand it herself? "It's like there's some part of me that is a warrior. I saw you in that chair my warrior inside got serious. I think it's like that mode that moms can do. You know, a kid is in danger and mom lifts a car off the little girl all by herself?"

"Like Superman?" asked Katie.

"More like amazon warrior mode. Zacke is our super boy."

Megan said, "You are growing up."

Katie didn't know what she meant. "We're all growing up. You too."

"Yeah," Megan struggled, "but you're growing up faster. You have a literal woman inside you. I'm not growing that fast. We finally like each other now. I don't want to lose that."

Katie put her arm around Megan. "I've always liked you. I just treated you like crap because you pulled mom's focus away from me." She stopped. "Wow. I didn't know I really felt like that until I just said it."

"I thought it was because Mom and Dad like me better," Megan smiled.

"Monster," said Katie.

Megan giggled. Then stopped. "Don't grow up too fast, okay?"

"I won't if you won't. Let's watch this movie. Plus, I'm starving. Saving your butt tired me out."

"Yeah, yeah," Megan said, getting comfortable on her bed. Katie laid beside her, pizza stuffed into her mouth.

"What do you want to watch?"

"Anything animated. No superheroes, please," said Katie.

Megan shrugged and picked the Disney version of The Hunchback of Notre Dame. A few minutes in, Katie's mind drifted. Notre Dame. A flash came of Zhanna having a running battle in the famous cathedral.

Zhanna was running, but she was not alone. Her friend Unna was there, torch in hand. The streets of Paris were alight, not with enlightened Republicans, but drunken fools looking for the next head for their guillotine.

Their prey was running through the front door, the church opened night and day to all of Paris. But to mock religion, not worship. Someone told her they'd even changed the name to the Temple of Enlightenment. Liars and idiots. Another excuse to loot and pillage from the church.

Unna pointed and Zhanna got the idea. She turned right while Unna went left. They both ran along each wall, around the rows of pews.

Even in the dark, lit only by candlelight, the cathedral was stunning. She always wanted to visit this place, but not like this. She spotted Tikeritus. He stopped, looking around furiously.

"Remember what he can do!" shouted Zhanna.

He turned toward the sound of Zhanna's voice. Mistake. Unna leapt over a pew straight for him. He lifted the heavy table covered in candles and flung it at Unna. She smiled. He clearly didn't know what she could do. Unna flung her hand at the candles and brought all the flames to life. The wall of fire pushed at Tikeritus. He shouted and dove for the alter.

Zhanna came around the last pew on her side and pushed a shield ball at him. It hit him in the chest, and he flung back. He landed by the grand altar, next to a pillar with a statue atop it. He ripped the statue off and flung it at Zhanna. She put up a shield and it bounced off and smashed amid the pews. Tikeritus ran at them, grabbing the first long pew and lifted in into the air.

"He's strong," said Zhanna.

"That won't save him," answered Unna.

"Indeed," agreed Zhanna. She darted behind him while he was distracted. The man roared at Unna when the pew flew past her, harmlessly. She walked up to him. To her right were half melted candles. Unna made the flames grow bright. Tikeritus backed up and hit something solid. He spun around to find Zhanna had thrown up a shield. He pounded on it fiercely, but it was too late for escape. Unna pushed the flame into the shield. Fire engulfed him. He screamed as he burned. Zhanna smiled.

Katie jerked out of her memory.

"Hey! You scared me," shouted Megan. "Where did you go just now.? You totally zoned out."

"Sorry." Katie readjusted to reality. *So real.* She tried to concentrate on the cartoon film, but her mind kept drifting back. Megan had asked if Katie could kill anyone.

Katie had just seen the answer.

* * *

Late that night, Zacke had finally told his brother everything, no details left out.

"That's crazy!" said Deke.

"I know!" said Zacke. "But that's the whole story. Dad knows too."

"You told Dad all that? Did he believe you?"

"He did." Zacke's face relaxed. Pressure had been on him for so long. Now, everyone he loved knew the truth.

"Aren't you..." Deke whispered, "... like afraid that some government agency will come take you?"

The thought had crossed Zacke's mind. He shrugged. "They can try."

Silence. Deke looked away.

Zacke narrowed his gaze. "You're going to ask me, aren't you?"

"What?" Deke still looked away. "I don't know."

"Yes you do," Zacke smiled, "just ask."

Deke shrugged, but didn't say anything. He simply pointed to the sky, shrugging his shoulders at the same time.

Zacke laughed, "Okay. Let's go." Deke smiled widely, following his brother out the door. Zacke had picked out a few spots around town where he could practice. No people, no surveillance cameras.

Deke looked around. "Okay. Good spot. How do we do this?"

Zacke walked behind his brother. "I'll stand behind you and lift you under the arms."

Deke pulled away. "Nah man, I don't like another dude standing behind me."

"I'm your brother. Don't make it weird."

"Nope," said Deke.

Zacke put up his hands. "Well, I'm not going to cradle you in my arms like you're a baby."

"Okay," Deke walked around his brother. "I'll hop on piggyback style."

"Like a five-year-old kid?" asked Zacke.

"Come on bro." said Deke. "Not strong enough, or what?"

Zacke rolled his eyes. "Hop on."

Deke tucked in behind Zacke and put his arms around Zacke's neck.

"Hold on tight," Zacke smiled.

"Okay." Deke asked, "Do you put your arm out, or... Hey. Hey!"

They were off the ground straight up in the air. Zacke kept an eye out for others, but it was so dark, he wasn't too worried. Deke held on tight.

"Dude," choked Zacke, "you're cutting off my air..."

"Sorry," Deke yelled too loudly, but relaxed his grip a little.

Make Out Point was at the crest of a hill on one side of Sea Valley. It used to be open to cars but was made just a pedestrian hiking trail some years before. Zacke imagined old 1950's teenagers going up there to "neck." Zacke had climbed it once by himself on the footpath. It was a steep climb, a real workout. Now, he didn't need to walk. He aimed for the summit.

"This is too high, bro!" yelled Deke.

Zacke accelerated his pace and felt Deke squeeze harder. They reached the summit where the paved trail ended. He set them down. Deke couldn't let go fast enough.

Deke jumped to the ground, "Wow. Wow. You do that every day?"

"Not every day. Come on. I wanted to show you the view."

"I saw it flying in," said Deke, pacing around.

"You had your eyes closed. I know you did. Come on." Zacke led his brother to the edge of the hill.

"Wow. Man. Wow! Is that really our little town?" asked Deke, staring out at the vista.

"Yeah. Not bad, huh?" The lights of Sea Valley twinkled below them. The classic city grid of lights made it look like an orderly constellation.

"This is awesome." Deke slapped his brother on the arm.

Zacke smacked back. "Wanted to share it with my big Bro."

"Thanks, Zacke. I know I've been gone, partying, trying to figure stuff out. I know I wasn't there for you when you were going through all that stuff. Fire Tower? Dragon? And Jesus, those spiders? I am never going back to that mission."

Zacke laughed, "Yeah. It has been crazy."

Deke's asked, "What happens now?"

"I don't know." Zacke looked out at the lights. "But I need a favor."

"Anything Bro."

"Leave town. Take Dad with you. I don't know what those guys are planning, but their friends promised to level this town if we didn't join them."

"Join them to do what?" a voice came from behind them.

Zacke whipped around, met with a flashlight beam in his face. He put his hand up in front of his eyes, blinking back the black dots in his vision.

Deke said, "Hey man, get that thing out of our faces."

"Calm down, Deke. Zacke. I just want to talk." The man flashed his light under his own face.

"Officer Jack?" asked Zacke.

Jack said, "Hi Zacke. Sorry to startle you. Hi Deke."

"Hi there Mr. Policeman," said Deke, an edge in his voice.

Officer Jack had given Deke a few warnings at some parties that had gotten out of hand. They were not strangers, but they were not friends.

"Officer Jack," Zacke repeated, not sure what to say. He tried a distraction. "What are you doing up here? Quite the hike, huh?"

"For some people, yes," replied Jack. "Maybe these will help cut through some of the crap." He handed Zacke his phone, opened to the picture files.

Zacke scrolled through them, his stomach churning with every swipe. The first was of Zacke on top of the Hotel downtown, another of a jet of fire on a hill. It was taken from far away, but Zacke knew that was taken when the dragon spit fire. The next three were grainy, dark photos of his friends around the fire tower. They weren't very clear. Zacke thought, *Does that matter? We're caught.*

"Did you take these all yourself? What are they?" asked Zacke, trying to play dumb.

"Games? Really? Okay, Zacke." Jack held up his phone. "These are snaps of larger photos at my house. They are from lots of different sources like security footage and stuff I shot myself. Next, I know you didn't pass me on the trail, so you either have a jet pack hidden in your pocket or you can fly."

"Fly?" said Deke weakly and laughed too loud. "Fly. That's crazy, crazy policeman."

Jack swiped and flashed his phone again. It was also far away, but it was Zacke in flight. He swiped and showed another, then another.

Jack continued, "Billy Miller told us some wild tales about the night on the fire tower. They were crazy, but consistent each time he told it. The five of you told a more reasonable story, but there were things that don't add up. Remember your training, Zacke. That inconsistent stories are red flags?"

"Officer Jack..." offered Zacke weakly.

His voice, always so controlled in every Junior Explorer class, rose now. "Not to mention dead bodies starting with the fire tower and ending with a severed head at the riverbed. One that was taken off cleanly with a blade, not some damned mountain lion. I'm tired of the lies, son."

Deke just stood there. Zacke didn't want to lie to anyone ever again.

Zacke stood there. He looked Jack in the eyes. "Okay, Jack. I'll tell you everything. But you aren't going to believe it."

* * *

Laughter rang out. John, Julien, Nestor, and Amina all had beer glasses in hand. The bar was deserted, except for the old warriors. Jacob's was a famous dive bar in the heart of the city, only two blocks from the old theatre, open for nearly 100 years. Décor of all sorts covered the walls and ceiling — old farm implements, highway signs and license plates, records, pictures of old movie stars and modern neon beer signs.

Instead of haunting the long old wooden bar, they sat outside in a covered area, open only to the sky. The smoker's hangout was deserted but for them.

John was in the middle of a memory. "...and you were left standing there surrounded by lava flows. I was battling an Elder on that schooner. What was the name of that ship?"

"The Merry Widow." Nestor raised his glass and drank.

"Right!" yelled John. "It was no use. Yarro had three good fighters. They cut me up and threw me in the water. I'm still not sure if I drowned before a shark got me. How was death by lava?"

Nestor said, "I've no idea. I jumped in the water. Lava had burned my foot, so I thought that drowning would be a better death."

"We both drowned that day!" John raised his glass.

Nestor raised his own. "Cheers to that?"

"Why not." They clinked their glasses.

"We never see each other," said John. "And when we do, we end up telling great death stories."

"Why not?" Nestor drank. "We live, we die, we live again, we fight, we kill, we die. To the struggle!" Nestor raised his glass again.

John grabbed his arm. "How about we end it this time, old friend. For good."

Nestor put down his beer and took another shot of Schnapps. "I will always fight by your side, my friend. But make no illusions that they will lose."

"When left that fighting spirit?" asked John. "I've heard your great rallying speeches before overwhelming enemies."

"Yes, and the last one was Gettysburg. A slaughter. I lost all my fighters but two. I also lost an eye and a leg. Not the best example." Nestor picked up his beer again.

Julien said, "We don't even know what they are planning, or how many they are."

Amina broke her silence. "I can't believe you are Unna. I thought you long gone."

Unna smiled through Julien. "Amina, you are just lucky you switched sides. I vowed to end you for good the next time I saw you. You killed my best friend."

"I remember," said Amina. "She died well, if that makes a difference."

"It doesn't." Julien's gaze bore into Amina.

"Unna," John put a hand on Julien's shoulder, "we must unite with good fighters that will help us."

Julien still had eyes on Amina. "How can we trust her, my love?"

Nestor laughed. "Unna, ever the doubter."

John said, "Zamma is dead. A true death. That still leaves three. We need warriors."

Julien replied, "You saw those warriors slink back to them. Warriors that were their prisoners."

"And I am here, with you," said Amina. "Pentoss is right. We must put aside these things."

Nestor said, "Funny. There were hardly any fights on the King's Road. Not sure why."

"Because we could finally take a rest," said Amina. "Why bother fighting when in prison? It was a welcome respite."

"But the fight is come again," said Nestor. "And we will join it!" Nestor raised his glass again, as did they all. They clinked and drank.

"Maybe this time will be different," said Julien. "You all made tight bonds on the King's Road. Recruit some more of those friends and trust will be easier."

"Contact the others that were trapped?" asked Amina. "Done."

Nestor offered, "Most of us exchanged cell numbers, believe it or not."

They all burst out laughing.

"Sworn ancient enemies for all of time," Julien laughed, "swapping phone numbers!"

"I know," said Amina, "We were bored. None of the phones worked, or course."

"It was more like," Nestor said, "Hey, when we escape, maybe have an epic battle — call me up, bro!'"

Peals of laughter.

Julien shook his head. "We used to send spies, have hidden compartments in our corsets. Even codes and disappearing ink."

Nestor added, "Now we text and say, 'what's up?'"

"To the modern world!" John offered the new toast. They all drank.

"Let's hope the River smiles on us all," said Julien.

Amina slammed her glass down. "I won't drink to that cold, wet bitch. Screw the River and her unknowable plans."

John said, "Let's make our own fate. I thought I was the very last Amartus. Now there is a chance." John stood up, a little unsteady. He hadn't drunk so much in a long time. "To friends here and gone. May we be victorious in the battle to come. Together."

They all toasted and thought of the bitter battle to come.

* * *

Caron looked in the mirror. His face was burned on one side, his left eardrum popped and useless. He steeled himself to meet the three elders and recount his tale. They would surely want him to bow, which would be one more painful indignity. He would be forced to hobble on his bad leg to get up off the floor.

He finished cleaning up, his formerly beautiful teenage face a ruin. It didn't matter. All that mattered was finishing them. Pentoss, the Witness. All of them.

He limped to the ballroom, where the three elders sat in mid-century modern chairs. They were arranged like thrones before him. He heard the whispering as he approached.

"...never happened before," said Ordway.

Yarro agreed, "Not possible."

Caron arrived and stood before the three Elders. Since it was Ordway's ballroom, she was seated in the middle. Yarrow was to her right, Sorrento on the left. They waited.

Caron bowed low. His leg protested. It was still in pain from the beating he'd taken on his journey, his gauntlet. He winced but completed the bow and finally stood back up.

"Thank you for showing us respect. The old ways are important," said Yarro.

Ordway spoke, "You say you are Caron. That is not possible. I was there when he died only a few months ago."

"I am Caron," he croaked.

"Then explain," said Sorrento, "make them understand your journey."

"I had a son," Caron began. "He meant nothing to me. He lived near San Diego, California. I was vaguely aware he existed, that he was a teenager. He was not in the struggle, a mere inferior. More human trash."

Yarro waved his hand impatiently. "How is this relevant?"

Caron swallowed bitterly, "The River shoved me into his body."

"Impossible!" said Yarro, standing.

"I thought so too," Caron said.

Sorrento spoke with a sharp edge, "Sit Yarro. You will want to hear his tale. It is significant." Yarro sat with a huff.

Caron continued, "It was only three days after that night on the Fire Tower, the night Pentoss and The Witness killed me."

Yarro interrupted. "The River does not place a warrior into a grown teenage boy. That is ludicrous. Warriors are inserted at conception." He spit, "It has always been so."

"Let the boy finish," said Ordway.

"It was very painful. There was no rest. I felt myself traveling on water, the way it always feels to me when I go back to the River. Normally, a cool place to rest." Caron swallowed hard, remembering. "This time, the River was on fire for me. It burned. It felt like forever, a torment, the Christian Hell. That pain was replaced with another when I suddenly found myself in a new body. It was like a childbirth."

"More pain?" asked Ordway.

"It was pain upon pain. Like an elephant being forced into the skin of a dog, my being was forced into the boy's mind. It ripped him apart. It ripped me apart. I felt his essence turn to shreds as I entered his mind. I felt my son as he was dying. I killed him."

The Elders didn't interrupt. Ordway shifted uncomfortably in her seat.

Caron continued, "My mind was unhinged, forced and rammed into another mind. In the first few moments, I couldn't see, barely think. I knew who I was, vaguely. Someone was there. I still couldn't see. I heard only white noise. This thing grabbed for me. In panic, I fought back and I threw it down, climbed on top of it. I beat my attacker with my fists until it stopped moving."

"Is this true?" asked Ordway.

Sorrento said, "Yes, my agents have checked out his story and confirmed all the details. A woman was found dead. We cleaned up the mess."

Caron blinked. Looking beyond the elders, he was lost in the memories. "It was only later, when my eyesight returned, I realized she was trying to comfort me. Her son. Our son. I only saw her one night, sixteen years before."

Sorrento prompted, "Tell the rest."

"Then I ran. I stole her car, but I crashed only a few blocks away. The boy's reflexes were bad. Mine hadn't fully returned yet. The crash hurt my back and bashed my face. Hit the steering wheel."

Yarro looked to Sorrento. With a nod, he confirmed that this happened too. "Continue." urged Sorrento.

"I ran on foot. The next few months were a living nightmare. I slept on the streets as I made my way north."

"Why north?" asked Yarro.

"To get back to that town." Caron growled. "The place that gave my brother a true death."

"Did you get there?" asked Ordway.

"No. I was beaten many times — by a gang once, by other homeless men older than me. Then, while sleeping I was taken by two men. They... they kept me as a prisoner for some time." He did not tell them what happened over those weeks. It was no worse than his own father had done in the last life, the one he so recently left. There were two of them. That was worse. "I finally remembered the correct spell." Caron stopped talking.

Ordway prompted, "What happened to these men?"

Caron responded, "Yes. The two men kept me underground. I knew the earthquake I created was my death as well. By then, I didn't care. We were all together and I rained death down on them both." He smiled sadly, "But I survived."

"And the River brought him to me," said Sorrento. "One of my agents was working in the area. Seems that Caron had killed her in a battle a few lives ago. She sniffed him out and it was confirmed. This is Caron."

Yarro announced, "You realize you are being punished by the River. Her brutal, strange justice, do you not?"

Caron nodded. He knew. His last life he'd been unbound. Caron knew the 2004 earthquake and tsunami alone would bring him untold miseries. He did not know the River would invent special suffering just for him.

"You are unique in history." said Sorrento, on the edge of his chair. "Your suffering is great. How does that make you feel?"

Caron growled, "Angry."

"No use at being angry at The River," said Yarro imperially. "She is unassailable. You can rage against her life after life. It is futile."

"No," said Caron.

"No?" shouted Yarro.

"No, it is not The River." Caron stared at Yarro. "My anger is with Pentoss and his brood. They were not supposed to win."

"They haven't," Ordway said. "Here you stand."

"Then they will pay for all my suffering," said Caron.

"We have a plan, and it just so happens you are the last piece to that puzzle, as though it was meant to be," said Yarro.

Ordway said, "Your brother was very clever. Too clever. His hubris got him killed. What we need now is a brute. A monster to be unleashed. Will you be our monster and help wipe them all out?"

Caron answered, "Yes."

CHAPTER THIRTY THREE

The Plan

John gathered his troops and they all met in Lucas' room. The converted garage brimmed with the new Amartus warriors. Including Nestor and Amina, there were twelve warriors now added to their numbers. Katie was forced to bring her sister along and Zacke brought Deke; neither would take no for an answer.

"Glad you all could make it, though the more civilians we bring in, the more I worry," John said.

Katie pointed, "Megan insisted that she's a part of this now. I've told her how dangerous this will get."

Megan crossed her arms. "I'm stubborn like you."

Deke spoke up, "And I'm here to support Zacke."

"We take all the help we can get," John said. "This is Nestor — Ness, what did you find out?"

"My fellow cellmates don't know what the Elders have planned exactly, but they know the location. There's a dam a few miles outside of this city. These are the coordinates," he held up his phone with the latitude and longitude and flashed it around the room. Those that were tech savvy punched the coordinates into their phones, the others shared screens.

"That's the Gibraltar-Bradbury," said Lucas.

"We are to fight in Gibraltar? I know it," said Amina. "The Spanish zone or the English side?"

"No, not the country of Gibraltar," said Lucas, going to the middle of the room. He read his phone. "The Gibraltar-Bradbury is the name of the dam. Here, I'll read what it says. 'The Gibraltar-Bradbury is a concrete dam built at

Cachuma Lake. It is a source of drinking water for the county and has a small hydro-electric power plant.' "

"Why there?" asked Amina.

Ariana said, "Wait. Isn't that the dam that feeds our riverbed?"

"You mean the dry riverbed?" said Cody.

"It's not always dry," said Ariana. "They have to release water sometimes."

"Right." Katie scratched her forehead. "Didn't we learn about this in school for some reason?"

Megan answered, "Yeah. A good reason. The siren system in town. We had to do drills in school because of the sirens."

"What's the danger?" asked John.

"Earthquakes," Lucas said. "They found out the dam would fail if there was a big enough earthquake. Sea Valley is a valley, obviously, and it's downstream from the dam. If the dam fails, it would wipe out the town."

"What about the drought? Isn't the lake really low?" asked Ariana.

Lucas said, "Not after all the rains last year. Nearly full."

"Are they going to destroy the dam?" Katie asked.

Amina nodded.

John said, "Caron is dead. Even if he was re-birthed the moment his last body died, we will have 15 or 16 years before we need to worry about him."

"They could blow the dam," said Nestor.

"I doubt it." Julien shook her head. "Rageto's greatest power is that they operate in the dark. An explosion would be too public."

"The fire tower was public," Cody said.

"Yes, Sazzo was bold this time around, but Zacke picked the fire tower for that battle," said John.

"Speaking of that," said Zacke, "can I talk to you outside later, John?"

"Sure. As soon as we form a plan." John turned to Ariana. "How public is this lake?"

Ariana answered, "Very. It's a campground and tourist lake. People are there all the time, even this time of year."

Julien added, "70 degrees in January. Not surprising it is popular."'

"It's a strange location for a battle," said Amina.

"Not at all. I know of battles on bridges, dams, lakes," said Nestor. "Hell, I was in most of them."

John put a hand on his shoulder. "You do attract danger, my friend. When will this battle happen?"

Nestor answered, "Tomorrow. 4 pm. They didn't try to hide it. They are setting the battlefield."

John rubbed his chin. "Okay everyone. We need to do reconnaissance before tomorrow. Know what we are up against. We'll get a team together and go to the dam now. Julien will break the rest of you into teams and train hard. We have the chance to end this tomorrow."

"John, can I talk to you, please?" asked Zacke.

"Sure. Just one more thing. If we are to win, we can't be protecting innocents at the same time. That means only warriors there tomorrow. Julien will take over. We need strategy." John said, "I'll meet you outside, Zacke."

The others did not seem at ease as John and Zacke left to talk outside, Deke trailing close behind. Zacke began speaking as soon as they turned the corner. "I told someone. In fact, I told a few people."

John asked, "What did you tell them?"

"Everything," said Zacke.

John didn't speak for a moment. "That was not wise."

"It felt right." said Zacke, "I'm not sorry." he waited for a blow up, an angry shout, that it was a terrible idea.

John's brow furrowed, but he spoke softly. "Who you choose to tell is up to you Zacke. That is your right. But there is more at stake than just you."

Zacke shot back, "I didn't do it because I'm selfish."

"That's not what I meant," answered John.

"Kinda sounded like it."

John responded, "I'm just concerned."

"Yeah, so am I with that weak ass plan," said Deke. "So, what? You're just going to go out there and 'figure it out'?"

Zacke added, "Deke has a point. John, that one elder showed up last time and we nearly died. It was last minute ideas that worked, but we were on the fly."

"Good one bro. Fly," Deke laughed.

"Not the time, bro," said Zacke.

"Yes, I remember," John nodded. "But now, two warriors are activated. You are much stronger, and David has the powers of an elder. And we have other Amartus warriors."

"Some. A few, really. And David? He has powers, John. Magic. You said power and magic corrupts. David's been holed up in some weird prison, mostly sick. He doesn't know how to use all that. They must be counting on that."

Deke interjected, "Or they're counting on you all showing up and winging it. Man, I made a flying pun too. Gotta watch that..."

John said, "That's why we need to get to the site and make a plan."

"That's the problem," said Zacke, "no offence, but you're thinking is stuck in the past."

"Are you calling me old?" John cocked an eyebrow.

Zacke paused, "Umm, I think you qualify."

Deke laughed.

"This is the twenty first century. Let's flip the script on them," said Zacke. "Let's go public."

John said, "We don't do that, Zacke."

"No. *They* don't do that. The Rageto hide. That's where a lot of their power comes from, right?"

"What are you suggesting?" John sputtered, "Hold a press conference?"

"Not exactly," said Zacke. "We need to show the world what they are, what is really happening."

"No," said John.

"Just no?" asked Zacke. "That's all I get?"

"No — for many reasons. Too many to go into on the eve of a large battle that could end this struggle. But I'll give you two: One — if the world knew about this, there is no going back. This changes humanity forever. All history gets rewritten."

"I think that's a good thing. What's two?" challenged Zacke.

"Two is that bringing innocent, defenseless civilians is an unacceptable risk. They might all be killed or used as hostages."

Zacke paused. "Okay. I hadn't thought of that. But..."

"The answer is no," said John.

Zacke knew there was a better argument. He could feel it swimming around in his brain. He just couldn't grasp it and it wiggled out of his mind.

John had fully dismissed Zacke's idea and gone back to his plan. "We need to get to that dam."

Deke said, "I'll borrow dad's car. I'm driving."

"Okay. But let's pick up David," said John. "We'll need Zamma's memories and strategy."

They left to plan the most important battle in all of their lives.

* * *

Katie chose the old field for training. It was at the back of her parent's property, well hidden from the road and the house. Her stepdad had not planted seeds in this small plot because it needed to rest this season, part of the crop rotation he was trying to teach her. It also stood behind a tall line of Eucalyptus trees. The only audience was Megan, who was excited to see a real battle.

Julien asked, "Are you fully activated?"

"Yes," said Lucas.

"I think so," said Katie, then thought of the last time she was training. "I mean, yes."

"Nope," said Ariana, "not even close."

"Okay. I will work with you, Ariana," said Julien. "Nestor, you work with Katie. Amina, you work with Lucas."

Nestor began, "I was hoping to work with..."

Julien cut him off, "You were hoping to go tumbling around in the dust with an old Viking friend. You nor Elgisard ever grow up. Whenever you run into each other, you become little boys."

"Do not!" said Nestor. And smiled.

"Amina will train with you," Julien told Lucas. "No playtime."

"Oh," Amina looked Lucas over, "I'm gonna have lots of fun."

"Just don't kill each other," said Julien.

Lucas laughed, then caught Amina's wicked smile. He smiled back. She stalked away, knowing Lucas would follow. She was right.

"Woo hoo!" shouted Megan. "Let's see some action!"

"Stop it Megan," said Katie. "Another cheer and I'll make you sit in the house."

That deflated Megan only slightly.

Katie began, "How hard can I be on you, Nestor?" She flung a small shield bubble, a perfect orb the size of an orange into his chest.

Nestor flew off his feet then stood, brushing himself off. "Zhanna. I thought that might be you. Come give us a kiss."

Katie let her warrior take over and launched at the man. She stopped in front of him, lowered her center of gravity and began punching. *When did I learn to do this?* She suddenly realized she was really good at martial arts, a mix of many disciplines. Unfortunately, so was he. He dodged her every punch, then surprised her with a kick to the stomach. She skidded back on the dirt.

"Ooohh," Megan said.

She came back and pressed, trying to ignore how much her gut hurt. She faked a left jab, then came back with a right cross. It surprised him, but he did something strange. He put up his hands and took the punch.

Megan cheered.

Her first hit landed above his right breast. Then he grabbed her hand with both of his. Katie screamed. She scooted backwards in the dirt, making a small cloud under her feet. She looked at her hand. It was metal, shiny like gold. It dropped to the dirt.

Megan gasped, "What did you do?"

"We all have two main talents," Nestor shrugged. "Zhanna just forgot one of mine."

Katie stared in horror. She tried to raise her hand, but it was heavy. She turned her gaze to Nestor. Zhanna smiled through her. "I remember the effect is temporary." Sure enough, the hand was already returning to the smooth pink teenaged skin. She balled her fists and ran back at Nestor.

Across the field, Lucas seemed worried. He was straining his warrior's memories to remember what this warrior could do. "Amina, right?"

Amina moved fast and slapped him across the face, then jumped back before he could catch her. She smiled, then nodded as they circled each other, less than five feet apart.

Lucas strained his memories. "Something about a warrior queen, somewhere in Africa?"

"Nigeria. Very good!" Amina laughed. "You are the Viking, right?" she looked over the skinny teenaged body.

"All Viking," Lucas smirked.

Amina said, "Somehow we have never tussled. I have seen you fight, however. Impressive. What a sad little body you got this time."

"I wish people would stop saying that." Amina was stalling and Lucas knew it. He thought to Elgisard, *Seriously. You are not very detail oriented. Can you remember anything about her?*

Amina lunged.

This was only training, so Lucas didn't want to hurt her.

Amina pulled back and delivered a round house kick to his face. No time to block it.

She smiled and ran down the field. Lucas chased her. Twenty feet away, she stopped and waited for him. What he didn't notice was that her left hand had been pointed at the ground.

The path in front of Lucas was suddenly perfectly flat. Too late, he went down and fell, like the ground was slippery glass. His momentum kept him sliding. His first thought was an air hockey table, him being the puck. Then he finally slid onto rough earth a dozen feet at the end. *Not air hockey*, he thought, *like a slip n' slide*. He swallowed some dirt, spit it out and got to his feet, fists up.

Amina said, "Two talents, remember?" She ran at him.

Back at the trees, Ariana was with Julien and he was perplexed. It was written all over his face.

Ariana knew why. "Yep, that's it. I can freeze things, make people throw up, and I linked us all mentally at the fire tower."

"That's why I'm confused. We only get two talents. Many times there is a low level ability like getting flashes, hearing someone's thoughts. But that has more to do with being in tune with the River."

Ariana looked down. "So, I'm useless."

Julien put a hand on Ariana's shoulder. "No child. Pentoss told me what you've all been through. I think it's harder on the new births. You have no inner voice to guide you, no memories or experience to fall back on. It was like this for all of us our first life."

Ariana raised her head again. "You said life, not body. Why?"

"That is an age-old debate among us. Some think that we put on different costumes of flesh. That is too simple. We are humans, we have complicated lives. Despite the body we get, each life is new."

"I like that," said Ariana.

"Good," said Julien. "Now, let's figure you out. Linking is a powerful gift, but it does not stand alone. I think your real talent is being in tune with the River. You saw where Cody and his father were. He spoke to you through The River."

"But how do I use that? That doesn't help me in the middle of a crazy battle." said Ariana.

"It could if the connection is as deep as we suspect. Maybe the River will show you the future, or the past at a moment that will give you the insight to defeat your enemy. It gave you the power to link many warriors."

Ariana said, "But John said that never worked before. He told a horrible story..."

"Yes. I know that story," Julien said. "The warriors died one by one in great pain, the link failing. I was one of them."

"You were?" asked Ariana.

"So was Pentoss. He was the last to fall."

Ariana didn't know what to say.

Julien looked deep into Ariana's eyes. "So, if he asked you to link warriors, he must have been sure you could do it. Okay, let's try a few things. You said a person you froze is unharmed after?"

"Yes, they just freeze," confirmed Ariana.

"Okay. Let's see it." Julien called across the field, "Megan, care to help?"

Megan had just cringed when Katie was thrown down to the ground in her own battle. Again. She ran over, eager to help. "Yeah! What do I have to do? Fight?"

Julien answered, "No, no. Something else."

Ariana smiled. "You okay if I freeze you?"

"Yes!" Megan exclaimed. "Where should I stand? What do I do?"

"Over there," Julien instructed. "Do nothing. Ariana — please freeze the girl. Megan — you can tell us exactly how it feels when she unfreezes you."

Megan beamed.

Ariana put out her hands. At the last second, Megan made a silly face. It froze that way. Ariana smiled.

"Concentrate," said Julien. "Now hold her there for a full minute. Let's move over here." They walked to the right, about ten feet.

Ariana concentrated. "Now?"

"Yes, bring her back."

Ariana dropped her hands and Megan unfroze. Her expression fell back to normal. She was waiting to see if she'd made them laugh, but they were gone. A comic look of confusion grabbed her face. Then she looked to her left.

"You were right there," pointed Megan. "Oh crap — can you teleport?"

"No," laughed Ariana, "It just seemed that way to you."

"Duh," said Megan, smacking her forehead. "You were standing in front of that tree. How long was I frozen?"

"About a minute," said Ariana.

Megan began jumping up and down. "I get it! You froze time. To me, it looked like one of those magic tricks on old shows. A witch snaps her finger, and the person disappears. Camera trick — they just stopped the camera, everyone else froze, the person walked off the set and the camera came back on."

"But what really happened was you froze and we walked over here," said Julien. "To you it looked like we blinked out, but it was you who stopped."

"Lucas was right. I froze time." Ariana asked, "But how? I mean can you freeze time in one little spot, or for just one person?"

"Let's find out," said Julien, "Megan — okay with more tests?"

"Yes!" Her tone was 'do you even need to ask?'

Julien instructed, "Okay. I want you to walk in front of us."

"Why?" asked Ariana.

"A hunch. Maybe a push from the River." Julien explained, "Vomiting is a reversal. Like the engine of digestion reversing. Maybe it's the same concept?"

Ariana started, "I don't see..."

"Megan, just keep walking and Ariana will freeze you."

"Okay," Megan began walking.

After about ten steps, Julien said, "Freeze her."

Megan froze. Ariana asked, "Now what?"

"Hold her there," said Julien, "and reverse."

Ariana looked at her hands, still pointed at Megan. The girl had been walking in front of them from left to right. Ariana slowly twirled her hand in a left-handed circle. She gasped as Megan started walking backwards.

"See the leaves?" Julien pointed.

It wasn't just Megan. In a small orbit around the girl, a few errant leaves fell upward as the girl walked backwards. Beyond that, Megan's facial expressions also ran in reverse, like a film in a slow rewind.

"What do I do now?" Ariana asked, excited.

Julien said, "When she returns to where she started, unfreeze her."

Ariana did. Megan came back to life. She looked around.

"What just... did you still want me to do it?" asked Megan.

Julien asked her, "How do you feel?"

Megan looked around again. "Weird. I just had Déjà vu."

Lucas came running up. Katie wasn't far behind. Their opponents came too.

"Umm, what are you doing to my sister?" asked Katie, breathlessly.

Lucas smiled. "Did you just... Ariana, did you..."

"I think I did." Ariana smiled widely. "Let's try again."

Katie asked, "Megan, what's going on?"

Megan shrugged.

Julien asked, "Katie, care to join her? This will help Ariana."

"I guess," said Katie. "What do I do?"

They repeated the experiment. Katie and Megan walked the same way, having a fake conversation. Ariana froze them and reversed them. Twice.

"I think I need to sit down," Ariana said. "What does this mean?"

"Ariana, it means your freeze talent is about time," said Julien. "You can rewind time in a concentrated area."

"Oh," was all Ariana said. Then she collapsed.

* * *

John, Zacke, and the others had all gotten the frantic texts about Ariana. When she collapsed, they had carried her into Katie's bedroom. Her stepdad Jason was on the other side of their property and her mom was at work.

By the time John and the others arrived hours later, Katie's mom was home and tending to Ariana. Her stepdad was confused by all the strangers. His wife said she would explain everything later. Of course, she knew only a fraction of what Megan knew.

"Thank you, Mrs. Jenkins," said Julien.

"It's Judith, please," she spoke to Julien, who seemed in charge. "I still say we should get her to the hospital. All of her vitals are fine, but she should have woken up by now."

Julien was sure it was the strain of using so much of a newfound ability. She's seen that happen enough over many lifetimes. But she did not know if Katie's mom knew anything.

Judith said, "Jason, can you get me a cup of coffee, please?"

"Sure," he said as he eyed them all, Julien especially.

When he was out of earshot, Katie's mom asked, "Is this to do with her powers? Or yours, Katie?"

Julien wanted to make the distinction between powers and abilities but know this was the wrong time. "We think she just overdid it. Using abilities can be exhausting, especially on the young."

"Do her parents know where she is?"

"We took care of that by text," ensured Katie. "Her parents agreed she could spend the night here. Is that okay, mom?"

Judith raised her brow. "You texted her parents pretending to be her?"

Katie resisted the urge to lie. "If I lie, you'll just figure it out anyway. Yeah, I did."

"Lie detecting is *my* superpower," said Judith, then looked at Ariana laying there.

"She will wake up soon," Julien said. If she didn't wake soon, Julien would try his healing ability.

"And what then?" Katie's mom looked around the room. No one answered. "How much trouble are you all in. Are we safe?"

"Yes," John lied. He couldn't stop thinking about the battle site he had visited. "I will keep them safe."

"The fire tower. I knew Katie's story about that night was fishy. But she was safe, so I chose to believe it. They found two men dead." Judith connected more dots. "Zacke was in the hospital recently. They found a woman's head for God's sake. What is going on?"

Katie put a hand on her mom's. "A lot, Mom. A lot. But these are the good guys."

Jason would be back with her coffee any second. He lowered her voice. "Okay. I will monitor Ariana's vitals every hour. If there is any change, she goes to the hospital."

John wanted to argue. He saw her mother-bear fierceness and said only, "Of course."

"Not to be rude, but now I want you all out of my house." All the teens had moms and knew that voice. Soon they had all left. Only Katie, Megan, and Ariana stayed.

Back at Lucas', they made their final plans. How they would get to the dam and all the logistics. They also talked over strategy. Not everyone was comfortable with the plan. They assumed Ariana would sit out the fight, but John desperately hoped she would be there. She might be the key to survival, like last time, he argued.

They all said their goodnights and made their way to their homes. John headed back to Julien's house where he'd been staying. Deke and Zacke finished dropping off the others and pulled into the driveway.

Victoria was waiting on the small bench on their front porch.

"Hey," said Deke.

"Hey," said Victoria.

On his way into the house, he passed Victoria. Deke said, "You break his heart and I'll be forced to kill you. You know that, right?"

"Got it," said Victoria.

Deke didn't say goodnight, just closed the front door leaving Victoria and Zacke alone.

"I got all your messages and pictures of the battle site," said Victoria.

"What do you think?" asked Zacke, sitting next to her.

"The plan is thin at best," Victoria said. "Hopeless at worse."

Zacke asked, "Just being honest, huh?"

"Always," Victoria answered, "from now on. I don't ever want to lie to you again."

"Good."

"You sure you want to do this?" asked Victoria. "Pentoss will be furious."

"Probably," Zacke reasoned, "but we need to get some control, or at least take some of theirs away."

"Will you..." Victoria asked, "...will you take me home first?"

Zacke eyed her carefully. "Really? You're going to let me see where you live? Isn't that breaking some secret Sect code or something?"

"Actually, it is. But I don't care. No more secrets."

"Deke's still got Dad's keys." Zacke looked back to the house.

"Mmm," Victoria said and cocked her head.

"I see," said Zacke. "You want another ride up there?"

"Yes," Victoria asked, "is that wrong?"

Zacke chuckled. "Where do you live?"

She put her arms around his neck and whispered the address into his ear. Warmth shot up and down his body.

Zacke looked around for neighbors walking their dogs. No one. Except for Officer Jack, his luck held. He scooped Victoria in his arms and took flight.

He soared high, straight up. She clung tight. Victoria only wore a light coat, and Zacke could tell she was shivering just a little. She didn't seem to care. Victoria beamed. That made Zacke smile too.

They arrived at a small apartment complex in a medium-dangerous part of town. All was quiet, but he set down in the alley just in case. They passed through the open-air design between rectangular two-story buildings. Victoria pulled out her keys and headed up a concrete staircase to the upper floor. She unlocked the door to apartment C. She flicked on the closest lamp.

"Hmm? No roommates?" Zacke said, taking in the scent of her space. Definitely smelled like Victoria. He wasn't sure if it was the barest hint of her perfume, but it made his warm again.

Victoria said, "Yes. That was a lie, too. Sorry. You want something to drink?"

"No, I'm good." Zacke looked at the walls. It was an eclectic mix of things. A print of what looked like a Roman scene, ruins. A pretty landscape painting of a meadow, a little old fashioned. An old Parisian advertising print with a black cat. He was pretty sure he'd seen one like it on the wall of the Friends TV show apartment.

From the other room, "Just turning on the heater. It's an old wall heater and even if I start it now, it still won't be warm for another hour."

She came back into the small, sparse living room.

"So, the plan," he began. She arched onto her tip toes and kissed Zacke long and hard, lacing her arms around the back of his neck.

He kissed back. Their bodies pressed together. It was actually painful when he broke off the kiss. "Victoria." Zacke unlaced her hands. "It's not that easy. I... I just can't trust you again so fast."

She came off her tip toes, flat to the floor. "I know." Her hand was flat on his chest. "Tomorrow will be hard and scary. I just wanted to forget that for a while."

"Yeah. Me too." He put his hand on top of hers. She looked into his eyes and he found himself kissing her again, his arms around her shoulders. Their tongues met and explored.

Zacke broke off the embrace and paced toward the front door, then back again. He almost kissed her again. "I'm in trouble here," Zacke said to himself, but the words came out aloud.

"So am I." she said. "Look. I just don't want to be alone tonight. Maybe that's not fair to you." Victoria decided. "I'm sure it's not."

Zacke didn't respond. He looked at the front door, knowing that if he saw those eyes again, he would probably stay.

"I don't want to pressure you into anything," Victoria said. "But I would like you to stay, even if nothing... nothing happens. Will your dad be mad if you stay out one night?"

"No. My dad won't care." He turned back to her, "But that's not the point. I'm still really pissed off at you. And confused."

Victoria put her hands on her hips. Then she folded them over her chest. Then they shot down to her sides.

Zacke asked, "Are you okay?"

"Yes. No," her arms crossed again. "I feel like anything I say with be that classic thing where I'm trying to trick you, or entice you, or whatever. I just... just..."

"Please just say it, whatever it is. Don't try to manipulate me. I don't know how to do any of this. And I really like you, even though I'm mad, even after all of this crazy stuff. I wish none of this was happening so we could just be a normal boy and a normal girl."

"But you are. You're a beautiful boy and I love you."

Zacke's mouth dropped open.

"Shit! I didn't mean for that to... I mean, can we just erase that part? Go back before I was so stupid and didn't know what to do with my hands?"

Zacke paced, trying not to look at her. Then he rushed to her and kissed her hard. She kissed back with equal force. After a moment Victoria realized they'd left the ground, Victoria's legs wrapped around him, like weightless star-crossed astronauts.

They floated back down gently, and her legs returned to earth, unwinding Zacke. The kiss ended and Zacke stepped back.

Victoria looked into Zacke's green eyes.

"I love you too." He looked at the floor. "That's why this is so hard."

Zacke turned and left out the front door.

CHAPTER THIRTY FOUR

The Battle

Ariana floated in another place. It wasn't cold or warm. It just existed all around her. It was a million sparkles of light. She was moving through them, but she couldn't tell if it was up or down, or any direction at all. It didn't matter. It was joy and harmony and she had no worries now. She knew she was The River.

Not in it, nor part of it. It was her and she was it and all was light. It was swimming in light, not the feel of water with its soul tied to gravity. No, this was motion without rules. She wasn't alone, though she could see no one else around her. The light was not a bright white, but mixed with blue, a memory of pure water. She peered ahead of her and almost saw a pattern.

She saw them now, her friends. For a moment she was each of them. She felt them sleep and dream and worry. Katie and Cody were having nightmares. Lucas slept soundly and dreamt of glory. Zacke tossed and turned, fitful and sad.

Then she was moving, as she traveled through her River of light back to the fire tower. The fight was over, and they were deciding on their story. She flashed to each brother. One laid crushed on the ground, fallen from the relic sword and a great height. The other brother, Caron, laid in a slurry of water in a concrete grave. She's never seen this before. Now she was back to the tower and her friends.

They were still linked, so were still in each other's minds. It felt warm and strong, but that faded as John and David left. The fear of the future that night pulsed through them all. Now the River moved again, and she saw tomorrow. Another concrete structure. This one held back a great body of water, too. The V shaped dam stretched hundreds of feet into the ravine. It stretched out farther than she could see, and behind it the vast waters. A blue light caught her eye. A square of light forming into a large rectangle. The rectangle held darkness. It sat silent, waiting. A strange teenage boy hobbled out. He stared straight into Ariana.

Ariana woke, the stars all around her winking out and leaving ghosts behind in her vision. The room was dark. She looked at the clock. 4:37 am. She didn't go back to sleep.

Not knowing how long she'd been out, she woke Katie.

Katie said groggily, "Oh, thank God you are okay. My mom has been coming in every hour."

"That's nice of her," Ariana said. "I think we have a problem."

* * *

They all met a few hours early, at a parking lot downtown. Zacke and Deke had their dad's car. Julien's company cars had been borrowed to convey John, Julien, Nestor, and Amina. Cody's van took David, Katie, and Ariana.

John stood before them. "You all know this will be hard."

"Pentoss, my love. Please, no speeches," said Julien. "They never go well."

John smiled. "We have no idea what to expect. How many Rageto? No idea. The Elders have a surprise for us if Ariana's dream is correct. We will arrive early to hide our numbers, but there is no guarantee of victory."

"Your wife is right. You suck at this," said Deke. They all laughed.

"Be careful. Do you best. I will fight hard for all of you," finished John.

Julien said, "We fight for each other."

They said nothing else and loaded into the vehicle. They drove to the dam.

Thirteen miles out of town, the road roughly followed the contours along the dry riverbed, until it finally diverged. They made a turn off the highway and took a service road to reach the dam.

No one spoke on the way, their thoughts occupied. Their solo thoughts co-mingled around the group. No one needed a flash to know worried and anxious everyone felt — about the future, themselves, each other. How strange, thought Ariana, that they were driving like families do — a road trip. But this destination was a fight. Blood. Pain. Death.

They rounded the last corner, and the dam came into view. Just as in her dream, the V shaped dam plummeted down the slope of the hill on either side, the riverbed in front of it. Behind it was the vast lake held back by the 300-foot-tall concrete V. The Bradbury-Gibraltar dam was over 600 feet long. The curved V is topped by a thick walkway for workers. Luckily, the modern equipment mostly ran itself. Maintenance was regular but not constant, no daily workers present. The curve ended in a control room, an enclosed circle of concrete with one door, like a bunker. Flanking out from there was the four spill gates. They were identical. On top of the gates was a metal walkway that ran over the gates.

They parked in a large field covered in short grass. It faced the dam and overlooked the dry riverbed. It was a large plateau overlooking the drop down to the riverbed below.

They all stared at the imposing dam.

Just then, Zacke's phone went off. All their phones did, except for David and Cody who didn't have phones.

"Zacke, is that you?" Katie said as a video popped up on her phone.

"Yes," said Zacke, staring at John.

John grabbed the phone from his back pocket. He watched the video. "Zacke. What have you done?"

"Given us a chance," answered Zacke.

John scanned the dam for enemies, then watched the video again.

Zacke was on all the social media platforms, racking up views everywhere. Underneath his video were the coordinates for the dam, both the physical address and GPS coordinates.

On the video, Zacke announced, "Yes, this will seem crazy. It's not. Today at 4 pm, on the central coast of California a battle with happen. If you ever thought magic was real, you were right. People with amazing abilities have existed for all time. The two sides, the Amartus and the Rageto are in an epic secret struggle. Until now." The camera panned out and Zacke hovered off the ground. "This is not special effects. It's real. I'm Amartus, one of the good guys. The world must know. See for yourself. Everyone, be a witness."

Zacke then lifted farther up into the air.

John couldn't tell where it was shot. "When did you do this?" demanded John.

Zacke shot back. "This morning. I timed it to hit right now. It's worldwide."

John stomped up to Zacke. "Why?"

"Best case, the Rageto see it and chicken out. Other best case, the world sees them for what they are."

John yelled, "This place will be flooded with victims and hostages!"

"Or an army to witness what they are," Zacke said. "You said they are scared of the light. We pull them out of the darkness on our terms."

John shouted, "And put a giant target on all those innocent heads! Stupid boy!"

"Stop!" said Julien getting between them. "It is done. Good or bad, it's done. Now we must deal with it. There is only this road in and out, yes?"

John said, "Good idea — stop them. Like the Greeks at Thermopylae."

"No Pentoss," Julien looked into his eyes. "We let them come."

"What?"

"It's dangerous, I agree, but all moves now are danger." Julien reasoned, "This has never been tried. Zacke is right. Rageto fear the light. This rips that away."

John didn't answer, just changed the subject. "Let's get into place. Teams, just like we planned." He added, "We need to clear the field before the innocent victims start showing up."

Zacke was going to argue, but John walked away with Julien. They all knew the plan. David and Cody paired off, so did Ariana and Lucas. David and Cody left for their spot.

Across the v shape drop to the riverbed was another field, much like the field where they parked.

Zacke flew across the expanse to the other bank and faded into a stand of trees. Deke stayed behind to direct traffic when the others arrived. He didn't know what to expect, but he and his brother agreed that he would be safer in the crowd.

It was nearly an hour before the Rageto was to appear, when the first civilian car arrived. Zacke watched from the far bank as Deke directed each car. He followed the plan and directed the cars to the outer edge of the field.

Deke muttered under his breath, "I told you we should have charged admission." He motioned and pointed. The cars dribbled in, a few at first then a steady line. He knew it was only a matter of time before some sort of authority showed up. *That will be fun,* thought Deke. The cars followed his directions as if he worked at a large stadium event or at a theme park.

People got out and had lots of questions. Deke kept it simple. "I just direct the cars. They didn't tell me anything. Live stream if you want." everyone seemed confused but complied. At first, they were total strangers, then people he knew started showing up.

A car full of his friends pulled up and rolled down the window, "What kinda crazy stunt is this, Deke? That was your brother, right?"

"Yep," said Deke, looking toward the dam. "Gonna be some show."

Soon the crowd was large. He lost count at 30 cars, some crammed full of people. He was a little worried when he saw some small kids among the crowd.

Twenty minutes early, A blue line appeared. It was clear day, but the neon blue could be seen by all. It started as a point of light then stretched to a line ten feet wide. Then the line doubled, and one moved up and one down. The gate formed exactly where Ariana had dreamed, on the roof of the concrete control room. Filling the gate was a deep blackness outlined in the neon blue.

The crowd spotted it and soon dozens of cell phones were recording video and snapping shots. Nothing happened for several long minutes, then shapes emerged. Three Rageto warriors came out. Zacke was on his own, among thick trees on the left bank, watching. He recognized the three — Janus, Cimo and Azoria — from the theatre. Right in front of them, Janus split into two people, the smirking twins. The crowds gasped. He saw all three were holding weapons. Relics.

Elder Ordway emerged from the dark. She wore a suit so dark blue it might as well have been black. To Zacke it seemed like some strange uniform. The middle aged-looking Elder had slicked back silver hair. Her eyes stared at the crowd, scowling. Then all emotion left her face. She didn't seem worried in the least. Zacke felt a chill.

Ordway stood in front of her gate, on top of the work room. Separated by three hundred feet or more from the crowds on the right field, she spoke. Her voice boomed out like she stood right next to them. "Civilians. Stupid."

She flicked both of her hands in either direction. Rageto warriors fanned out from the dark gate. Janus One stationed himself to her left, over the dam itself. The top of the dam was a wide concrete walkway ten feet wide. Janus One stopped, waiting. The other Janus climbed down the caged metal ladder from the work tower and stationed himself halfway over spillway gate number two. Azoria joined him there. Cimo stood next to Ordway.

Another figure emerged. A teenage boy. Ariana's blood turned to ice. *The boy from my dream.* He didn't look at her like in the dream, just jerked his head and hobbled over the dam on the left, past the first Janus. He moved slowly but looked determined to reach the edge of the dam.

Lucas and Ariana were waiting there. A dozen feet from them, the boy stopped. He looked up. His one good eye ignored Ariana. He stared at Lucas. The boy growled.

Ariana stood side by side with Lucas on the edge of the dam. She heard the "Shlickt" sound of Lucas' twin batons locking into place. The other boy was too fast. He raised his handgun with his left hand and fired. Ariana froze the bullet in midair. Lucas was already running at the boy. He knocked the bullet out of the air with a baton and charged. Ariana ran to keep up. She froze the boy in place. He wore a mask of frozen hate. Lucas shoved the frozen boy to the left, off the dam and into the reservoir behind. He stayed in the frozen pose, like a statue and hit the water with a splash. Ariana unfroze him out of habit. She didn't see the boy surface again. Ariana kept watching the water, ready to freeze him again.

Lucas charge Janus. He shouted, "Which one are you? The coward or the fighter?"

Janus smiled and assumed a fighting stance. Lucas smiled back. "Good."

Lucas swung his right baton. Janus tried to block it with his left arm. It crashed into his upper arm and Janus let out a howl of pain. Janus clamped his right hand onto Lucas. Lucas hadn't seen a weapon, but Janus tore his hand away and Lucas felt the rip of the kakute ring. The iron ring had two spikes, hidden within the man's palm. It tore two rough gashes into Lucas' arm, just above his wrist. One baton flew into the reservoir.

Before Lucas could recover, Janus swung his other hand back at Lucas. This ring was pointed up, on top of the man's hand, two spikes protruding like a serpent's tongue. He'd aimed for the face, but Lucas ducked. That made Janus lose his balance, overextending his arm. From the crouch, Lucas came up, slamming his right-hand baton. It caught Janus under the chin, whipping the man's head sharply with a crack. Before he could counter, Lucas pushed the man to the right, off the dam. Janus One fell down the long, slopping concrete. He tumbled and flipped as the concrete dam curved down.

Lucas jammed his left hand, bleeding, under his right armpit. Ariana rushed to him. She ripped the bottom part of her blouse away, a thin strip about three inches. As she bound Lucas' wounded hand.

Ariana focused on the wound, but looked down where Janus had fallen. It slipped out, "You killed him."

Lucas replied, "I... yes, we did." They were fighting for their lives. They'd prepared for death mentally, but to see it happen was different. Ariana and Lucas heard a shout of rage. Their heads snapped to the other side of the dam, to the walkway over the spill gates. The second Janus shouted another diatribe of hatred at Lucas across the curving dam. He began to run over his walkway, toward Lucas. Ordway raised her hand and he stopped, fuming. Janus two, now half himself, held his position.

John and Julien walked across the long steel bridge toward Azoria who held a two bladed knife, the haladie. A semi-circle guard encircled her hand, a serrated spike protruding, while two curved blades extended from either side.

"Relic on relic action," Azoria said.

John held his own blade in front of him, in both hands.

Azoria smiled. "Been a while Pentoss. I've been training hard."

"Never seems to help. I just keep sending you back to the River." John touched his sword to his forehead his eyes locked onto hers. "Last trip for you."

She laughed and attacked. She jabbed with the serrated spike. John met her with sword and twisted his blade. It caught her serrated edge and twisted Azoria's wrist. His blade was in control of her weapon. That gave John the moment he needed. He kicked with his left leg and connected with her hip. She went down. She rolled away from John, her weapon still in hand. She seemed awkward with the weapon, being careful not to cut herself on the three blades of her haladie.

Azoria stood up and Julien stood in her path. She held a simple zippo lighter, lid open. Azoria almost laughed but realized who stood before her. Julien's thumb hit the strike and fire exploded from the small flame. Julien pushed the flames with his ruined hand. Azoria was engulfed. She screamed, dropped the haladie, and leapt into the water. John did not see her come back up. They turned their attention back to the elders.

Lucas and Ariana stayed on the far-left side of the dam, waiting for John and Julien to make their move on the elders.

The crowds were vocal, like they watched a performance. It was a complicated mix of gasps, groans and cheers when the mini battles unfolded. Deke watched the battles from among them and realized the crowd had no idea who the bad guys were. He looked for his brother but hadn't seen him yet. *Must be holding back*, he thought. That's when he heard the first siren. It was faint at first, then closer. *It must be from the highway.* Either Officer Jack or a bystander had called the authorities. Movement caught his eye and Deke looked back to the action.

Zacke flew at the dam. He aimed for Cimo. Zacke spotted the weapon he held, the relic axe. But Cimo didn't see him coming, busy waiting for John and Julien to attack. He slammed into Cimo. One moment he was standing next to Ordway, the next he was not. He's caught the man in the stomach with his shoulder, doubling him over and latching onto him tight. Zacke raced into the sky, now headed straight up. He had the man doubled over his shoulder, so Cimo's arms were free. Zacke knew he would try to cut him with the axe, so he simply stopped and released him. The man flew away at terrific speed, swinging his arms and legs wildly as he flailed. Cimo slashed into the water hundreds of feet away.

The crowds all cheered when Zacke appeared. He touched down next to John and Julien, on the walkway above the spill gates. Just as he touched down, Janus two erupted from the reservoir side.

"Look out" was all Julien could manage.

Janus leapt at John. He had the Madu, the fierce animal horns sticking out each side. He slashed at John hard. John ducked back and misjudged. He flew over the railing. John landed hard, suspended over the spill gate. John realized his predicament. He'd landed on a steel girder, one of many laid out like a grid above the spillway. The square openings between crisscrossing girders were easily large enough for a man to fall through. He looked around frantically, any way back up to the fight.

Zacke landed by Julien and grabbed Janus from behind. He lifted him by the back of the pants and flung the man off the dam.

Zacke looked over the edge. Janus had fallen to a girder, only a few feet from John.

A massive wave came over the reservoir edge. It washed Zacke and Julien over the edge. Zacke flew out of the path of water, looking for the source. Julien fell onto the same metal girder with John. More water splashed over the side, and the wave hit Julien.

John yelled, "No!"

Julien just caught a girder with his good hand. He dangled, gripping the slippery steel edge. John sheathed his sword and walked over the slippery girder. He bent and reached for Julien's hand. Another wave came and covered them. John grabbed Julien's hand but it was too wet.

Their hands slipped apart. Julien fell.

Then she stopped, in mid-air, sopping wet.

Katie stood on ground above the parking field, facing the dam. Zacke realized what she'd done and flew under the shield bubble, lifting Julien and depositing him back on the sidelines, next to Katie, onto solid earth again. The bubble disappeared and Julien fell to the strip of ground just above the field of spectators. The crowds cheered. Julien stood, peered down at the field of spectators. He gave a small salute. Julien stood next to Katie and quietly said, "Thanks Zhanna"

Ordway scowled. John and the second Janus were standing over their respective girders, standing over hundreds of feet of air.

John drew his sword again. "What happens when one half of you dies a true death and one doesn't? I've always wondered that."

Katie stood next to Julien. "I can help him." she raised her hands to throw shield balls.

Julien stayed her hand. "He can handle himself. Watch."

Janus growled and leapt for John's girder, but John scrambled back, slipping a little, but recovered his footing. John asked, "Was he like a brother? Or a shadow? You have always puzzled me, Janus." John looked down to when Janus one had fallen. "Guess we'll never know."

Janus attacked. He leapt to John's girder. Stepping back, John swung his sword down. Janus' arm outstretched, it was sliced through and flipped away with his weapon. Janus' face went white and he missed the girder, smashing his head on the steel. He fell between the girders to the emptiness below. Both Janus' were gone.

At the parking field, two deputies had gotten through. By now there were hundreds of people. Cars could no longer get through the snarl of heavy traffic blocking the only service road in. The officers arrived on foot. They'd gotten through the crowd asking who was in charge. No one really knew, but a few remembered Deke telling them where to park. They waded through the dense crowd to Deke.

Deke asked, "Why you asking the black guy? I'm just watching the show." Deke pointed to the dam.

The cops looked. They'd been called out with some crazy claims. What they saw was impossible. One officer said, "That kid is flying, right? You see that?"

The other confirmed, "Uhh. Yeah."

They assessed the scene. They couldn't reach the dam from here by foot. If they got through the crowds, the field ended in a dense layer of bushes, but was separated by a steep incline to the next plateau, where Katie and Julien stood. Not an impossible climb, but difficult.

The older officer said, "We could go around to the service road that leads directly to the dam."

"We saw on our way in, there was a locked gate, remember? Besides, what do we do, arrest the flying kid? Disperse the crowd?" He looked at the large gathering. "Just us two?"

The other cop shrugged. "We don't even know who the bad guys are."

"Right. We call for backup. For some reason, my hand held is acting up." They both agreed and split up. One headed back to the car on the highway shoulder to make the crazy call. The other officer stayed and watched the crowd. Of course, he was also watching the show.

Zacke sped toward the Elders. He saw there was only Ordway. He hoped to simply push Ordway back into her gate. He flew straight at her. She saw him coming and a wall of water came over the dam's edge and walloped him. She waved her hand and the water pushed him off course, onto the left side of the dam wall. Zacke landed hard, tumbling over and over until he finally stopped. Ariana and Lucas ran to his aide. Zacke sputtered and coughed.

"You okay?" asked Ariana.

"Yeah," Zacke said and stood up slowly. "Just banged up."

John ran along the girders toward the front of the structure. There was a central pipe that ran along all four spill ways. He ran over it and joined Julien and Katie on solid ground.

Ariana closed her eyes and reached out her mind to John. "Is it time?" Before John could answer, she sent another thought. "Wait, what is that? Do you hear it?"

John did. By now they all heard it. A helicopter approached over the water. Zacke assumed it was a police chopper. *Who else could it be?* He knew what to do. It crossed the dam and hovered halfway between the field of onlookers and the dam itself. It stayed above the fray some fifty feet. Zacke acted.

He flew slowly to the helicopter. He approached from the side. He reasoned they would not shoot him, since it was not clear what was really happening. *Plus, they probably don't see flying teenagers every day,* he thought. He hoped they would listen.

About twenty feet away, the chopper still hadn't moved, just hovered there. Then the side door opened.

"Victoria?" shouted Zacke.

"Hey fly boy. Come over here," she shouted back.

He approached carefully, flying up and under the loud rotors. Victoria said, "The Sect High Council wants me to give you these. Maybe it will even out the fight."

She handed him a case. He took it. Heavy.

"What's in here?" asked Zacke.

"Relic weapons. To balance the fight."

Zacke smiled, "I do love you."

"I love you too," said Victoria and kissed him. "Be careful. Lots of people watching. It could go bad fast."

"I will," said Zacke. He flew towards John and the others.

A giant column of water shot up into the sky. It hit the helicopter from the bottom, slamming it upward. The pilot tried to right the copter and went spinning, round and round. It spun over the dam, over the Elder, and out over the dry riverbed. It was safe from more water attacks. The pilot was able to keep it relatively level, but the endless spinning continued, pushing it toward the field, right over the crowds. The police officer started to shepherd people slowly out the only road, but it was hopeless.

Zacke rushed to the chopper, then remembered the relics case in his hand. He shouted, "John!" and flung the case. He hoped it was as sturdy as it looked. John heard the shout. Zacke didn't have time to see where it landed and headed for the chopper. The spin had gotten worse and the copter continued toward the hill, right over the crowds. Zacke raced. He had no idea where to grab the thing. It was a giant metal and glass machine with rotors going at full speed. Those rotors were inches from the hill side now. He looked down, the crowd in a panic. They were too packed together to go anywhere. *This is my fault. I made this public. All these people will die because of me.* He was almost to the spinning beast.

He dove under the chopper. The skids were easier to grab. He roped his arm around one and pushed the opposite direction of the spin. The rotors sliced at the springy grass on the hillside, sending dirt and grass to the crowd below. The spinning slowed. He flew hard, dragging the helicopter's momentum slowly away from the hill.

He had no idea how a helicopter worked. He was afraid to do too much more that would hurt the pilot's ability to steady the aircraft. It was no longer over the crowd. Zacke let go. The helicopter wobbled, but the spinning had stopped. It finally steadied.

The crowds were wild, cheering, shouting. The police officer cheered too. He couldn't help himself.

Through the window, Zacke and Victoria made eye contact. She nodded. She was okay. The helicopter made its way to the left side of the empty riverbed, safe from the crowds and Elder attacks, and landed safely. Zacke was getting tired. He didn't know he'd have to do the helicopter thing. *How am I going to make it? I need to land soon.* So tired.

His thoughts were cut short. A lance with a huge triangle shaped blades came at him. He shifted his body in mid-flight and it whizzed by. He felt something hot on his chest. He looked down at his shirt. It was sliced. A thin red line appeared. The sharp sting of pain erupted across his torso.

Zacke looked back toward the Elder. Someone else had joined the fight.

Standing next to Ordway was a tall man with a gray beard. He wore Bermuda shorts and his upper body was covered in leather armor.

What the hell is that? thought Zacke.

Elder Yarro had joined the fight. He put his hand out toward Zacke. The lance returned to the tall man and he caught it.

On top of the work tower, Ordway looked Yarro up and down. "You look ridiculous. This isn't Troy," she looked at his shorts, "or Bermuda."

Yarro replied, "I haven't fought for a while. Thought I'd do it in style"

"The style of a pensioner with dementia," said Sorrento as he came through the gate. He held his relic book in one hand.

"You're both late," said Ordway.

"How many have you lost?" asked Sorrento but seemed preoccupied by the book.

Ordway replied, "Four, if you count Janus twice, as I do."

"That all?" Yarro asked, leaning on his spear.

"Lost Four warriors and three relics. Two are dead for certain, though not true deaths. Two may still be alive in the water behind us. They have not returned yet, so they are useless. The sect girl brought something to the fight, but we don't know what yet. None of the Amartus have fallen."

"And them?" Yarro pointed to the hundreds of people standing on the field, watching.

"Our enemy used social media," Ordway sniffed.

"Not good," said Yarro.

"I know. I've got big plans with several world governments," said Ordway. She turned to Sorrento, "Where are you going?"

Sorrento just walked away, over the walkway above the flood gates.

"I've brought my warriors as agreed," Sorrento called back. "Use them as you like. I have my own part to play in the battle." He kept walking.

"It is time, then. Proceed as planned," said Ordway. From behind her, warriors appeared out of the gate. Seven warriors walked out, all armed with weapons, relics among them.

The main crowd gasped. The solid block of bodies had slowly dissolved as the danger had come closer to them. The helicopter overhead had made many decide to leave. People streamed out slowly. Dozens had left, but others stayed, filming and some even giving play by plays on social media.

More Rageto warriors came out of the gate, now an even dozen. Their elders ordered each to go left or right. Julien recognized two of them from the King's Road. Apparently, they had chosen the wrong side again. On the left side of the dam, Ariana and Lucas stood ready. Zacke headed toward them when he saw Rageto warriors running for them. To the right, past the floodgate walkway were John, Julien, and Katie. They too ran for the dam to engage.

Ariana heard the voice of John whisper in her head. "Now, Ariana, now."

She alerted the others with her mind. From among the crowd of onlookers, aluminum folding ladders appeared. Hidden no longer, they were being unfurled against the steep hill next to their clearing. In an organized line, the first cars to arrive were doling out weapons: swords, daggers, crossbows, and bows with quivers of arrows.

Deke panicked, but didn't know what was going on. They didn't tell him this part of the plan. The officer still on the scene yelled, "Hey!" and pushed his way through the remaining crowd to reach the new players. The new warriors, half of whom were on the ladders to reach the next plateau where John and the others had been, just ignored him.

A woman helped another person up the ladder as the officer arrived. His hand was on his gun, but he hadn't drawn his weapon. A woman on the ladder pointed to the dam. "Have you been watching? You have no idea how to deal with this. We do."

"Who the hell are you?" asked the officer.

"The Amartus, of course," she smiled.

The police officer searched his brain for a gang by that name. Didn't sound familiar. He threw up his hands and wondered how soon back up would get here.

The Amartus warriors crested the hill and ran for the dam. Ariana ran back to land, toward the Sect helicopter on the left clearing. She spotted Victoria and three other big men with her. The men were running to the fight. They met up, but Ariana saw something out of the corner of her eye. Something was moving in the brush, near the dam. A boy was laying by the edge of the dam. He was struggling to get up. He hobbled very slowly. He looked pathetic and beaten. Ariana ran to Victoria and pointed out the boy.

"You guys, go help fight. I'll take care of that one," said Victoria. The Sect men ran to the dam to help Lucas. Victoria ran toward the boy and Ariana followed.

Over the flood gates, John, Julien, and Katie ran with the new Amartus warriors. The two from the King's Road, Nestor and Amina, got to them first.

The Rageto group were over the spillway. The Amartus army drew near. The walkway was narrow, no wider that two large men.

One of the Amartus yelled, "Death to slavers." She charged ahead and leapt into the Rageto bunch with a sword held high. It came down and sliced two Rageto warriors. One went over the dam. The other fell back.

All the warriors ran and crashed into each other. Swords sliced, axes swung, and Nestor caught a crossbow bolt in his arm. No one knew which weapons were relics, but they were weapons that cut and sliced. True deaths would be sorted out later.

John and Julien led the fight. Julien raised a relic sword of her own; Zacke and Victoria's gifts were helpful.

David and Cody were the last ones to crest the ladders.

Elder Yarro then, "Is that him?"

"Yes," said Ordway, staring at David.

David felt the power surge in him. He launched his ability. Controlled single bolts of lightning came down and struck Rageto warriors. They fell on either side of the dam, some off the side and some in the water.

Yarro growled and flung his spear. The head of triple blades glinted as it flew. It was half the distance when Zacke swooped in and grabbed it. He stopped and hovered, facing the Elders. Blood still ran down his shirt. He flung up one leg and smashed the weapon's wooden handle in two. He let the two ends drop to the riverbed below. It did not return to the Elder.

Yarro screamed, "That was priceless!"

"Now it's garbage," Zacke yelled back.

Yarro screamed and held up his hands. A wall of intense heat washed over Zacke and made the skin on his arm blister. Zacke screamed and flew back.

Yarro directed his super-heated Simoom toward David and Cody.

Ordway turned to the clash of warriors. She raised her hand. A huge wave began to form.

David saw the wave. He knew she was going to wash all the warriors over the dam, her own included. The wave was twenty feet high now, coming down. David's hand shot out. The water sprayed straight up, like hitting a glass wall. David's mind grew dark. He remembered battling Ordway many times. The old tricks.

Yarro's simoom hit the wall of water and it became super-heated, steam exploding outward and upward.

David pushed the water back at the Elders. Ordway's shocked face was seen only for a second as she disappeared back into her gate. The gate disappeared and Yarro was alone, scalded with the boiling water. Thousands of gallons hit him. All exposed skin blistered. He was swallowed by the wave and he disappeared into the reservoir. As the hot water hit the cool lake, more steam rose. Yarro didn't come back up.

The fierce fighting continued on both sides of the dam. Lucas bit his tongue. The blood rage rose within him. He and the Sect held their own while they fought six Rageto warriors on the left side. David was single handedly taking care of his side when a blue light appeared behind him. Julien saw an arm appear, then Ordway emerged.

David turned, but before he could react, a Rageto warrior leapt passed Ordway and came straight for him. Cody raised his hands, about to release an electric charge. Just then, the warriors' arm caught on fire. He dropped his long knife and was consumed in flame. Ordway stumbled back.

John looked to Julien. She shook her head. Wasn't her.

Just then, a Rageto warrior dropped his blade and clutched at his throat. He fell dead, his face turning red as he fell.

On Lucas' side one female warrior stabbed herself in the heart. Another leapt off the dam side, tumbling over and falling to their death.

In the distance, Sorrento chuckled to himself. He spoke aloud into his device, naming warrior after warrior. The device amplified the spell. "You gave me the book, you fools. Did you think I would forget we are at war?"

More warriors dropped. The Rageto were falling by the hand of Sorrento's killing spells.

Yarro climbed out of the water, onto the dam, barely able to stand, his face and arms of ruin of sloughed off skin. He searched for Ordway and saw her among enemies, across the field. Something was wrong. He looked at their armies, nearly all fallen.

Ordway still stood on the sidelines, backing out of the falling warriors. She growled to herself. "The book. The damned book."

* * *

On the left bank, Victoria had the damaged boy pinned to the ground. "No weapons, at least."

"He had a gun. I think it flew into the water," said Ariana.

The boy laughed mixed with a strange wheeze. "I remember you."

Ariana blanched. "I don't know you."

He shifted under Victoria to see her face better. Ariana gasped at the battered face. *He must be my age, maybe younger, but his face...*

The boy turned to Victoria, his one good eye blazing. "Plucky little restaurant girl. I wanted to get back and kill you so badly."

"Who is this?" asked Ariana, backing away.

"Nobody," Victoria said, desperately trying to keep him down. He was surprising strong for his size. "Help me keep him down."

Ariana went to help, but the boy threw Victoria off and struggled to get up. He reached down and stood. Victoria lunged for him again. He thrust a small blade into Victoria's stomach and then out. He jabbed it in again and left it there. It was a tiny pocket knife, but it did damage.

Victoria grabbed her belly and fell to her knees, throwing the knife far away. Ariana rushed to her.

The boy stood, lopsided and looked at the dam, ignoring the girls.

The boy shrieked a terrible sound and sank his hands into the earth. He shrieked again, gibberish flying out, filled with rage. "Toke lurrikara tresti. Toke lurrikara tresti. Toke lurrikara tresti."

Then Ariana remembered.

The earth began to shake.

CHAPTER THIRTY FIVE

Forever Change

They all felt it. Everyone stopped. A massive earthquake began. Before Ordway could reach Sorrento, she was shaken to the ground. On the dam itself, Lucas and the other warriors were nearly shaken off, but managed to stay on their hands and knees.

On the clearing Ariana was helpless. She watched the disaster unfold, cradling Victoria. The boy laughed wildly. He said through his laughter, "die fait accomplis." His laughter grew wilder as the cracks began. His hands still in the ground, he watched the dam crack.

Ariana held Victoria's wound the best she could. The shaking stopped, but the cracks continued. The first one sounded like giant sheets of ice cracking. Then Ariana flinched. An explosion, then a crack appeared straight up the dam. Water squirted out as through two front teeth of a child. Then another crack brought the flood. Ariana stood and ran. She saw Lucas and some other warriors trying to run. The dam crumbled below them. A wall of water erupted as the concrete sheared away.

Ariana screamed. She pushed out her hands.

Everything froze.

The whole scene in front of her, hundreds of feet of crumbling dam and warriors falling.

It. All. Stopped.

She heard herself breathing, her lungs working like bellows at a huge fire, in and out. She closed her eyes. The weight of all that water and all the concrete was on her. She felt that weight like gravity had tripled. Her lungs burned with the weight. She felt underwater with no breath. She stared at the frozen destruction.

She reversed it.

She didn't rewind her finger with a flourish. She pushed her essence, all that she had into reversing time. But nothing happened. Sweat poured off her brow, her clothes drenched in an instant. She pushed harder. Ariana screamed.

The freeze held, but nothing happened. She thought of that room of light, being in the River, one with it. She pushed again. Lucas looked so small, mid fall. She pushed. She screamed and screamed and pushed.

The wall of water reversed. The chunks of dam reformed. The figures fell up and not down, the concrete re-knit and the water fell back behind thick, whole walls of concrete.

Ariana collapsed.

Caron screamed and screamed.

Victoria and the boy were outside the time reversed area. They saw it all. Caron struggled, trying to dig his hands into the earth again.

Victoria ignored her wound. She grabbed something from the copter and ran. She tackled him; his arms free of the earth. Victoria presses a button and her taser stopped Caron.

John and the others slowly got back on their feet. Sorrento picked up the book again and began to speak. A giant wall of flame engulfed his book and his hand.

Sorrento screamed, his hand ablaze. His device dropped and rolled away. He dropped the book. It fell to the ground unscathed.

Julien closed the zippo lighter. John raised his sword and took a step toward Sorrento.

A small blue gate appeared. An arm shot out and John's sword flew from his hand to Ordway.

The gate disappeared and a bigger gate reappeared over Sorrento. Ordway stepped out and ran the sword through Sorrento's heart. She screamed, "Potestatum Niri!" Over and over. She gave the blade a twist and slid it out. Sorrento laid dead. A fine green mist left his body and swirled around Ordway.

Blood covered her pant suit and John's blade as she backed away from the others. No longer her regular cool demeanor, her face was a mask of hatred and rage. A blue gate appeared behind. She stepped back into it and it closed. Ordway was gone.

Lucas felt strange as he ran off the dam. He knew he had to get to Ariana. But he didn't know why. He felt out of step, like a moment was missing from his mind.

By then, Victoria had Caron bound with zip ties and gagged by duct tape, tucked away in the helicopter. The others all made their way to that side of the dam. Yarro too was gone, but no one saw where or how.

Ariana was unconscious. Lucas got to her and held her in his arms. She had a heartbeat and was breathing shallow breaths. Those in the time reversal were still working out what had happened to them. Those unaffected by the reversal knew what Ariana had done. They all gathered: John, Julien, Katie, David, Cody, Zacke, Lucas, and Ariana, seven warriors and two sect men. Loud sirens were wailing on the other side of the dam, official vehicles pulling up from the other service road next to the dam.

Victoria explained the helicopter could only fit six people and still fly safely. The crowds were overrun by police. More officers poured in. It would only be a matter of time before they were reached and overwhelmed by the authorities.

Lucas had more important things to think about. He cradled Ariana, willing her to wake up.

Julien said, "Lucas, let me try. I can heal her."

Lucas relented and Julien took Ariana in her arms. He closed his eyes and concentrated. He said, "She is healing. Her body will be whole soon."

Ariana was still, eyes closed.

"What do we do?" asked Katie. She looked to the approaching sirens. The life she knew was gone forever.

Zacke said, "We tell the truth."

"What choice do we have?" asked David. "Everything is probably going viral as we speak. There's no hiding this with a flimsy story."

John sighed, "I agree. For better or worse, there is no more hiding."

"The struggle will now be a public one," said Julien, still cradling Ariana.

Cody said, "Let's hope they don't make us lab rats."

"Or secret government agents," said Zacke.

Ariana was once more surrounded by light. She knew what it all meant now, and why the River chose to show her this. It was all about currents and flow. She could be inside that current. It would be so easy to stay there. No time. No worries. She felt the minds of all her friends, heard their conversation around her and she also felt their essence, their true hearts. She decided.

Ariana's eyes slowly opened. "Or we could just be a family."

Everyone cheered. Lucas rushed to her side again. They all tried to hug her, but she was too weak.

They tended to Victoria's wound. The rest only had minor injuries. They were together. They waited in the field for the authorities to reach them. Whatever came next, they would face it all united.

Epilogue

The relic sword sat propped against the desk.

Ordway kept it by her at all times now. She sat before her twin computer screens. Her new habit of scanning around every few minutes was necessary. She's moved to another safe house across the country. Yarro didn't know about this one. The magical protections around her current location was unassailable. Still, she scanned the air around her.

Ordway stared at her twin screens. Mini video boxes dotted the monitors, each of a different country's newsfeed. A new dialogue box popped up. It was a black box with old fashioned DOS-like white letters.

It read: I can help you.

Ordway smirked. She scanned for all traditional viruses, worms or any other nasty ways this insolent intruder had invaded. Then she magically scanned for invasive spells.

She spoke to herself, "Hmm. Just a fancy hacker." Ordway turned on her voice recognition software and voice translator for incoming text.

She began the unexpected conversation with this new, mysterious stranger.

Ordway: "Perhaps. That depends on who you are."

The ghostly white text appeared and spoke aloud at the same time.

The stranger said: "I can help you find them all."

Ordway: "I'm going to skip over the boring part where you refuse to tell me who you are and I threaten you, and we do this dance. I'm too tired — no one knows where they are. It's been three months. Even highly placed Government officials all over the world don't know. They apparently couldn't hold them, the cowards."

Five small video boxes popped up. Ordway scanned. One showed Zacke in flight, though it wasn't clear where he was. The others showed various groups of two and three people: Cody, David, Katie, and Lucas were clearly visible in different locations all over the world, in various disguises.

Ordway: "Those can be faked. The battle videos at the dam nearly melted the internet. Deep fake videos have been ubiquitous ever since." She hit a button. A video popped up of Zacke from the dam battle carrying a large cartoon cat with sunglasses. Words superimposed over the boy said, "McFly!" and he was suddenly dressed in an orange vest.

The stranger didn't answer immediately.

Then another video popped up. It showed a clear picture of John and Julien. It panned out and showed they were in the streets of Prague, near a specific street that Ordway knew very well.

She snarled involuntarily.

Stranger: "They are after bigger secrets now. The world knows so much, and the Sect is cooperating with world governments. Unchecked, the Amartus will bring down the pillars of the Rageto. Unless I help you."

Ordway: "I'm listening."

The stranger's breadth of knowledge surprised the Elder. She picked up the relic blade and played with it while she listened. They conversed through her screen for nearly an hour. At the end she burst into laughter and leaned back in her seat. "What a dark, delicious plan."

END OF BOOK TWO

Author Note

I'm not one to pontificate about a book's meaning. I set out only to tell a not-super hero story. The germ of the idea began when I was a teenager and culminated in Forever Warriors, published in 2016. Sequels are tricky and I didn't know if this book would ever happen. Often my characters demand to be heard. And mine were very patient. As always, I put them through a lot in this book and it took me four years to do it. Thank you also, patient reader.

Again, I used fictional versions of real places in Central California. Most names are inventions, though Cachuma lake is real and does have a dam. Those familiar with the area may spot a few fun twists on reality.

Historical note: There was a real Simoom reported in Santa Barbara, Ca. in 1859 — the same day as the prologue of this book. Temperatures spiked to 133 degrees Fahrenheit. It was the hottest recorded temperature on earth (until Death Valley beat the record in 1913).

If you liked, or even better, *loved* this book please leave a review on anywhere you want to tell the world how amazing it is. If you hate my stories, you can always yell and throw things at me at mjsewall.com or e-mail me directly at mjsewallwriter@gmail.com

Thanks for taking another journey with me.
M J Sewall,
November 2020

Thanks and Acknowledgements

To everyone that helped me with this weird little sequel, thank you.
  But especially:

My wonderful editors, Mindy T. Conde and Natalie McDermott. Thanks for your patience amidst a languid writer, life challenges, and a pandemic.

The amazing team at Next Chapter Publishing. Thank you for all you do.

Aidan McCalister, Carol Weible, Chelsea McKinney, Danielle O'Brien, Hillary Frye, Janet Wallace, Jennifer Honey Moore, Nellie Sewall, Preston Frye, Robert Lee, Rose Torres and Alice Palm.

Thank you!

Author Biography

M.J. Sewall is the author of six novels and a short story collection that everyone should read immediately. Overly fond of all types of stories, pizza, chili, and his children and grandchildren, he will leave it up to the reader to put those things in the proper order. He is surrounded by heavy books of all kinds. When the earthquake comes, he is in serious trouble. Living in the naturally climate controlled Central Coast of California, he thanks the universe each day for all the wonders on display.

For more information, please visit mjsewall.com

and the publisher's Author Page at:

https://www.nextchapter.pub/authors/mj-sewall-fantasy-author-california